MW01077140

A Midsummer Night's Scheme

Also available by Harper Kincaid

The Bookbinding Mysteries
To Kill a Mocking Girl

The Wonder of You
Bind Me Before You Go
You Do You (I Just Want to Pee Alone, #6)

A Midsummer Night's Scheme

A BOOKBINDING MYSTERY

Harper Kincaid

CROOKED
LANE

NEW YORK

PUBLISHER'S NOTE: The recipes contained in this book are to be followed exactly as written. The publisher is not responsible for your specific health or allergy needs that may require medical supervision. The publisher is not responsible for any adverse reaction to the recipes contained in this book.

Published in the United States by Crooked Lane Books, an imprint of The Quick Brown Fox & Company LLC.

Crooked Lane Books and its logo are trademarks of The Quick Brown Fox & Company LLC.

Library of Congress Catalog-in-Publication data available upon request.

ISBN (hardcover): 978-1-64385-630-8
ISBN (ebook): 978-1-64385-631-5

Cover design by Mary Ann Lasher

Printed in the United States.

www.crookedlanebooks.com

Crooked Lane Books
34 West 27th St., 10th Floor
New York, NY 10001

First Edition: March 2023

10 9 8 7 6 5 4 3 2 1

Dedicated to the good men in my life,
past and present: my beloved Uncle
Richard, Lenny Cohen, Phil Cohen
(not related to each other) and, for always,
my heart, David.

Chapter One

All the world's a stage, and all the men and women merely players.
They have their exits and their entrances;
And one man in his time plays many parts.
—Shakespeare's *As You Like It*

When a gal's treasured childhood home of Vienna, Virginia, has two murders in six months, it makes her realize there really is no place like home—and maybe that's no longer a good thing. Quinn Caine had been born in this town, raised here too, only leaving for college and, after graduation, to teach English overseas. She knew she was still young, but that didn't mean life hadn't touched her. Quinn was old enough to realize that hometowns, just like people, are complicated; simultaneously wonderful and terrible and never quite as predictable as they'd like you to believe.

She was sprawled across a cotton blanket with her German shepherd, RBG, aka Ruff Barker Ginsburg, pressed close to her side. *At least my dog is pure goodness.* She smiled to herself. *Whip-smart too.* If there had been a Mensa society for dogs, RBG would totally have qualified. Glancing around at the crowd of young families and old souls, Quinn seemed to be the only one still thinking about what had happened earlier in the summer, how one of their own—and a newcomer—had been murdered. The Vienna Police had caught the killer, who was sentenced to life in prison without parole, and the whole town expelled a long-held sigh of relief. Tensions melted away from her neighbors' collective shoulders and life went on.

But not for Quinn, not really. For one thing, she thought of her murdered frenemy often. Tricia Pemberley was beautiful, intelligent, and had spent the entirety of her young life as a Nellie Oleson incarnate, a truly awful reboot of the *Little House on the Prairie* character. Spoiled. Entitled. Mouthy. But Quinn couldn't shake how her childhood nemesis had shown a hint of vulnerability and maturity on the last day of her life. That's what haunted her, knowing Tricia had been on the precipice of redemption, only to be killed—and in such a strange, unexpected way.

She kept petting RBG's fur, surveying all the seemingly sparkly happy people around he. And why wouldn't they be? Most people just wanted to forget what happened and have a good time. But no amount of sunshine and sweet tea could fully take the sour out of her mouth.

Quinn knew from watching too many documentaries that the human brain was designed to forget pain in order to remain hopeful for the future, the proof being right under her tush. The Town Green, where she and her fellow Northern Virginians were lounging carefree, had once been a makeshift Civil War campsite for both Union and Confederate soldiers. She tried to imagine being beaten and bloodied by war, only to find oneself convalescing mere yards away from the son of a gun who shot you.

Quinn and half the town were perched like a mob of meerkats in front of the Town Green's open-air stage, eyes wide as they waited for the festivities to start, under twilight skies tinged with dusty pinks and sun-soaked umbers. Vienna's own All-Star School of Rock band was slated to play, and they were a town favorite. The school might have been a music education franchise across the country, but the Vienna branch had a nationwide reputation for graduating future rock gods and Broadway icons.

RBG was panting, but not because she was getting all worked up over the rock 'n' roll lineup. She was thirsty, so Quinn retrieved a portable water bowl out of her bag and poured her some much-needed refreshment, whacking the side of the lined bottle so the ice cubes would slide out and plop into the water. An arctic-chilled drink with an icy crunch—that's how RBG liked it, and Quinn, the same as any other pet parent, lived to serve her canine charge. "You overindulge your girl," her mamma always said to her, which was rich, considering the woman kept a magically refilled supply of liverwurst doggy treat "cupcakes" in her jacket pocket at all times. Just in case, just for RBG.

Meanwhile, her dog exerted as little physical effort as possible, scooting and stretching her neck forward just enough to reach her bowl. RBG slurped her water—and she did it loud enough to trigger anyone with a bad case of misophonia to cringe all over.

Quinn scratched RBG's black-and-tan rump. "See? This is why we can't go to nice places. You forget your table manners."

Some of the people sitting close by laughed along with her, but one cackle stood out from the rest. Quinn glanced around because she'd know that laugh anywhere.

Sure enough, there she was, her buoyant, fiery-red curls lifting off her shoulders a half beat behind due to her light-on-her-feet gait: fellow Prose & Scones bookshop employee Leah Grover, with her husband, Ryan. She had started off as a part-time "book matchmaker" and then been promoted to social media manager. A great call, in Quinn's opinion, especially since Quinn was the one who had been singing Leah's praises to the owners, who just happened to be her parents, Finn and Adele Caine.

Quinn was madly in love with everything to do with books. She even sniffed them when no one was looking because—really—what was more heavenly than that new book smell? Leah felt the same way, which was why they were such good friends. Maybe not as close as Quinn was to her cousin, Elizabeth—now church novitiate Sister Daria—but she certainly saw more of Leah these days. Her cousin lived only three miles down the road at Saint Guinefort House, the church's abbey and dog shelter, but it might as well have been a continent away. Quinn was learning to live with Daria's calling, but that didn't mean she didn't miss the cousin she'd grown up with like a sister as if she were a phantom limb.

Meanwhile, Quinn's friend had now maneuvered her way through the crowd, dragging her husband behind her. Judging by the lopsided grin on his face, Ryan didn't mind; he'd let his cherubic bride schlep him wherever she wanted to go.

Leah stopped right at the edge of Quinn's blanket. Her toes were painted a shiny rose gold. "Well, look at you! That chicken wing of yours is all healed up. 'Bout time too."

Quinn glanced down at her left arm, which was about eight shades lighter than her right. She crooked her elbow and flapped it up and down as if testing for flight. "Yeah, the doc sawed the cast off on Friday, and I can't tell you what a relief it is to finally be out of that thing."

Ryan scrunched up his nose. "Bet it was stinky too."

"Ryan!" Leah play-slapped his upper arm. "I'm sure that's not true."

"Oh, it's totally true. There was an entire season of summer sweat encased in there. You should've seen how my skin was peeling off in places, and—"

Leah's rosy cheeks turned an unflattering shade of green as she shooed away Quinn's words. "Please, *please* stop—I've got quite the vivid picture burned in my brain now," she gagged. "Thanks for that."

Oops.

Ryan draped his arm around her, giving his wife's shoulder a reassuring squeeze.

"Well, we're just relieved you're all better. Every time I'd come to pick Leah up from work, I'd talk with your family, and—trust me—they were worried sick."

Quinn couldn't blame them for feeling overprotective. After her kidnapping earlier this summer, Tricia's killer had done quite a number on Quinn's arm and shoulder during an attempted escape from the Vienna PD. Quinn had sustained a fractured wrist, a broken humerus, and a shattered scapula, the latter requiring extensive surgery on her shoulder. Recovery had taken months, which meant she had missed out on her favorite warm-weather pastimes—usually involving a body of water and an alcoholic concoction with one of those pastel-colored paper umbrellas stuck into a piece of tropical fruit swollen with sugary juice.

The color returned to Leah's complexion. "So, is it just you and RBG here? Or are you waiting for uh, hmm . . . someone special?"

Quinn coughed into her hand. "Wow, that wasn't even subtle, like not even a little bit."

Leah squinted up at Ryan. "Honey, am I even *capable* of being subtle?"

He barked out a laugh. "I'm not answering that one."

Leah wasn't the only one curious about Quinn's love life. Everyone was. Quinn even noticed a few ears around them perking up the minute Leah's question left her mouth—and she knew why.

They all wanted to know how Quinn and Aiden Harrington, the town's lead detective and her older brother's best friend, were faring as a new couple.

It was Aiden who had rescued her from the murderer's backyard crypt. Most of what had happened remained fuzzy, but what Quinn could remember from that day was pain: soul-sucking, blinding agony so piercing, she fainted as soon as she cleared the doorway. According to reports from the press and police, Aiden had swooped in and scooped her up in his arms, carrying her to safety like a hero from a Marvel comic book. When she regained consciousness, her blurred gaze locked with his.

"We got the suspect, Quinn," he told her. "You're safe now."

She let out a sigh. "For the record, they are totally off the Caine Christmas card list."

Then she passed out, and the last sound she heard was Aiden growling, "You'll get justice, Quinnie. I promise."

A Midsummer Night's Scheme

Later, the local paper read "Vienna Killer Caught—and One of the Kidnapper's Victims Gets the Ultimate Meet-Cute to the Town's Most Eligible Bachelor."

Those headlines had been enough for her to wish the killer had finished her off. Who knew *The Vienna Patch* had its own Yente on staff? Of course, Quinn had known Aiden all her life, harboring a secret crush ever since he, at age eleven, had taught her, age five, how to tie her shoes with the bunny-ears method.

At least she'd *thought* her feelings had been a secret. But as soon as the info got out that they were dating, everyone—meaning *everyone*—called, texted, or stopped by to visit while she recovered at her parents' house, saying it was "about time these two kids got together" and how they'd all been praying he would "*finally* notice her." She even found out Eun and Greg Hutton, the owners of her favorite grill, Church Street Eats, had had a betting pool going, with customers throwing down good money on how long it was going to take Aiden to "get his head out of his ass and ask her out already."

Quinn vacillated between wanting to crawl into a deep, dark hole and fighting the urge to go postal with a hot wrath o' vengeance for being embarrassed. Of course, in the end, she did neither and pretended not to notice the stares, gawks, and questions.

Thank sweet baby Jesus all that drama had ended months ago. Now she was trying to soak in all the vitamin D left in the season, shielding her eyes from the sun while gazing up at the Grovers.

And while she had to give Leah props for her creative, if not-so-subtle, "fishing" expedition, Quinn opted for the redirect. "So, hey, are you two staying for the concert? I heard there was going to be a special guest with a 'once in a lifetime' announcement, whatever that means."

Ryan nodded. "Oh, yeah, have you heard them? They're really good. Hard to believe they're just kids."

Quinn couldn't have agreed more. "I grew up going to their concerts, mostly because my brother's girlfriend, Rachel, used to sing with them in high school. In fact"—she pointed toward the stage to the right of the Town Green—"she's over there with Bash. Rachel's a lawyer now, but she still gives singing lessons to the kids on weekends."

Bash must have felt their eyes, because he glanced up, smiled, and gave a chin lift. Rachel was in a huddle, probably offering the kids a last-minute pep talk. Quinn couldn't help but grin wide and bright. She had prayed for years those two would get back together. Frankly, she thought her brother had been a dozen different kinds of idiot for breaking up with Rachel in the first place. Whatever "oats" he'd needed to sow back in college hadn't been worth losing the love of his life. It had taken some doing, but now Bash and Rachel were back together and closer than ever.

The three of them waved back at Bash.

Through her plastered-on smile, Leah muttered, "For the record, I am onto you, Ms. Q. And let me state, again for the record, it's not going to work."

"I have no idea what you mean," Quinn lied.

Leah chortled. "Uh-huh, so tell me. Did you come here with someone, or are you and RBG flying solo?"

A deep, rough-edged voice vibrated right behind them. "For the record, she's here with me."

A Midsummer Night's Scheme

Just the sound of him generated tiny earthquakes everywhere. Quinn twisted her torso while sitting in place, her gaze climbing up slow and high. Aiden towered over her, the sun beaming right behind his jet-black hair. Haloed with a gentle smile, just for her.

While the town might have known Quinn harbored a not-so-secret-crush for years, she was now careful not to reveal much more than that. They were taking their time with this new romance. Quite daunting when one considered how long she had waited to be his, but not so much since she had to recover from shoulder surgery at her parent's house all summer. Hers had been a real nasty injury, a rare one too, and she'd been under the knife for over eight hours. Half her side had remained immobile in an arm and shoulder cast for eight weeks. Aiden had come by twice a day to walk RBG, and they'd spent their time on the Caine compound. Even when Finn and Adele would give them room for a private dinner for two, Quinn had been hard-pressed to feel romantic when, glancing down at her plate, she found her mother had already cut her meat for her.

Before Quinn had a chance to give Aiden a proper hello, RBG snapped out of her hot-weather stupor and jumped up to greet him, front paws on his chest, tail wagging close and fast enough to almost slap Quinn on the side of the head.

"RBG! Get down!" she commanded.

Her dog wasn't listening, but then again, Quinn always lost her alpha status when Aiden came around. RBG stood on her hind legs, batting her long lashes like a schoolgirl.

Quinn tried not to take it personally. "I swear, this dog thinks you two are the couple—not you and me."

He offered a playful wink. "That's because she hasn't seen Rueger in a couple of weeks. Your cousin's been keeping that beast all to herself." Aiden turned his attention back to her dog. "Down, girl."

And just like that, RBG sat down, gazing up at him, panting hard with her tongue lopped to the side. Quinn didn't even try to hide a snicker.

"You'll have to excuse my girl. She's fixed but can obviously still go into heat. I'm actually quite embarrassed for her."

If RBG was bothered, she hid it well. She barely gave her guardian a glance.

Leah let out a hoot. "Well, can you blame her? Your man brought sustenance!"

That's when Quinn noticed he had a sizable basket in his hand— the old-fashioned kind made of wicker stained the color of sand.

"Whoa, what's this? I thought we were going out for dinner after the concert."

He smiled, a teasing glint in his gray eyes. "Yeah, there's no way you'll be able to wait for food until after nine o'clock. I'm not new here." Aiden glanced over at Ryan and Leah. "Quinn gets seriously hangry if not fed on a regular basis. I'm just doing my civic duty to prevent a local incident. Less paperwork that way."

Leah blushed. "Oh my, aren't you considerate."

If Ryan was bothered by his wife tittering over Aiden, it didn't show. He leaned forward to shake his hand, a genuine grin on his face. "Hey, man, good to see you."

Aiden reciprocated. "Same. Thanks for keeping Quinn company," he said, folding all six feet of himself down onto the blanket. He placed the basket in front of them and started to open it but stopped and glanced up when he realized Leah and Ryan were still standing there.

"Would you like to join us? There's plenty," he offered.

Before Ryan could even begin to formulate a response, Leah did a combo squeal-jump, dropping down into a perfect crisscross-applesauce formation on the blanket.

"Thanks! This way we can catch up." She looked to her right, only to find she was staring at her husband's calves. "Ryan, don't be rude." She patted the space next to her. "Come sit."

He let out an amused snort before doing what he was told.

Leah clapped her hands. "Oh, this is so great! Since you've been cooped up all summer, we hardly had a chance to see you. You haven't worked a shift yet at the shop, have you?"

"So much for a romantic meal in the park," Quinn muttered to herself.

Although who was she kidding? They were surrounded by almost everyone they knew in town. The minute Aiden showed up, Quinn had noticed everybody peering in their direction, trying to be sly as they spied.

Aiden's hand reached inside the basket. "Actually, Quinn just got off her first shift. How'd it go, babe?"

Okay, so Quinn and Aiden were now an item, and phrases like *How'd it go, babe?* were expected boyfriend lexicon. Hearing such words outside her active imagination further enhanced their velvety effect. Perhaps that was to be expected when the man you'd been pining for since you were in pigtails and braces suddenly became yours. For the first month, Quinn had often secretly pinched herself, just to make sure she wasn't dreaming.

"Babe?"

Quinn refocused to find Aiden, Ryan, and Leah staring at her—concern times three.

"I'm sorry, what were you saying?"

Aiden grimaced, taking the wineglass out her hand. *When did that get there?*

"None of this for you, then," he told her. "I had a feeling, after your first full day back on the job, that going to this concert may be too much for you."

"That's silly. Studies have shown creative, neurodivergent people fall into dissociative states on a regular basis, especially when we're processing a lot at once."

"The same is true for trauma victims." Aiden studied her pupils. "Was today not a good day for some reason?"

Note to self: redirects don't work on whip-smart detectives.

Quinn took back the wine he had poured for her. "I am totally fine. And today was great, although everyone acted like they'd just seen a ghost when they caught a glimpse of me working in my office. But on the bright side, I made these adorable mini journals—made with handmade aged paper and recycled leather. I'm hand stitching the bindings, so it's taking a little longer than I'd like, but it'll be worth it. We're going to start selling them this week."

Her man beamed at her. "I bet they'll sell out in no time." Aiden, still holding the wine bottle, glanced over at their unexpected guests. "I'm sorry, guys, but I didn't bring extra glasses."

"Not a problem whatsoever," Leah piped in, rummaging through her mammoth satchel. Her face lit up as she produced two foldable metal cups. "We just got these in the store. Aren't they adorable? Forget eco-friendly; these are eco-*licious*."

Quinn chuckled while biting her lip, sneaking a peak over at Aiden. She could tell from one look that while he was being amiable—because his mamma would've slapped the hair off his head otherwise—he wasn't stoked about the extra company, even if he did genuinely like the Grovers.

Leah further made herself comfortable by peering into the basket. "Wow, Aid . . . this assemblage is extra in the best possible way."

Ryan coughed into his hand. "You'll have to excuse my wife. I swear I take her out and romance her the way a thoughtful husband should."

Quinn smiled. "What's ours is yours."

Leah's face emerged from the depths of spelunking, and she fanned herself. "Whoa, Aid . . . not only do you have your own basket"—she reached inside—"but you brought along a book of Mary Oliver poetry. I mean, come on. Are you even real?"

He was smart enough not to respond with anything more than a polite chuckle, but something inside Quinn expanded, the way your heart does only when the person you love honors the words another person has been gracious enough to write upon your soul.

She leaned over and gave him a soft kiss on the cheek. "You remembered?"

His eyes warmed. "Of course I did. She's one of your favorites. Now one of mine too."

Just then, someone tapped the now-live microphone onstage, breaking the spell between them. A rail-thin little body stood on her tippy-toes to reach the mic and squeaked out, "Testing. Testing, one, two, three. Can everyone hear me?"

They all looked up in unison. Some of the audience started cheering.

"Woo-hoo!"

"Play some music!"

"School of Rock *rules*!"

"'Freebird'!"

Quinn shook her head. "That same dude *always* screams 'Freebird' at these shows. And they never play it. It's time to give up the dream."

The girl onstage was undeterred, sporting an impish smile. No longer the shy mouse, she started talking again, and the band members walked onstage, taking their positions. Soon six teenagers and one tween girl were ripping steel on their guitars and pummeling the skins on their drum kits in beautiful rock 'n' roll unison. And they were playing an old favorite.

Ryan, however, appeared confused. "What's this song?"

Aiden polished off his wine. "You don't know Jane's Addiction? Please don't make me feel any older than I already do."

Ryan's face was still blank, so his wife piped up. "It's not his fault. My man was homeschooled and not allowed to watch television or listen to rock music growing up. He's learning."

Aiden handed Quinn a Tupperware container filled with treats he had picked up from the Magnolia Dessert Bar, sliced up into bite-sized pieces. She brought the container of soft Nutella crepes right up to her nose to take in its aromatic, pan-fried doughy goodness. "Ooh, I love this! And sweets for dinner? It feels wrong in all the right ways."

He smiled again. "I know."

"Ryan, come to a couple of School of Rock concerts and you'll get all caught up on the musical canon of the late twentieth century in no time. They cover almost everything."

It was true. In the time they had been eating and drinking, the band had already played Jane's Addiction, Radiohead, Fiona Apple, and Duran Duran—and they weren't done yet. Quinn scanned the crowd off to the side of the stage, which was buzzing with performers and school staff. Then she spotted someone unexpected, a man zeroing in on Rachel.

And whoa, whoever that guy was, Quinn wouldn't have been surprised if he had been magically transported right off the big screen into their not-so-little town. He was too pretty for her taste, born with the chiseled jawline and sharp-angled cheekbones meant for shiny show posters and other two-dimensional virtual realities. Broad shoulders. Lustrous dark-brown hair. Whoever he was, it was obvious, even from a distance, he was attracted to Rachel. But then again, he was also checking out his own reflection in her sunglasses.

She couldn't quite recall who he was, but there was something familiar about him. He kept positioning himself in Rachel's dance space—enough for Quinn to notice her taking a few steps back—before Bash came over, wrapping one arm around Rachel's shoulder while shaking the guy's hand with the other.

Classic Sebastian "Bash" Caine maneuver—making his claim on his girl but doing it in such a way that the other guy could save face.

A strong arm now curled around Quinn. Aiden leaned close to her ear. "Should I be jealous?"

Quinn tore her gaze away from the stranger. "Never. Why?"

"You've been staring at Broadway for a solid five minutes."

"Broadway?"

Aiden's brows shot up. "You don't know Chad Frivole?"

She did a quick memory scan. "Nope. Should I?"

He shrugged. "Not necessarily. I think he had already graduated by the time you got to high school. But Chad's the local kid who made good. He just finished a hit Broadway show."

Recognition ignited the lightbulb filaments over her head. "Ah, *that's* who he is. There were a bunch of articles about him in the *Washington Post* and the *New York Times* after he won the Tony. I *knew* he looked familiar."

"Wait a second," Ryan's eye rounded. "You read both papers?"

Aiden chuckled. "Uh, no, she reads *three*. She forgot to mention the *Wall Street Journal*." He placed a quick kiss on her temple. "My girl likes to keep up on all aspects of the news."

Leah sat up, stretching her neck to catch a glimpse. "Huh. I thought he'd be taller."

Quinn agreed. "Objects in the mirror are often shorter than they appear."

"All right, all right, all riiiight," the lead singer drawled to the crowd, doing his best Matthew McConaughey impression. "That happens to be one of my favorite songs on our set list. Is everyone having a good time?"

The crowd cheered and screamed.

"Cool, cool. We want to thank the town of Vienna for having us out here tonight. It's always good to come back home . . ."

A Midsummer Night's Scheme

Again, the crowd went crazy. It was easy to forget most of them were aging parents with federal government jobs.

"We're going to switch gears now, because we happen to have a very special guest. Like . . . really, really special. He's a huge star, raised right here in Vienna, but this man used to be me—I mean, he was the lead singer for House band and the All-Stars. Give it up for last year's Tony Award winner for best lead actor in a musical for his performance in *Shake the Roof Right Off*—Chad Frivole!"

The prodigal celebrity walked onto the stage with something between a strut and a saunter, waving to the crowd with the perfect aw-shucks demeanor. He patted the teen singer on the shoulder.

"My mother couldn't have given a better intro—thanks, man."

The singer nodded in a trance before one of the school staff grabbed him by the sleeve to coax him off the stage.

Chad kept sprinkling out the charisma for free. "Y'all sure know how to welcome a guy home! Makes me wonder why I ever left. In fact, what would you think if I stayed a while?"

Collective suburbia lost their ever-loving minds. All the soccer moms clapped, bouncing up and down, a twenty-first-century Saint Vitus dance. Their unbridled enthusiasm earned them an even bigger grin from the town's star.

The roars around Quinn grew deafening. She cursed under her breath for forgetting to bring her noise-cancelling headphones along. She's always been sensitive to loud noises.

"Dear Lord, if these women start throwing their bras and panties at him, I am moving back to Southeast Asia." Quinn stuck her pointer fingers in each ear.

Her boyfriend stared at the scene, shaking his head. "It's like watching him spoon-feed catnip to a clowder of cats."

He was right. What once had been a crowd of respectable citizens had now transfigured into something feral. And Chad was just getting warmed up.

He beamed a gleaming Oscar-worthy smile. "I cannot tell you how good it is to be back in my hometown, especially since Vienna's School of Rock's the place that gave me my start. If I wasn't playing in a rock show, I was playing a solo acoustic set over at Jammin Java. If I wasn't doing that, I was in one of Mr. Henderson's productions at Madison High. This place *made* me, and I think it's time to pay it forward.

"That's why I'm stoked to announce I am opening a new theater company. I'm talking new plays, reinvented musicals . . . we're going to change the future of theater as we know it!"

Leah clapped and shrieked at the same time. "Can you imagine? Our own theater company? What a fabulous thing to do for the town!"

Quinn smiled at Leah but leaned close to Aiden's ear, keeping her voice down. "Actually, we already have one."

"I know, the Vienna Theater Company. They're great. My mom used to perform with them."

Quinn stared, taking her fingers out of her ears. "She did? How did I not know this?"

He shrugged. "Before your time. Come to think of it, before *my* time."

Quinn tried picturing Mrs. Harrington as a young thespian. "Why'd she stop?"

"I don't know. Life got in the way, I guess." He popped a gooey chocolate bite into his mouth, the thought melting away faster than the chocolate on his tongue.

The applause kicked back up, becoming even more deafening than before. Quinn covered her ears again, wishing she had her noise-canceling headphones with her. From what glimpses she could catch over the heads of the crowd, she could see Chad was basking in the warm glow of the local limelight, pacing back and forth onstage.

"Man, I cannot *wait* to bring a world-class theater company to this town. You deserve it, all of you. Imagine, being known for theater that *means* something. We're going to bring reimagined productions of Shakespeare, Moliere, Williams, O'Neill. You and me, Vienna, we're going all the way!"

That got the town's favorite son another round of applause and whistles. Leah was fanning herself with a paperback copy of some young adult novel she must have brought with her.

But not everyone was singing Chad Frivole's praises tonight. Close to Rachel and Bash on the sidelines was a trio of young women. Like MacBeth's storied coven, they whispered curses under their breaths, their focus sharp as a dagger's blade.

Even from afar, Quinn could spot the alpha of the group—a natural stunner, with something indiscernible behind her gaze.

Ella Diaz.

Heartbreaker. Short-tempered. A genius in the kitchen. She was a Michelin-star chef, a local gal who brought cuisine from the far corners of the globe back home.

Next to her was another beauty, Corri Rypka, a nurse practitioner who had served in the military until a bomb blast near her MASH unit took one of her legs from the knee down with it. Quinn had always thought she resembled Sarah Connor from those vintage Terminator movies—windswept blonde hair, sun-kissed cheeks, biceps sculpted out of granite.

The last one was never last in anything in her life: Senya Petrova.

She was a woman rumored to have a family lineage peppered with KBG spies, then CIA operatives after they defected to the United States. All before Senya was born, of course, but she hadn't stepped too far from the Petrova Justice League: she was one of the best defense attorneys in Northern Virginia.

Quinn knew all of them—not well, but enough to know the three of them didn't have much in common. "I've never understood why Ella, Corri, and Senya are tight, but they've been friends for years."

Aiden studied them. "True, but you're right, they've always been close friends, probably because of their differences. Opposites attract and all. That said, they did have something-or someone-in common—and he's giving everyone quite a show."

Leah tugged at Ryan. "Honey, do you mind if we get a little bit closer? I can hardly see Chad from way back here."

Ryan glanced back and forth from where they were to the stage. "We're only about thirty yards away. How much closer do you need to be?"

She blushed. "Just a *little* closer, honey."

"You two go on," Quinn insisted. "I want some alone time with my man anyway. You'd be doing us a favor."

Leah mouthed *thank you* and dragged Ryan away before he had a chance to complain.

Aiden's eyes glittered with mischief. "Finally, semi-alone at last." He went in for the kiss. Quinn placed two fingers on his lips.

"Wait a second. What did you mean when you said they have Chad in common?"

He let out a grunt. "I should've known you wouldn't be able to let that comment go."

"Indeed. Now explain."

Aiden looked around and over his shoulder, but for once, no one could care a flying leap about him and Quinn—they were all mesmerized by Chad Frivole. Keeping his voice low, he said, "He dated each of them in high school—at different times, mind you, but still. And if memory serves, he broke up with all of them."

"But that was years ago. No way they'd hold a grudge for this long."

Aiden frowned, his eyes never leaving the huddle. "Usually you'd be right, but Chad didn't just date them and break it off. He humiliated them. I don't know what he's like now, but back in the day, he had a big mouth and an even bigger ego. It's one thing to harbor a broken heart in private, but it is quite another when half the town knows your business."

Quinn sat there, gobsmacked. "How did I not know any of this?"

"Why would you? He's five years older than you and hung with a different crowd. Plus people know better than to talk trash around you—you've never been into town gossip, thank Christ."

Chad must have finished with his announcement, because everyone got to their feet for a standing ovation. Quinn started packing their stuff into the basket. "Perfect time to bolt before everyone leaves and the traffic gets backed up."

"A girl after my own heart." He hoisted the basket and blanket in one hand and grabbed her free one with the other. "Let's get out of here."

Aiden zigzagged through the crowd, Quinn's short legs ramping up to a sprint to keep up with his long strides as he made his way toward Rachel and Bash to say good-bye. On the way they passed Chad's ex-girlfriends, who were still talking among themselves but doing it loud enough for her to catch some of their words:

"That weasel made a big mistake coming back here. I told him he'd be sorry if I ever saw him again."

"You're not the only one," Corri growled.

Senya's face turned beet red. "He's a plague upon this town."

Ella didn't even try to keep her voice down. "He may think there's no place like home, but this here's not his home. Not anymore. He needs to go—and never *ever* even think of coming back."

Chapter Two

By the pricking of my thumbs,
Something wicked this way comes.
—Shakespeare's *Macbeth*

Before she became Sister Daria, when she was just the scrappy girl everyone knew as Elizabeth "Lizzy" Caine, she was obsessed with all things *The Sound of Music*, which everyone—including Lizzy herself—thought off-brand. She was the kid with the sweaty mess of hair and scabbed-over knees who'd zoom past you on her skateboard and flip you the bird if you got in her way. Back then, Lizzy didn't even *like* going to church, because why be stuck inside when you could be whacking a softball out of the park or knocking a bully off his feet?

But then again, Fräulein Maria didn't start off as Baronin von Trapp either. People change, usually in ways they could never have anticipated. Sister Maria began as an abbey outcast, annoying the older nuns like it was her God-appointed job to do so. Lizzy could still remember watching *The Sound of Music* with her parents, singing along with Julie Andrews about raindrops on roses and whiskers on kittens, thinking, *Thank you, Jesus, no one can see me now.* She'd lose all her street cred, which, in hindsight, was ludicrous: she was from a tony suburb outside of Washington, DC.

But years later, when she became obsessed with BBC's *Call the Midwife*, it dawned on Lizzy that the crux of her favorite musical's appeal didn't reside in Dame Julie Andrews's sonorous pipes or how the hills were alive with the sound of music. Elizabeth was wholly transfixed by the tenacious, enigmatic spirit of the nuns and the religious orders in which they served.

And who could blame her? They might have been solely devoted to the son of God, but that didn't mean they were meek church mice: these ladies had moxie and took care of their own. An apt example was the nuns of Nonnberg Abbey. They certainly high-fived each other when they married off Governess Maria, but there was no way they were going to let the Nazis get to her and her new brood, even stealing car parts to make sure they couldn't go after the von Trapps. Saving their lives was totally worth the extra Hail Marys.

And what about the sisters of Saint Raymond Nonnatus? Pedaling their little hearts out around Poplar, London, alabaster wimples flapping like dove wings in the breeze as they brought new life into the world. The only comparative that came close, from Elizabeth Caine's perspective, was social worker pioneer Jane Addams and her girl gang at Hull-House, who lived among the immigrants on the West Side of Chicago during the early part of the twentieth century. They weren't perfect, by any means: a bevy of middle-class, white women who assumed they knew best and inserted themselves into spaces they weren't invited-a tradition kept alive and unwell into present day. But Lizzy still adored them. They dared to live their lives outside the comforts and expectations of their prescribed roles. It was no wonder her heroes growing up were Jesus, Jane Addams, and Henry Rollins. In that order.

She had tried finding that same sense of purpose in her own life, through jobs in lockdown psych wards and teen homeless outreach centers, but those colleagues—while laudable—didn't come close to embodying the solidarity and calling for which she was searching. And then, as she was driving down Vale Road one day, Guinefort House had caught her eye, its Carpenter Gothic architecture both regal and homey at the same time. Why had it taken her so long to notice an abbey—just like in *Call the Midwife*—mere miles away from where she had grown up?

The memories of *why* she had left the Anglican church years ago didn't make an appearance that day, nor did they surface for many moons afterward. What once had been a huge reason for her exit, the church's anti-LGBTQIA stance, had been reduced to an annoyance easily ignored—heady, heteronormative privilege she didn't bother examining. Loneliness and a desperate need for purpose could be just as dangerous as blind ambition.

"Everything in my life has led me here." She lifted the suitcase up, to prove she was all in.

The Reverend Mother's mouth quirked. "You do realize, most of our days are spent shoveling feed in one end while scooping poop out the other?"

Nothing the Reverend Mother said could dissuade her. She would live at Guinefort House, a home built during the Reconstruction era and designed to heal a bifurcated nation. She would spend her life resting in the comfort of serving her canine charges in Jesus's name.

And *He* was perfect, always listening. His loyalty was absolute, and He'd never, ever leave her. The only other men she could say that about were her dad and Rueger, who actually wasn't a man but a dog—part German shepherd, part Rottweiler—but he still counted. Besides, he was the unofficial mascot of her abbey, so while he was technically not hers, try telling that to either Daria or the dog.

Now she was walking down Church Street, the historic charming hub of her town, on her way to meet Quinn. Sister Daria slowed her pace as she strolled past the Middle Eastern bakery, hoping to catch a sugary whiff of delectable goodness. Maybe a fresh batch of buttery, melt-in-your-mouth ghraybeh cookies or the scent of toasted pistachios being sprinkled onto mafroukeh. "Another time," she promised herself.

Down a bit farther, sunlight hit her hard. Sharp silver. Shielding her eyes, Daria approached the consignment store window. Knee-high black leather boots with polished chrome tips, serpentine laces shimmied up and through the grommets. Daria was never one to feel attachments to material possessions, especially designer. *But those boots*, she sighed inside herself. The longing was still there, as if her old self had stomped back into town, parking itself in her path. Just to taunt her.

Rueger licked her hand.

"Not worth it." She forced her legs to move on.

"There you are!" Quinn was standing on the corner with RBG at her side. She couldn't wave with her hands full, but she still managed to offer a greeting by wiggling her elbow in Daria's direction like a fluttering chick unable to catch the break of a breeze. Daria would've waved back, but she was too busy being yanked forward by Rueger performing his perfect rendition of a Mack truck barreling down the street.

As soon as they were closer, both gave each other a happy bark and proceeded to sniff each other's butts—the dogs, not the cousins.

"Get over here and give me a hug!" Sister Daria leaned in, giving Quinn an extra squeeze, taking in the sweetness of her apple-blossom-scented hair. "It's been too long. My heart hurts when we don't see each other for weeks."

Quinn sighed into her ear. "Same here. Who knew you becoming a nun would be so time-consuming?"

True story, Daria thought. "Yeah, I'm proof of the phrase *Be careful what you wish for*. I kept pushing to run a training for emotional support animals, and whoa, they took me up on it. You wouldn't believe how many are enrolled now."

Quinn handed her a cup. "Sounds like you need sustenance."

She brought the lidded container of heaven right under her nose, its gossamer wisps of coffee aroma sparking her back to life. "Thank you, sweet Jesus, for this blessed gift. Which one did you get this time?"

"Uh, excuse me, but Jesus wasn't the one standing in line for fifteen minutes. You can also thank Nicki for that cupful of joy." Quinn took a sip, her shoulders dropping with a contented sigh. "She personally recommended the Papua New Guinea hand-pour. Her dad spent the next ten minutes bragging how she just won yet *another* Golden Bean award."

Daria snort-laughed. "Poor Nick."

"Seriously. If Mr. Amour could make her wear the medals around the shop, I think he'd do it."

Anyone who lived in Vienna for more than a minute knew Caffe Amour had the best coffee around, but the residents would be lying if they didn't admit to having more pride than a pack of lions that the rest of the country knew it too.

Sister Daria glanced at the cup in her hand. "Wait a sec, why did you get coffee from them when your bookshop buys their beans? You could've gotten the same thing for free."

Quinn lifted the cup in salute. "Just supporting another local business is all."

Likely story. "You wanted one of your princess fancy-pants drinks, didn't you?"

Quinn chortled. "What are you, ninety? You sound like the old biddies at the abbey."

Another true story. Sometimes Daria felt like she was twenty-seven going on extinction.

Rueger let out a bark. RBG rubbed her face against Quinn's leg.

"Let's roll. The canine children are restless."

They started walking, side by side, both dogs ahead of them on a courtship stroll. "It's a shame you missed the concert last night." Quinn told her about Chad Frivole coming back to town, his plans to start his own theater company, and how his exes had looked primed to run him out of town with the force of their molten fury alone.

"Darn it! Why does all the good stuff happen on Sundays? Don't y'all know that's my busiest day of the week?"

Quinn didn't even try to hide her amusement. "I know. So rude."

"I remember Chad from high school."

"Didn't he ask you out?"

Sister Daria coughed. "Uh, *yeah*, but trust me, that was far from rarefied territory. He asked almost every girl out—and most of them said yes before he was even done with the asking."

They had arrived at their destination, the place guaranteed to brighten even the gloomiest Gus—at least of the four-legged variety—out of a bad mood. RBG let out a series of happy yelps while Rueger licked Daria's hand—his version of a thank-you kiss. They knew they were in for a special treat.

Quinn pulled on the handle shaped like a dog bone, letting the others through. Three bells rang from the top of the door, announcing their arrival.

"Sister Daria, Ms. Caine. Welcome back. What can I get you?"

It didn't matter that both cousins used to babysit Luke Jovanović, the young man behind the counter, when he was a stuffy-nosed toddler; he still called them by their more formal titles. But that was Luke, an old soul disguised as a teenage boy.

In the Doghouse was his mom's newish canine bakery. The freestanding dog treat business, built on Church Street right by the W&OD Trail, was constructed to look like a giant doghouse, with the inside decor rivaling Willy Wonka's Chocolate Factory— except without the actual chocolate. Swirls of rainbow lollipops, bone-shaped cookies, tacos stuffed with "meat," and tiny hot dogs were on display, all edible to the culinary canine. There was a flowing water fountain in the shape of a fire hydrant with an attached bowl at the base where dogs could come over and get a drink. The walls were painted turquoise with fire-engine-red trim, which made the black-and-white doggy caricature wall stickers pop. The owner, Sarah Jovanović, had many of the town's most popular dog breeds on display—French bulldogs and Yorkshire terriers, Labrador retrievers and Irish setters. But there was no doubt her personal favorite was the mini Australian shepherd. Sarah's dog Skipper was the inspiration for not only the logo but the whole business. While she was certainly busy raising three kids, being wife to the local pastor, and serving as a member of her Clink-n-Drink social group, the time had come for her to get back into the workforce, and the idea of leaving Skipper home alone all day had been too much for her to bear. So she'd become her own boss instead—although Sarah would be the first to say Skipper was the one really in charge.

As soon as Quinn and Sister Daria walked in with Rueger and RBG, they could see King Skipper sitting on his throne—a dog bed shaped like a giant, plushy lamb chop. He lifted his head, his stunning heterochronic eyes—one brown and one blue—taking them in before he went right back to his late-morning nap.

Daria chuckled. "Good thing your mom has you here for customer service."

Luke glanced over at Skipper, shaking his head. "That's because my mom's been having him taste test her latest recipe all morning. Even if the place was on fire, I don't think he'd be able to move."

"Stuffed like a Christmas goose." Quinn reached down to pet Skipper. He groaned in response, ignoring Rueger's and RBG's friendly sniffs as well.

Sarah flew through the swinging doors from behind the counter, her long hair up in a bun covered with a hairnet, her apron dotted with white flour. "Hi, girls! Great to see you! Is Luke helping you out?"

Daria nodded. "Of course. We were just about to order."

Sarah's eyes rounded as she put a hand up. "Wait! Before you go for your usual liverwurst cupcakes, I've got something I want them to try." She ran back, returning with two mini bagels. "It's a new recipe I'm trying out. These here only have cream cheese filling, but I'm going to make a version with lox as well. Here, they're on the house." She handed the bagel treats over to each of them, watching in anticipation as Quinn and Daria fed them to their dogs—who didn't so much eat them as inhale them.

Sarah studied the dogs. "Well? Any good?"

Rueger's tongue made a full sweep, licking the last of the crumbs off his face before nibbling for crumbs on Daria's fingers.

RBG nudged Quinn's hand for more. "I think that's a yes."

Daria grabbed a napkin. "Seriously, Rueg . . . you almost bit a finger off."

Sarah's expression brightened. "Oh, good, they're a hit! Because if I feed any more to Skipper, he's headed for a canine coma."

Sarah's dog let out a drawn-out groan, just to prove his mamma's point.

Luke scratched the back of his neck. "Yeah, it's a good thing you came in here, because my mom was this close to making *me* try one of those things."

Sarah ruffled his mop of umber hair. "No need—you already have a beautiful shiny coat."

He blushed as he used his fingers to comb his hair back into place.

Sister Daria decided it was time to save him from further mom embarrassment. "We'll get a half dozen of the cupcakes and another half dozen of the tacos. When you make more of the bagels, we'll add them to the weekly list."

Just then the sounds of tiny bells flitted through the air, and none other than Chad Frivole sauntered in. As soon as he cleared the door, he peeled off his Ray-Ban aviator sunglasses, just like they did in the movies—all smooth moves and masculine grace.

"Just when I think this town can't get any better, something changes and I'm proven wrong all over again. A canine bakery called In the Doghouse? Now *that's* genius."

"What's really genius is how, for years, my mom convinced us she couldn't really cook," Luke said, filling up a bag with treats. "Only to discover—now that I'm almost grown and out of the house—that she actually *can* cook and likes to cook—but only for dogs, not people."

Everyone in the store laughed, even Sarah, who rolled her eyes and elbowed her son. "That's because Skipper actually likes my cooking and gives me lots of kisses."

Luke tossed a couple more treats in the bag. "I'm very happy for you both."

Sarah pretended to scoff before turning her attention to Chad. "How can I help you today?"

Chad seemed to notice Daria with her cousin and their dogs. He did a double take. "Holy shhh . . . Liz? Is that you? Lizzy Caine?"

She was surprised he remembered her. "Hey, Chad. I heard you were back in town."

With arms out, he was ready to hug her, but Rueger blocked his way and emitted a low and menacing growl. Chad's arms went back, his hands up in surrender. "Whoa there, killer. Just trying to say hello to an old friend."

He was going for casual *no big deal*, but seeing him visibly swallow, his face fading to pale, Daria felt bad. It was obvious Chad was freaked by big dogs.

"He's just naturally protective. He won't hurt you."

Chad offered a shaky half grin, all while still moving backward. "If you say so . . . gotta tell you, Liz, I think he's more horse than dog. How the heck can a little bitty thing like you even handle such a beast?"

Daria shrugged. "What I don't have in size, I make up for in attitude."

"Now that's the truth," Quinn said, noting her cousin's stink eye. "What? I'm agreeing with you."

Whatever.

Chad might have been keeping his distance, but his green eyes were fixed on her.

"Wow, I can't believe it: Elizabeth Caine. How've you been, anyway? I haven't seen you since high school." His eyes traveled the length of her, from head to toe. She suddenly felt the need for a long, hot shower, with a scrub brush made by Brillo.

"I'm fine. Really good." Suddenly Sister Daria remembered her manners. "Oh! And this here's my cousin, Quinn Caine. Quinn, meet Chad Frivole."

Quinn offered a half wave, the kind she gave when she was feeling awkward. "Hi. Nice to meet you."

His brows went north. "Whoa, this is your cousin? How did I not know about *you* when I lived here?"

Daria got a kick out of watching her cousin blush bright pink. Since childhood Quinn had been a natural beauty, but she'd never been comfortable with attention, at least the kind centered on her appearance. Meanwhile, Bash handled any attention he got with ease.

Daria could see she'd have to rescue Quinn. "Chad, you'd already graduated and left town by the time she was in high school, so there's no way your paths would've crossed back then."

Luke cleared his throat, their treats all sealed up. "Here you go, ladies. That'll be eighteen dollars even."

"Allow me, Liz," Chad handed over a twenty. "Oh, and keep the change."

This was not an option as far as Sister Daria was concerned. She might have taken a vow of poverty, but she still had her pride—something the Reverend Mother often told her she needed to pray over.

"Chad, really. There's no need. Thanks, though."

"But I insist," he went on.

Daria shoved a twenty into Luke's hand, imploring him with her eyes to take it. Luke glanced over at his mom, who gave him a slight nod.

Quinn piped up, "Save it for the theater company you're starting, which, by the way, sounds like an amazing project. Congratulations."

Chad put the money back into the pocket of his shorts, rocking back and forth on his heels. "Well, good, at least the people of this town like the idea. My manager thinks I've lost my mind. He's even flying down here to talk some sense into me."

"Well, I'm sure he's just looking out for you," Quinn offered. "I'd be surprised too. Didn't you just finish a successful Broadway run? Why would you want to start something here when everything is happening for you in New York?"

Chad grimaced, his frustration evident as his jaw and neck tensed. "I have both personal and professional reasons for my decision. Don't get me wrong, the show was a huge break for me, but having to perform that dreck eight times a week, a production with no real substance or story line—and, trust me, I recruited my own dramaturge to find one because I was that desperate—and now everyone is only offering me parts just like this it, typecasting me . . . I just"—he blew out an exasperated breath—"I can't anymore."

"What would you like?" Luke asked him.

His expression brightened. "I want to play Jean Valjean in *Les Misérables*—at least when I'm older. Or Alan Strang in *Equus* . . . maybe even Jerry Mulligan in *An American in Paris*, for when I want something lighter."

Luke blinked several times in a row. "Uh, no, I mean, what can I get you from our store."

"Oh, right." Chad seemed to have forgotten why he had come to the bakery in the first place. He skimmed the contents of the display case, scratching the stubble on the underside of his jaw, leaning his forearm against the glass. "I don't know. What do dogs like?"

Sarah's expression was nonplussed. "Well, what does yours like to eat?"

"Oh, they're not for me. I'm not really a dog person."

It only took six little words to suck all the oxygen out of the room.

Sister Daria cleared her throat. "I knew celebrities go on a lot of crazy health kicks, but Chad, these aren't the petit fours you're looking for."

"That's a good one. I forgot how funny you can be," he said, before scanning the room. Taking notice of everyone's reactions, Chad realized his mistake. "Oh, don't get me wrong. I love animals—just more of a cat guy. In fact, I've got a gorgeous blue Burmese. Shame you don't sell treats with catnip in it. My girl would love some of that." Then he turned his attention back to Daria. "You should come by my new place and meet her. She actually likes people."

Yeah, that wasn't going to happen. "What's your cat's name?"

Without a hint of irony, he said, "Cindy Clawford."

"You named your cat after the supermodel?"

"If you met her, you'd get it." He turned his attention back to Daria. "What do you say? Want to come by and meet her?"

She was just about to let him down gently, but Quinn beat her to it. "It seems you haven't been home in a while, because Liz isn't Liz anymore—she's Sister Daria, as in the latest postulate over at Guinefort House."

Chad let out a sound between a bark and a cackle. "A nun? You, Lizzy 'Heading for Larceny' Caine? Please tell me your cousin is messing with me."

Daria turned to Quinn. "Why does everyone react that way? I was not *that* bad!"

"I'm sure he didn't mean it like that." Quinn seared Chad with a heated glare. "Right?"

He froze for a half second before busting out laughing. "Oh, c'mon now, Liz. Aren't you the one who knocked that Bollero girl out cold, after she made someone cry?"

Daria grumbled under her breath. "Well, yes, but that was middle school."

"And didn't I hear somewhere that you hot-wired your daddy's car and drove it across Fairfax County when you were only fifteen?"

Sarah coughed. "You did *what* now?"

Quinn's ears burned red. "The only reason she did that was because her friend called, drunk as a skunk. If Liz—I mean, Daria—hadn't gone out to get her, her friend threatened to drive drunk in order to get home for curfew."

The bells on the shop door rang.

If Chad sensed Sister Daria's discomfort, he didn't demonstrate a smidgen of awareness.

"Explain to me, then, how someone goes from being the town's firecracker homecoming queen to a *nun*, of all career-day choices?"

She opened her mouth to respond, but someone else bellowed forth, "Actually, why don't *you* explain to everyone how, after all these years, you're still casting judgements and causing trouble wherever you go? That's what I'd like to know."

The people in the shop turned around, all of them probably thinking the same thing: how did such a roaring foghorn come out of such a tiny body?

"Whoa, Sennnn-yaaa," Chad drew out, as if his mouth was trying to catch up with his brain. "I haven't seen you since . . . since . . ."

Senya opened her hand then snapped it shut like a sock puppet. "Nope, I do not want to hear my name in your mouth. I cannot *believe* you slithered back here after everything you did!"

He took a step forward. "C'mon, Sen-Sen, that was a long time ago. We're both not the same peop—"

She wasn't having it. "Why are you even here in a shop catering to dogs? You hate dogs—ever since that corgi bit you while filming that dog food commercial."

Sarah bit her bottom lip. "You got nipped by a little corgi and *that's* why you don't like dogs?"

Chad's mouth pressed into a thin line. "Now that's not fair. That dog was possessed! Pure evil. Trust me, inside that mongrel resided the soul of the devil himself. Besides, I was only nine at the time. The incident left a mark."

Luke fanned out one of the treat bags. "So what can I get you? Since you don't have a dog, we can give you a sampler so you can see what your friend's dog likes?"

Chad eyed Senya and swallowed, his Adam's apple bobbing up and down like a buoy in rough seas.

Senya's nostrils flared. "Oh, wow, she actually agreed to go out with you again . . . and now you're trying to get in there through her dog. Am I right?"

Chad rested his hands on his hips. "Listen, I don't mean to sound like a di . . . a jerk, but what happened between us was a long, long time ago. I've moved on. I suggest you do the same."

If Sister Daria thought *she* had anger management issues, well, they were nothing compared to what she was witnessing with Senya.

Her left temple throbbed.

The corner of her eyelid twitched.

"It's on me? Am I hearing you right? You think what *you* did is on me?"

The more wound up Senya got, the calmer Chad seemed to be, like they were on some weird psychological seesaw.

"It's not healthy, all this anger. You should see a therapist. Would do you a world of good. I did. Changed my life."

Now the muscle in her right cheek was beating in time with the vein down her neck.

"You did *not* just say that to me." Her voice was low. Not the kind of whisper someone lets out when they're trying to be quiet— the type that comes when white-hot fury has traveled down their throat, scorching the life out of their words.

"Well, Chad, considering you're the one who hit on Phee three days after you broke up with me, maybe you're the one in need of the psychiatric tune-up. Or an exorcism."

Sarah walked from around the counter, wiping her hands down her apron. "Senya, why don't you and I get a coffee and talk? It's my treat."

Quinn was still trying to play catch up with the cast of characters. "Who's Phee?"

"Pheona. My sister." Senya's ocher-brown eyes flashed pain. "My twin sister."

Quinn gawped. "Oh noooo."

Senya blew her bangs out of her face. "Oh yes . . . and then, when I found out and went off on him, do you know what he said—what he *actually* said to me?"

Daria took one glance at Quinn's expression and knew she was regretting asking about Phee. She had triangulated herself between Chad and Senya.

"He said I should take it as a compliment because we're twins, so obviously he still thought I was hot. He was just going to make sure next time around he went for the 'less needy' sister."

Daria could see that Quinn needed a rescue. She grabbed her sleeve, giving it a tug. "Maybe my cousin and I should leave you two to it."

Senya went on as if Daria hadn't just spoken. "How you haven't been struck down with some sort of venereal plague by now is beyond me—and proof the devil plays favorites."

Chad cracked his knuckles. "Yeah, my behavior back in high school? Totally my bad. That wasn't cool."

She stared at him, waiting for something else. "Annnnd?" she drew out.

He went blank before shrugging his shoulders. "Well, obviously I regret my behavior . . . listen, it was a different time back then. I'd never say something like that now. So, are we okay?"

One look at Senya's face and it was obvious she wasn't going to let it go, let it slide, or let him off the hook in any way.

"Obviously that therapist of yours never role-played how to offer a sincere apology."

Chad's head tilted.

"Ugh, whatever. I can't be in the same room with you." She met Sarah's flummoxed gaze. "I'll come by later for my usual order."

Senya threw herself against the shop door, the bells above ringing in a sharper key. The rest of them stared at the space she had just vacated as if there were a life-sized cutout of her left in the drywall.

Daria was the first to speak. "Wow. I don't think I've ever seen her that ticked off."

Chad rubbed a hand over his face. "Oh, I have. When we dated, her being pissed at me was a daily occurrence. She's fiery, passionate—that's what first drew me to her."

"Is what she said really true?"

His eyes darted around, reading the room again. "Hey, I know. I was an ass. I'm not proud of what I did to Senya—and many, many others. But I apologized."

Luke threw out a much-needed redirect. "So I'll get you the sampler?"

Chad gave a grateful smile. "Oh, right. Sounds great."

"Well, that's our cue." Quinn lifted her purchase. "Thanks for the goodies, Sarah. We'll see you next week."

"See you soon!" Sarah called out, already sauntering back toward the kitchen. Luke gave them a wave.

They opened the door and walked outside, the late-morning sun momentarily blinding them.

Just before the shop's door shut, Chad called out, "Hey, wait a sec!"

Daria glanced at Quinn. "And we almost made it."

"Keep the change," he said to Luke while barreling through the door, bag in hand. "Hey, listen, no hard feelings. Just an initial shock to the system. I really do wish you the best of luck."

"Thanks, I appreciate that. And best of luck to you with the new theater company. It sounds like a heck of a project, one that could really benefit the town."

"Oh, it will. It's going to be my legacy, a great way of giving back." He turned to her cousin. "Nice to meet you too. You're not becoming a nun anytime soon, are you?"

RBG barked, pressing her long, strong body against Quinn's leg. "Not a chance. Jesus is awesome, but I only go to church to appease my parents and support my cousin."

"She's dating a detective—built like a brick house, that one."

Quinn jabbed her cousin hard.

"Ow! Was that entirely necessary?"

Quinn *tsk*ed. "You're fine." She offered Chad a weak smile. "His name is Aiden Harrington. He was a year ahead of you?"

"Oh, yeah, I remember him. He's one of those salt-of-the-earth types." Chad chuckled to himself, his crooked smile broadening. "Such is my luck . . . all the good ones are taken." He lifted his bags of treats. "Well, I'm off! Senya may be madder than a swarm of mosquitoes, but she was right: I got 'em for a date. See you two around."

They watched him walk to his car—a midnight-black Alfa Romeo Giulia.

Daria let out a low whistle. "Nice wheels."

"Thanks. You know, every time I get in this car, I can't believe she's mine." He smiled just like a kid, eyes squinting in the sun.

He hit the button on the key fob, but there was no clicking sound. "That's weird; I thought I locked it. Anyway, I'll see ya around."

They both said good-bye as he folded himself into his car. Daria gave Rueger's leash a quick tug, all four of them falling into step with each other.

"I can't believe he said that to Senya."

Daria blew out an annoyed breath. "I know. Can't unsee *that* show."

Chad's car had pulled out of the shop's driveway and was headed down Church Street. It didn't get very far before he started swerving, jerking his car left, then right, and then sharply left again.

They stopped walking. Rueger and RBG started barking.

Quinn tossed the rest of her coffee in the trash bin on the street. "He's driving like he's drunk, but he was totally sober, right?"

Instead of slowing down, the car accelerated.

Daria held her breath, the scene in front of her playing out in slow motion. Down the block, a small group of parents with baby strollers were emerging from Church Street Eats. Two of their older children were skipping out in front, giggling loudly and playing tag.

And Chad's car was headed straight for them.

Without thinking, Daria dropped everything in her hands and started running toward them, yelling and waving her arms. "Get out of the way! Get out of the way!"

That's all it took. Rueger took off, his leash flapping behind him, with RBG bolting after both.

"Stop! Noooo!" Quinn screamed. "RBG! Rueger! Come back!"

Chad was gaining speed. The kids had stopped skipping, all of them frozen like pillars of salt, the car a moving Gomorrah. And Daria kept screaming. "Get out of the way! Get the kids out of the way!"

But then suddenly the car made a hard right in the opposite direction, barreling over the sidewalk, headed for a new business, A Space for Vape.

The parents snapped out of their stupor, yanking their kids forward, running in the opposite direction.

Meanwhile, Chad's car gained speed. There was no stopping the disaster about to happen. Daria skidded to a halt, her hand on her forehead.

The car crashed into the storefront. Glass shattered like a supernova, the rest of the building cratering into itself, Chad's car the only thing standing between their world and a dusty black hole.

Thankfully, the shop was closed and no one seemed to be inside.

"Whoa, did you see that?"

"It's like something out of a movie!"

Once Daria had stopped running, RBG and Rueger changed course and headed straight for the crashed car, both scratching at the driver's side door. There was broken glass everywhere.

"Rueg! RBG! Get back!" Daria whipped her head around to Quinn. "They're going to get their paws cut from the glass!"

Quinn caught up and grabbed their leashes, using every ounce of strength she had to pull them away from the crash site.

Meanwhile, Chad was screaming, banging on the glass, his body writhing like he was either dancing or seizing—it was hard to tell. "Help me! Please! I can't get out!"

Daria tried opening the car door. Once. Twice. Three times. "It's locked, Chad! Unlock the door!"

Even with the dark window tinting, she could see Chad's expression was panicked. "I . . . I can't! It won't unlock!"

"Try the other side!" Quinn yelled out, tying the leashes to the nearby dogwood tree. Daria nodded, running to the other side of the car. She tried to open it several times as well, using her weight to pull on the handle as hard as she could. "It's locked too!"

"Make it stop! Make them stop!" Chad cried out as his body jerked around in his seat.

Daria had never felt so helpless in her life. "I think he's having a seizure!"

Quinn called out, "If he's still talking coherently, it's not a seizure."

"Then what is happening to him?"

Quinn peered through the driver's side window. "Chad's not talking anymore. He's lost consciousness!"

Sister Daria kept trying the handle on the car door, banging on the passenger window in frustration. "I can't get in! Chad, wake up! Reach over and unlock the door!" His windows were tinted dark enough that it was nearly impossible for her to see in. She looked around and saw some bystanders. "Call an ambulance! The fire department! We can't get him out!"

"They're on the way!"

It was Pastor Johnny, running from the church's office in the next building. followed by one of his parishioners, Holly Berry.

"What can we do?"

Daria was breathing heavily, her adrenaline in overdrive. "He's locked in! We can't get him out!"

Holly tilted her head, ear out. "What's that noise?"

Daria and Quinn hadn't noticed it, their panic making their hearts beat too loudly in their ears, but the minute Holly said something, they caught it too.

Johnny's face was blank. "I don't know. It sounds like a rattle."

Daria could hear it now. "It's like a hissing. Maybe something with the engine?"

Johnny ran over toward the vape shop, where there was a standing cylindrical trash can. He picked it up over his head. "Get out of the way!"

They jumped back, just in time, as Johnny slammed the can into the passenger-side glass.

It barely made a scratch.

"Try again!" Holly called out.

He did. Same result. He tossed the can down, breathing hard. "What on earth are those windows made out of?"

Now that Holly had pointed out the hissing sound, it was all Daria could hear. "The car is rattling louder now. What if it explodes with him inside?"

An ambulance, followed by the fire department, blew down Lawyers Road and turned onto Church Street, with the firefighters dropping out of the trucks before they had even come to a full stop.

"Out of the way! Firefighters coming through!"

Daria and everyone else obeyed, standing off to the side with the dogs. Pastor Johnny and Holly joined them, watching Fairfax County's finest do their work.

One of the firefighters yelled to her crew, "We got to get him out! Something's up with the engine. It's hissing really loud."

The firefighter slid a long bar between the driver-side glass and the door, shimmying it around. "There's something stuck in there! Something's keeping me from getting the door opened."

"We're going to have to break the glass," the lead firefighter called out.

"I tried breaking the glass with that trash can," Johnny let them know, "but it barely did a thing."

The lead firefighter shared a knowing look with her unit. "It must be polycarbonate bulletproof glass. Get the hammer!"

The bystanders watched as the firefighters swung at the glass, lightning fast, to get to Chad. After a few swings, they finally broke through and yanked the car door open. And that's when the hissing got even louder.

The leader of the crew jumped back. "Oy vey—is that what I think it is?"

Quinn hugged RBG closer to her. Rueger started to whine. Daria scratched the back of his neck, trying to soothe him.

The head EMT cursed under her breath. "Everybody get back. We've got snakes! Lots of snakes."

Johnny prayed. Holly crouched near the dogs, her eyes fixed on the rescue effort.

And that's when they all saw them: one, two, three . . . it seemed like there were endless snakes slithering all around the floor and seats of the car. There was one coiled right in Chad's lap, its tail vibrating fast like a baby rattle on a bouncy spring.

More sirens sounded, piercing through the air the closer they got.

"Someone radio animal control," shouted one of the firefighters.

The lead firefighter growled. "We can't wait that long. Call Inova so they have antivenom ready in the ER." Without warning, she dove into the car and yanked Chad's body out—all in less than six seconds.

"Close the door! Close the door!" she yelled. Her crew complied, also grabbing some canvas tarp and shoving it into the hole where the passenger window used to be.

Meanwhile, Chad was hoisted onto a gurney, his skin fading from a warm olive to a cold ash, his eyes without focus. Daria couldn't tell if he was still breathing or not.

"He's lost consciousness, but I've got a pulse! We've got to get him to the ER."

They hoisted him inside the ambulance, slammed the doors, and took off. That's when Daria felt someone next to them.

"Are you two all right?"

It was Aiden and he was on his phone, seemingly waiting to talk to someone. Beside him were Officers Ned Carter, Shae Johnson, and a few others.

"We're fine," Quinn reassured him.

Before he could respond, Aiden was back to his call, and whoever was talking to him was not telling him what he wanted to hear. "No, they haven't arrived . . . No, that's *not* acceptable. We've got a—" Something caught his eye from down the street. "Never mind, I see them . . . right."

He hung up, his gaze on Daria's cousin. "Are you sure you're not hurt?"

"Yeah, we're fine. The dogs have a couple of cuts, but it's nothing, considering all the glass. Go do what you have to do."

Aiden nodded and met up with the animal control unit. He pointed over at the vehicle.

"Everyone needs to back up! We don't know how many are in there!"

Two animal control employees, dressed head to toe in protective gear, slowly released the canvas tarp from the hole. They had brought a bunch of thick burlap bags and long poles with pincers at the end to grab the snakes. They took hold of the slithering reptiles one by one and finagled them into the sacks. Each time they'd call out the name of the snake.

"This one's a copperhead!"

"Got ourselves a timber rattler over here! There's also a bunch of rattlesnakes!"

"Whoa, whoever did this wasn't messing around. I think this one's a black mamba!"

The reptile opened its mouth, hissing at the handler. Inside, its mouth was the color of pitch.

"Yep, definitely a black mamba." He shoved the snake in the bag.

Daria noticed the officers writing each one down. By the time they were done, they had captured seven snakes, each one more deadly than the last.

Aiden looked at the list, his expression like stone. "Ned, call over to the ER. They're going to need to know exactly what kind of snakebites they're dealing with."

Officer Carter nodded before walking to the side to make the call, while his partner, Shae Johnson, jotted down more notes.

After the animal control officers secured the snakes inside their truck, one of them walked back over toward them. "Listen, Detective, you should know, whoever did this thing, they went far and wide to get them snakes."

Aiden flipped a page in his notebook. "Be more specific."

He adjusted the bill of his cap. "Well, some are local, but a couple of 'em aren't even from this continent. I'm no herpetologist, but I do know for a fact it's illegal to keep a black mamba. Some of the others, well, I'd have to look up. Let's just pray that guy didn't get bitten by that one."

"Thanks, Mike." Aiden shook the animal control guy's hand. "Going to need a name of a good herpetologist, if you've got one."

"Yeah, it's in the truck. Follow me."

As Aiden and Mike went off, Ned and Shae returned with yellow tape, sealing off the area.

"Can't believe we're seeing this kind of crime scene again this soon," Quinn mumbled under her breath.

RBG and Rueger were dog-tired, both lying on the ground in front of them. If they had been tweaked earlier, they weren't anymore.

"Something like this doesn't just happen," Daria told her. "This was planned. This is attempted murder."

"I know it, but I still can't wrap my mind around it."

A Midsummer Night's Scheme

After finishing with animal control, Aiden had his team scour Chad's vehicle for evidence. It didn't take long. Right under the driver's seat they found an opened burlap sack, similar to the kind animal control had but without the agency's logo. With gloves on now, Shae rooted around inside the car. Her eyes rounded as she stopped and took out a handwritten note. She unfolded it and scanned the words.

Her partner, Ned, interrupted her reading. "Well, what does it say?"

Her tawny eyes met his gaze. "Someone here went old-school. Listen to this:

"O serpent heart hid with a flowering face!
Did ever a dragon keep so fair a cave?
Beautiful tyrant, fiend angelical
Dove feather raven, wolvish-ravening lamb!
Despised substance of divinest show
Just as you return, it is time for you to go."

Ned rubbed his bald head and the back of his neck with a kerchief. "Now, what on God's green earth does all that mean?"

Standing near where Chad's body had been on the ground, Aiden grimaced. "It's a passage from *Romeo and Juliet*. The perpetrator is calling Chad Frivole a snake, saying he should've never come back to town . . . and he deserves to die."

Chapter Three

To die, to sleep—
To sleep, perchance to dream—ay, there's the rub,
For in this sleep of death what dreams may come . . .
—Shakespeare's *Hamlet*

Quinn had always known that Aiden was sharp, but he had just demonstrated a whole other level of theater geekdom. "You have *Romeo and Juliet* memorized?"

His brows furrowed. "With everything happening, *that's* what you're asking?"

"Oh, I have a lot of questions, but that's the only one I think you can answer at this point."

"Fair enough. No, I don't have Shakespeare memorized per se, but Grace played Juliet at her college's production last season and I ran lines with her."

Grace was one of his younger sisters, currently finishing up at James Madison University's musical theater program.

Aiden rested his warm hand on the crook of her neck, his thumb stroking the underside of her cheek. "Are you sure you're okay? What happened here was extreme."

She rested her hand on top of his. "I mean, all things considered, yeah. But Chad? Not so much. He did not look good."

"Yeah, I better head on over to the hospital, see what's up."

"Okay."

He gave the curve of her neck a gentle squeeze.

She searched his eyes for a clue. "What?"

Aiden let out a vexed grumble. "Just promise me, Cagney and Lacey, you two won't start poking around this case."

Quinn tilted her head. "Cagney and Lacey?"

He looked skyward, muttering "Deliver me" under his breath.

"I'm *kidding*, Aid. I've seen their reruns on Nick at Nite. That show's even older than you."

"Babe, your charm is appreciated, but I need you to promise me your involvement in this case ends here."

Daria shuddered. "If she won't, I will—for the both of us. We were out the minute someone brought snakes into the picture."

Quinn swallowed the lump in her throat. "Yeah, the only place I ever want to see snakeskins is on my belts and boots."

Aiden's shoulders dropped. "Good." He gave her a quick kiss on the cheek. "I've gotta run. I'm probably going to be late tonight."

"No worries. Should I bring some dinner over later?"

Daria gagged but covered it up by pretending to cough, pounding a fist to her chest. "What? I have allergies."

Aiden ignored her, turning his attention back to Quinn. "Nah, I'll grab something. Call you later."

As soon as he was out of earshot, Quinn elbowed her rude cousin.

"What?" Daria feigned innocence.

Quinn gave her the stink eye.

"Listen, I know you two becoming a couple is your girlhood wish come true," Daria said. "But c'mon . . . we used to make fun of such PDA."

Quinn crossed her arms. "Well, that's a big bucket of bull crap."

"Excuse me?"

Quinn didn't hesitate. "It'd be one thing if we were smashing it up in front of you, but we were being totally appropriate. So what gives?"

"It's just . . . I don't know." Daria blew some stray hair out of her eyes. "Aiden's awesome. You know I think he's the best. But remember . . . he's a guy. He's *just* a guy."

Quinn was confused. "I don't understand. Did he do something to tick you off?"

"No, of course not!" Daria said in a rush. "I'm just saying, he's human."

"I know that."

Daria let out a grunt. "That means he's not the superhero you've built him up to be. He's going to make mistakes. He's going to leave the toilet seat up or forget to put the cap back on the toothpaste."

"I'm not *that* anal-retentive."

Daria's countenance softened. "I know you're not. What I'm trying to say—badly—is that I don't want you getting hurt, or setting him up to fail either. I want you to be realistic and not look at him like he's your own personal savior."

"Says the woman literally marrying Jesus."

Daria stiffened. "That's different and you know it."

Quinn studied her cousin: shoulders tense, an impenetrable shield. The tough girl with the gaze of steel and a heart fragile as glass. It hurt to witness her pain.

And Quinn knew exactly who was responsible for breaking something in her cousin, something that had yet to heal.

"Not all guys are like Raj, you know. There are good ones out there."

Daria's head reared back, like she'd been slapped. "What does he have to do with anything?"

Oh, he had everything to do with Daria's current reaction, at least in Quinn's opinion. Raj had been her cousin's boyfriend back in grad school—the first guy she'd ever brought home to meet the family.

"He's the one," Lizzy had whispered in Quinn's ear over Sunday dinner. "Isn't he something?"

And the commitment seemed mutual, with Raj inviting her cousin not once, but twice to India with his family over school breaks. By his last year of law school, they were practically living together, with him using her place as his quiet space to study for the bar exam.

Her apartment wasn't the only thing he used, Quinn thought.

Two weeks after he passed his exam, Raj took Elizabeth out to celebrate.

She thought he was going to propose. She had bought herself something fancy, a dress meant to be noticed without begging for attention. She'd let her hairstylist magician, JoDene Dewey, work her sorcery on her straight-as-an-ironing-board locks, even splurging on one of those deep-conditioning treatments to give her hair a shimmering glow.

Raj picked her up at her parents' house, dressed in a vintage Armani suit and bearing flowers for both his girl and her mom. Quinn had been over to help her cousin with makeup, so she was there to witness the whole exchange, including a moment between her aunt and uncle where they acknowledged the gravitas of the occasion.

They were happy for their daughter.

It had taken some time, but Aunt Johanna and Uncle Jerry had grown to care for Raj too. After three years, the family agreed: it was time for an engagement.

"We won't be too late," Raj let them know before leaving. "I'll have her back right after dinner." He stopped, his dark-brown eyes warming as they locked with Lizzy's mom's. "I want to thank you for everything, for always making me feel like part of your family."

Okay, so those last words were a tad strange, but at the time both Quinn and her aunt Johanna thought he was trying to give them a signal of what he was about to ask. The minute they heard his car leave the driveway, Quinn's auntie jogged over to the back fridge, grabbing a bottle of champagne along with the ice bucket she and Uncle Jerry had received on their wedding day.

Her uncle only griped a little. "Don't get me wrong. That young man is all right. But would it have killed him to ask for her hand?"

Quinn filled the bucket with ice. "Uncle Jer, that's so old-fashioned!"

"Humph. Well, so am I," he said, before snapping his newspaper open and hiding himself behind it.

For all his bluster, when he was done with the international news section, Uncle Jerry hoisted himself out of his favorite La-Z-Boy chair to give the champagne glasses an extra wipe-down so they would gleam in the candlelight. Then the three of them sat and waited, pretending to read until Raj and Elizabeth came back home.

Raj was a man of his word and had Quinn's cousin back in under two hours, right after dinner. When Quinn and her aunt and uncle heard sniffling on the other side of the front door, they assumed Lizzy was crying from happiness. Uncle Jerry even started twisting the champagne cork.

But when they heard car wheels ripping through the gravel road, the three of them were confused—until Elizabeth opened the door. There was so much black mascara running, it was as if Raj had left his tread marks all over her face instead of the street outside.

The cork accidentally popped from Uncle Jerry's hands.

They couldn't believe it. Raj had pulled a *Legally Blonde* maneuver, choosing a fancy restaurant so he could orchestrate the breakup in public.

"I don't understand. What about the flowers? His vintage suit?" Quinn voiced what her aunt and uncle couldn't.

Not even bothering with a tissue, Lizzy lifted the skirt of her dress to wipe her tears and runny nose. "He said he wanted to give our time together the respect it deserves, to give me and my family a proper good-bye. When I told him I thought he had been gearing up to propose, you know what he said?"

The three of them shook their heads in unison. Uncle Jerry handed her a tissue.

"He said he loved me, he wished he could marry me, but not enough to go against his family's expectations. Family came first, and what they wanted was for him to marry a more appropriate match—a proper Bengali woman, someone who went to an Ivy League university and has a 'real' career.

"Oh, and the only reason why they took me on those trips was because he had insisted, and they figured it was better for him to be with a *maagi* they could keep an eye on than the alternative. The last thing he said to me was, 'Well, at least you got to see the world outside your little town.'"

When Aunt Johanna asked what *maagi* was, her daughter told her it was better if she didn't know. Quinn had looked it up later. She vowed to punch Raj in the face if she ever saw him again.

The break-up wrecked her. Shortly after that night, Elizabeth quit her job at the homeless shelter, gave up her apartment, and then didn't leave her childhood bedroom for over a month.

The "incident"—as everyone in the Caine family called it from then on—had occurred years ago, and it still stung fresh just thinking about it.

"Forget what I said," Quinn insisted. She knew Daria wasn't ready for this particular conversation. "Are you hungry? Because I could chew my own arm off. I've only had that coffee today."

The tension drained from her cousin's face. "Yeah, I could eat. Let's go."

They walked around the crime scene toward their favorite lunch spot, Church Street Eats, run by Greg and Eun Hutton.

The girls tied up the dogs to a nearby post, making sure they both had filled water bowls, which were always kept at the ready right outside the door of the restaurant. Most of the businesses on Church Street offered the same courtesy; Vienna was a true-blue dog town.

As soon as they walked in, tiny bells signaled their arrival, and Eun stopped in the middle of taking an order. "It's about time you two got over here! I thought I was going to have to drag you in myself!"

Daria and Quinn exchanged a glance before sitting down in their usual spots at the counter. Eun shoved an order into the ticket carousel and automatically filled a glass with ginger ale for Daria and one with seltzer for Quinn.

"All right, so what happened? Was Chad drunk? You know, I was at the doctor's office the other day, and I read in *People* magazine one of his castmates just checked into rehab. Of course, they didn't actually say 'rehab.'" Eun emphasized with air quotes. "They said it's 'exhaustion,' which everyone knows is"—she glanced left and right before loud-whispering—"*drugs*."

Quinn knew Mrs. Hutton was being serious, which is why she sucked in her lips to stop herself from letting out a laugh.

Daria answered for her. "It was nothing like that. We saw Chad at the dog bakery just before he got into his car. He was fine. Sober. Really."

Eun narrowed her eyes. "So what made him swerve all over the road like that? I think his car destroyed that new vape store. Not that I'm complaining."

Greg Hutton balked. "Good riddance, if you ask me. This town doesn't need that kind of business here."

Eun called out over her shoulder, "Preach it, my king! Vaping is no good!" Her gaze darted back and forth between the cousins. "It's like putting microscopic glass shards into your baby-pink lungs. You girls never do that, right?"

"No way, Mrs. H," Daria told her. "My most controversial coping mechanism of choice these days is biting sarcasm. I'm as dull as dirt."

The tiny bells above their door rang again—and two familiar faces walked in.

"Should've known I'd find you two here—getting ready to stuff your faces while only a stone's throw away from a crime scene. The Caine women's idea of a good time has always been really twisted."

It was Bash, hand in hand with his girlfriend, Rachel.

Daria chuckled. "Says the guy who runs *towards* and not away from burning buildings."

"Yeah, but it's my job to save lives—not like you two."

Something in Quinn's stomach dropped. The conversation was taking an acrid turn.

Daria's face fell. "What the heck is *that* supposed to mean? Are you suggesting your sister and I are looking for danger?"

Rachel's cerulean eyes rounded while Bash ran a hand through his sandy-brown hair in frustration. "No, of course not, but what are you doing at the scene of an accident where there's venomous snakes?"

Eun dropped a handful of empty plates, the ceramic shattering into pieces. "Snakes? Chad's car had *snakes* in it?"

A collective hush fell over the restaurant. Bash cursed under his breath.

"It's all fine now, people," Quinn told everyone. "Animal control got them all."

Greg lowered the heat on the grill before grabbing the broom and pan. "Bash, you could've brought up mice, ants, cicadas, spiders, even an alien invasion, and Eun wouldn't have flinched. But snakes? That's the one thing my bride cannot handle."

"Why did you have to say the *s* word?" Bash shuddered.

Rachel bit back her giggle. "He means spiders."

"Babe, really? You know I can't stand them, even though Mom is always harping on how good they are for her garden."

Quinn nodded. "They eat mosquitoes and earwigs and flies."

"And lions and tigers and bears, oh my!" Rachel teased.

Eun grimaced. "Ugh. For me, it has and will always be snakes. They used to be all over my parents' farm." She turned to her husband, who gave her a kiss on her forehead. "Sorry I made a mess."

Gregg shushed her in a gentle way. "Don't worry about it. I've got it."

Meanwhile, Quinn had questions for her brother. "How did you know about the snakes, anyway?"

He gave her an *Are you kidding me?* look. "I'm second in command for the county's fire department. Of course I'm going to know about what happened—even on my day off and especially when the people under my command are called to the scene. Want to explain to me why you two are at another crime scene in town?"

Daria's back straightened. "Hey, we had plans for a peaceful stroll with the dogs. That's all. Talk about blaming the bystanders."

"She's right, Bear-Bear." Rachel tucked her long, brown hair behind her ear. "I know it's upsetting they were this close to danger. Maybe tell them that instead?"

Bash let out a loud sigh, throwing his arm around his girl. "Yeah, you may have a point."

"Is that an apology?" Daria tried hiding her grin. "Bear-Bear?"

He rolled his eyes. Daria snorted.

All was forgiven.

Quinn swung around on the stool. "Hey, want to grab a table with us?"

In unison, Rachel said, "Sure," while Bash answered, "No, thanks."

"Oh, come on, we haven't hung out with your family in a while," Rachel said.

Bash chortled. "You're kidding, right? We see our families all the time!"

"Correction: you've been spending a lot of time with *my* family. We've seen yours more in passing." She leaned over, grabbing Daria's and Quinn's drinks. "Mrs. Hutton, we're going to eat together at the booth by the window."

Eun nodded. "Sure thing, Rach. Two patty melts?"

Rachel beamed. "You know it."

A dark rumble came from Quinn's belly. "I guess I'll have the same. The stomach has spoken."

"Me too," Daria added, sliding off the stool. She and Quinn followed Rachel and Bash to the booth.

Once they were settled in, Eun sauntered over, placing Cokes in front of Bash and Rachel. "Can I get you anything else? We have fried pickles on special today."

"Yes, please. Those are my favorite." Rachel licked her lips in anticipation.

Eun patted her own back. "I know! Why do you think I make Mr. Hutton put them on the menu? As soon as I heard you two were back together, I *knew* I'd be seeing you around more." Her eyes darted back and forth between them. "And you're welcome."

As she walked away, Rachel leaned in. "I think she knew we were back together before even *we* did."

Bash gulped half his Coke down. "Seriously."

Just then, a police siren blared in short spurts. Outside the window, Officer Ned Carter was repositioning his vehicle while his partner, Shae Johnson, held off traffic to let the officers and criminalists finally leave the scene. Of course, the neon-yellow tape and orange barricades remained.

Quinn couldn't get over the damage. "Whoever owns that vape shop has one heck of a reno in their future."

"That's all fixable." Daria stared off toward the scene of the accident. "Chad's a hero. If he hadn't swerved his car at the last minute, he would've hit a bunch of kids and their parents."

"At least the fool did something right, for once."

All four heads turned in unison. It was Ella Diaz, one of the women who had been part of the concert huddle the night before. Like Senya and Corri, she had dated Chad back in the day and it had not ended well. Another woman was with Ella, but for the life of her, Quinn couldn't recall her name.

Her nameless friend looked aghast. "Don't say such a thing!" She turned to the four of them. "Forget what she said. Ella didn't mean it."

Meanwhile, Ella brushed off her friend's apology with a wave of her hand. "Oh, please, they know I'm just teasing. There's a reason why jerks like Chad adore felines—both species have nine lives. He'll be fine."

Eun butted in, with a full platter. "Fried pickles up!"

As soon as the plate went down, Rachel snatched a couple, popping them right in her mouth. "Thanks, Mrs. Hutton." She closed her eyes and moaned. "These are soooo good."

Eun smiled in acknowledgment but went off without a word. It was officially the start of lunch rush, and she didn't have time for her usual chat fest.

"Yeah, no worries, by the way," Daria chimed in, addressing Ella's friend. "We know her humor is dark but not her soul."

Ella's gaze locked on Quinn's brother. "I heard you were back in town. Still playing with fire?"

"That's like me asking if you're still playing with your food for a living."

"I'll be having a side of awkward with my pickles, thank you very much," Rachel muttered while pretending to read something on her phone.

Quinn and Daria shared a knowing look, because they both remembered: Ella and Bash had had a fling years ago too. It had been casual, with no hard feelings on either end when they broke it off, but it was obvious Rachel felt uncomfortable. Bash offered his girlfriend a reassuring hand squeeze.

Meanwhile, Quinn went for her favorite conflict mediation strategy: the redirect. "When did you two get here, anyway?"

Ella was fishing around for something in her purse, the electric-blue tips of her hair fanning forward. "Oh, actually, we were just leaving."

Her friend piped up, "Yeah, we were sitting in the back, grabbing a bite before visiting her latest restaurant location. She's letting me pick the tile colors."

Ella threw her hands up. "Good going, Jenny! That info is supposed to be on the down-low."

Jenny's hazel eyes widened; her mouth gaped open. "Oh shoot, that's right! I forgot! I'm so sorry, Ella."

Eun called out, "Move it or lose it, ladies! I've got hot plates coming through."

Ella and Jenny scooted off to the side so Eun could give everyone their lunch. As soon as her hands were free, Mrs. Hutton took out her pad while scratching her scalp with the tip of her pencil. "Refills? Anything else?"

All the Caines had their mouths stuffed with juicy patty melts, so Rachel answered. "We're all good for now. Thanks."

Eun went to another table. Bash swallowed a lump of meat, wiping his mouth with a napkin. "Hey, don't worry about it. We won't say a thing."

Rachel reached out, touching Ella's sleeve. "Absolutely—and that's a promise. Besides, I know my whole family will be your first customers. We love your food."

Any hardness in Ella's expression mollified. "Wow, gorgeous *and* smart. Bash, you better seal the deal with this one." Ella gave them a wink. "And as a thanks for not flapping your lips, I'll make sure you all get invites for the grand opening. I'm hoping to open in six weeks."

"Very cool of you, Ells. Thanks," Bash said.

Ella radiated. "Sure thing. It was good to see all of you. We've gotta go—bye!"

Jenny followed behind, giving the group a sheepish grin while hiding behind her mop of dirty-blonde hair.

Quinn watched them through the window as they walked to Ella's car—a new Tesla Model X. "I don't know anything about cars, but even I know that's a spiffy ride."

Bash shrugged. "Not surprised. Family trait."

A line creased between Rachel's brows. "What do you mean?"

"She comes from a family of motorheads."

"A family of what?"

Daria cough-laughed. "In English, cousin." She flicked her wadded-up straw wrapper before smiling at Rach. "He means they're into cars."

"That makes sense." Quinn tossed a fry in her mouth. "Ella's brother, Lucas, owns Frankie's Garage in town. He was a huge help to me when I was trying to figure out the kind of car the killer drove. He had this whole setup where he was able to—"

Bash interrupted. "Uh, I don't think he'd be cool with you sharing how he gets his info."

"But he said it was all legal."

He frowned. "Yeah, well, don't get me wrong. Lucas Diaz is a good guy. I'd trust him with my life, but what he considers legit and what's actually cool in the eyes of the law are sometimes two very different animals." He eyed Daria. "You too have that in common."

Rachel pretended to cover her ears. "I'm not hearing any of this. Remember, I'm a lawyer. An officer of the court. Lalalala."

Bash kissed the top of her head. "Don't worry, I'm done talking."

His phone began to ring, vibrating the four-top.

Daria couldn't resist talking with her mouth full. "Spke tww suuun!"

He grabbed the phone. "Caine speaking."

Usually he'd slide out of the booth to take the call outside, but Rachel had the outer seat, so he stayed in place. Quinn finished the rest of her drink as Bash listened more than talked—if you could call *mm-hmms* and *uh-huhs* talking. And even though he was sitting with the three people who knew him best—not including his parents and best friend, Aiden—Quinn could tell none of them could read Bash's reaction or surmise what was happening on the other end of the line.

Quinn mouthed to Rach, "Who is it?"

Her expression was blank as she shrugged, mouthing back, "I have no idea."

Eun came over, slapping the check down on the table, her face scrunched in the shape of a scowl. "You may be a firefighting hero, but you still know the rules, Bash Caine: no cell phones inside the restaurant!"

Bash eyed her, still talking into the phone. "Anything else? Right." Then he hit the button to end the call. "Apologies, Mrs. H. Won't happen again."

Rachel rested her hand inside the crook of his arm. "Everything okay?"

He tossed the phone on the table, rubbing a calloused hand up and down his face.

"That was my hospital contact. You're not going to believe this, but Chad Frivole is dead."

Chapter Four

Though this be madness, yet there is method in't.
—Shakespeare's *Hamlet*

No television. No radios on. All cell phones kept in a hand-woven basket hanging off a peg in the vestibule. There was a black telephone perched on a slim wooden stand at the entrance of the living room, but only a handful of people ever called on the landline. They had Wi-Fi, but only one laptop for everyone to share, and the Reverend Mother had strict rules on how long anyone needed to, as she would say, "surf the interwebs for nonsense and frivolity."

Sister Daria had to admit, the lack of access to technology was one of the biggest adjustments she'd had to make regarding monastic life. She had been a typical millennial before taking her first vows, her phone having been almost surgically attached to her ear since she was in high school. Talk about missing a phantom limb.

However, after hearing the news of Chad Frivole's death over lunch, she was relieved to be able to walk into her abbey, Guinefort

House, without having any means of modern communication. She had thought Rueger would want to come inside and snuggle for an afternoon nap, but as soon as Daria unlatched his leash, he trotted right over to the kennels, where Sister Theresa and Sister Lucy were letting the adult dogs have some playtime in the fenced yard. They offered a quick wave and went back to talking among themselves, which was another relief because she didn't have it in her to chitchat—and she certainly wasn't ready to share the news of yet another person dead in their town.

Cold, clammy dread coated her skin like a fever, making her shiver even in the heat of late summer. And she knew it was because she had witnessed the machinations of pure evil. What kind of sick mind would orchestrate such an ending? Sure, Chad could be a real tool. Full of himself. He was vain with a mean streak; at least he had been in his teen years. His past cruelty was exacerbated by his present determination to not fully own his bad behavior, if the scene with Senya at the dog bakery was any indication of how he conducted himself.

She knew she was young, but a truism Daria had learned the hard way, in her twenty-seven years, was to understand no one was all good or all evil, no matter how determined she had been to reduce everyone and everything in black or white terms—an unfortunate Caine trait.

"It's the reasoning of a child, not a grown woman," the Reverend Mother had told her, her words pointed but delivered with a soft touch. "But perhaps working with dogs will suit you. They respond well to hierarchy and straightforward commands. People? Not so much, my dear, dear girl."

Her words had stung, which was Daria's first clue they held truth.

Chad had been a player, and not just on the Broadway stage. Nothing new there. Everyone also knew he could be generous, giving his time and money to the causes he cared about, specifically organizations combating child abuse. Raised by a troubled widower, Chad wanted to do everything in his power to assuage the suffering of others, a passionate mission to which he offered boundless energy. Just like everyone else, he was a mixture of the best and worst of his experiences.

"All boys need the guidance of a good woman in order to become the men they're meant to be," was something her mamma was fond of saying. Hearing her mother's voice in her head made Daria scoff as she ascended the stairs to her room. If she wanted a project, she'd go to a craft store, not on a dating app.

Jesus might have often spoken in parables, but His messages were always clear: stop judging others, actions count only if your heart is in it, and love everybody, even the wankers.

She still couldn't wrap her mind around Chad being dead, especially since he had been taken straight to the hospital. Did snake venom kill that fast? How would she know? She'd been too busy trying to hook up with her lab partner the year she took high school biology. It didn't make sense, and Daria hadn't been shy about sharing her doubts over lunch.

"Maybe those snakes have the kind of venom that only *mimics* death."

Rachel side-eyed the others. Bash shook his head.

"Seriously, guys! Don't certain kinds of snakes release a venom that only paralyzes its victims and then they're brought back to life?"

Quinn coughed into her hand. "Uh, I think you've been reading too many Bible stories."

Daria scoffed. "There is not one story in either the Old or New Testament about someone being bitten by a snake and coming back to life. Anything is possible. Besides, what does anyone in this family know about snakes? Ever since we found one coming out of the shower drain, a Caine goes running the other direction at the mere sight of one."

"That's true," Rachel added, glancing over at Bash. "You can throw spiders on that list as well."

"Babe, why'dya have to go there?"

Okay, even Daria had to admit, her suggestion was one standard deviation away from crazy pants, but leave it to Bash to humor her and call his contact at Inova Fairfax Hospital to ask anyway.

Because she was family, and when a young man had been murdered right in front of her, her cool-as-a-cuke firefighter cousin was willing to embarrass himself with an asinine question to a professional colleague.

She wasn't ready to one hundred percent let go of the fantasy-land notion that Chad was in the midst of playing the role of his life, Lazarus-style. It was the only reason she sneaked her phone past the abbey entrance, keeping it on vibrate and tucking the device under her pillow after closing her bedroom door. Just in case Bash got news from the hospital and needed to reach her.

If the Reverend Mother caught her breaking house rules, it wouldn't be good; she was already on paper-thin ice. With all the time Sister Daria had spent trying to help her cousin solve those murder cases from earlier in the summer, the abbess had summoned her to her study for several heart-to-hearts.

"You did God's work," the Reverend Mother had shared, elbow perched on the chair arm, chin resting in the curve of her palm. "Now you must decide if you want to continue His work with us or if you are being pulled in other directions."

"I don't need to decide! It was a special circumstance, that's all. What's the likelihood my cousin's going to stumble across another body?" She let out a nervous laugh. "Or that there's going to be another murder in town? Nothing ever happens here."

That conversation had happened only two and a half months ago.

She toed off her sneakers. "Not the first time you've been wrong," she mumbled, folding herself between the sheets of her bed. She needed a nap. Actually, she needed a medically induced coma, but that wasn't going to happen anytime soon, especially with all the time Daria had taken to help Quinn solve the Pemberley murder. And now Chad Frivole—barely in town seventy-two hours, at the prime of his life—was probably dead.

No wonder she couldn't sleep. Of course, her room being a thousand degrees wasn't helping. Most of the sisters were on the other side of menopause and thought air conditioning was an optional home feature. Daria crawled out of her bedsheet cocoon to open her window a crack and turn on the portable fan she kept by her bedside. Little relief, but it was something. The older nuns were fond of sharing stories of serving in Africa or in the heart of the Amazon in their youth, without the luxuries of electricity or clean water, never mind central air. Even Quinn had once lived in a hut in Guatemala, a dirt floor beneath her feet in a tiny space she and three other English teachers shared. Every story served to confirm what Daria already knew about herself: for all her bravado, she was a big baby when it came to creature comforts.

The air blowing right on her wasn't cold, but it provided enough of a breeze to let her settle back under the covers and attempt a li'l cat nap on her day off. She was lucky to have been given a west-facing room in the back of the abbey, which meant it was cooler there than in the rest of the house. And while she could still hear the dogs playing in the yard, their noises usually traveled in the other direction.

The same, however, couldn't be said for the rest of the domicile.

Guinefort House was a vintage gem, but like any aging beauty, she was vocal about what ailed her. The pipes groaned when the hot water hit. The catawampus roof housed more wildlife than the National Zoo. After dwelling 912 or so days in the Carpenter Gothic landmark, the novitiate had learned old houses would talk to you if you knew how to listen. The floorboards in each room of the house creaked in their own pitch, the volume determined by which nun was walking across the aged oak planks. The walls let out sighs when there was weather.

Just as she was about to drift off, Daria felt and heard the front door slam—the first clue that whoever had entered didn't live there, since they'd all been conditioned to enter and exit quietly.

Voices carried inaudible tones through the house as the visitor talked. Judging by the sound of leather slapping against the floorboards, Sister Theresa was the one receiving company, since she was the only one who liked to wear ballet slippers at least a half size too big. Whoever had come calling sounded like they had on rubber-soled shoes, the thick bottoms squeaking and clunking down hard as if marching off to war.

Perhaps they're running from one.

The sliding door leading to the garden in the back unlatched and slid open and shut, which meant Sister Theresa and her guest were parking themselves right below Daria's window. Daria climbed across her narrow bed so she could shut the window. At least that's what she was planning to do, until Sister Theresa started talking.

"You really should be going to the police—not to me."

"Why *not* you?" The young woman had tears in her throat. "Aren't you glad to see me?"

Daria could hear them moving their seats before sitting, the ironwork scraping against the stone patio near the garden. She knew it was wrong, but she perched herself on the edge of her bed near the window. The aging lace curtain blocked her view, but she was too afraid to move lest she be spotted.

Sister Theresa let out a sigh. "You know I delight in a visit from you. But this is different, and you know it." Then she couldn't seem to help herself, adding, "If you'd bothered going to church once in a while, you'd know that nuns can't hear sacramental confessions."

"Well, that rule makes about as much sense as a screen door on a submarine."

"True that," Daria mumbled to herself.

Whoever this woman was, she was getting cranky. "Who else am I going to go to?"

"On the phone you said you had been with him last night. What does that mean exactly?"

The young woman let out a sardonic chuckle. "What do you think it means?"

"Dear Lord, do I need to stuff cotton in your ears? Because all the common sense's leaking out of you like a sieve."

"I've just been . . . I hate to admit it, but . . ." The woman's voice wavered. "I was tired of being alone."

"Now *that* I understand. Loneliness wreaks havoc on common sense. It'll convince you the best cure for what ails you is to go back to the poison that almost killed you in the first place.

"Listen, if you didn't do anything wrong, then letting the police know you were with him last night will be seen as helpful— and take you off the list of suspects faster."

The young lady didn't respond. Her cell phone rang.

The elder nun cleared her throat. "You didn't do anything to harm him, now, did you?"

The blaring alarm stopped. "My lunch hour's almost up. I've gotta get back to the hospital."

Take a quick peak, Daria. This is your only chance to see who it is.

The metal chairs grazed across the flat stones as Sister Theresa and the visitor got up to leave. Daria uncurled herself while moving the curtain panel aside just enough to peer down below. But all she could see was the top of the gal's head—dark, grown-out roots, the rest highlighted a warm golden color. She was wearing navy-blue scrubs and carrying one of those purses big enough to fit a bowling ball inside.

Suddenly, Daria's wafer-thin mattress began to vibrate. "What the—"

It was her phone. She had totally forgotten all about it. Sister Daria shut her window, slid her hand under her pillow, and looked at the display.

Bash Caine.

Oh please God, let him be calling me to say Chad woke up. She slid the bar, making sure to keep her voice quiet.

"Hey, what's up?"

"Why are you whispering?" he asked.

"Because I'm not supposed to have my phone upstairs in my room."

"What are you, twelve?" he groused.

She had no patience for him today. "Tell me you've got some good news for me."

Bash paused. "C'mon now, you didn't really think he was going to pull a Lazarus, did you?"

She emitted a held breath. That was enough of an answer.

"'Fraid not. I'm calling for another reason."

Bash sneezed into the phone. Once. Twice. Then again.

"Bless you, times three. What's up?"

He sniffled. "We need your help. I'm going to text you an address. You can walk to it; it's close to the abbey."

She had to admit, he had piqued her curiosity. "Why? Whose house am I walking into?"

Another sneeze, then a pause.

"Chad Frivole's."

Chapter Five

The cat will mew, and dog will have his day.
—Shakespeare's *Hamlet*

The minute Quinn spotted Sister Daria in the doorway, she couldn't help but let out a sigh of relief. "You have no idea how good it is to see you!"

Daria thanked Officer Ned Carter for escorting her inside Chad's house. Quinn watched as her cousin took the gloves and booties he offered, putting them on before coming closer.

"I just saw you earlier today. What was so urgent?" Daria glanced over at Aiden. "I thought our days of crime fighting were kaput."

Aiden gave his usual chin-lift greeting. "I hope they are. We need you here for your feline prowess."

"Um, news flash, Aid. I'm becoming a *nun*. My prowling, flirty days are over."

"Not prowling," Quinn corrected. "Your prowess—with cats." Daria's face was blank. "I don't understand."

Aiden went on, "We called the county's animal control units again, but because they're dealing with all the snakes from this morning, they don't have anyone to spare to come over and get this cat."

Quinn piped in. "And I called a bunch of cat rescue groups, but because it's a holiday weekend and they're all volunteer run—"

Daria finished Quinn's sentence. "No one picked up your call, and they probably won't respond until tomorrow morning at the latest. Okay, I understand, but why didn't one of you just take the cat home with you? Guinefort's a dog rescue. Don't get me wrong, I love all animals, we all do, but I don't know if I can just bring her back with me without getting the request cleared by the Reverend Mother." She glanced over at Quinn's brother. "What about you?"

Bash used his knuckle to wipe under his red-rimmed eyes. "That's why I came over. Rachel was so excited to adopt a kitten, but look at me. My schnoz is about to fall off my face, I've been sneezing like crazy. This house is sweet, but it's covered in cat dander and, obviously, I'm still allergic. I had hoped I'd outgrown it." Suddenly, he stopped talking to sneeze—once, twice, three times—grabbing a clean tissue out of his pocket. "Ugh, that's my cue to leave this den of horrors. I'll talk to y'all later."

They waved good-bye. Meanwhile, Quinn stuck her arms out. "Don't be fooled by her cuteness. That cat is Freddy Krueger incarnate. Look at what she did to me."

Quinn knew she was being extra, but she was desperate. She was determined to have Daria rehome this adorable fur ball of ruin.

Her cousin's eyes widened at the sight of all the long scratches up and down her arms. They were already turning an angry shade of red. Aiden had long sleeves on, but Quinn saw Daria eyeing the claw marks across his neck. As far as she was concerned, the kitty had been aiming for her man's carotid artery.

"In fairness, she's probably scared out of her mind," Aiden said. "We were hoping you'd have better luck?"

Daria shrugged. "Sure. Where is she?"

They all stepped aside, as if they were making way for her to capture one of Carole Baskin's ravenous carnivores.

"That's your she-devil? She's, what, nine pounds soaking wet?"

"She's stronger than she looks, with a hard swing to boot," Quinn muttered.

"Yeah, but admit it: she's a stunner."

Oh, great. Now Aiden was melting like a tub of Crisco in a cast-iron skillet.

After impersonating a thrasher movie villain, the kitty had somehow crammed herself into a tiny gap inside the dilapidated fireplace, right between the brick and the marble molding. She would occasionally peek out her little head, then take a quick sniff around before retreating just as fast, those two celadon eyes staring wide at the humans.

Daria threw up her hands. "This is ridiculous," she said, leaving the group to walk into the kitchen.

Quinn couldn't believe it. "Heck of a time to grab a snack."

They heard her opening and closing cabinet doors before coming back out with something in her hand.

She held it up. "Observe."

Curling her forefinger through a ring, Daria pulled back the metal top in one dramatic sweep. "Cindy Clawford! Lunch is served!"

Daria plopped the can of cat food down on the floor. A blur of gray fur rocketed out of the brick and parked herself over the pungent morsels, making growly happy noises as she ate.

"I suggest you find her pet carrier and stick her in there before Ms. Fancy Princess Froufrou finishes her vittles. I'm going to get her some water."

Another blazing trail of black-and-tan fur streaked into the room, almost knocking Officer Johnson off her feet. "Whoa! What was that?"

"Not what—who." Quinn frowned. "RBG, what are you doing? I swear, she was hanging in the cab of my truck. It's not like her to jump out like this."

Aiden grinned. "That's before she heard the universal sound of mealtime—the cracking open of a food tin."

Daria went back into the kitchen and came back with a small bowl of water, placing it next to the cat food. Her cousin was even able to sneak in a couple of strokes down the kitty's back before straightening her legs. "Chad's girl here really is quite beautiful—and so soft too."

If RBG had come running inside for the promise of sustenance, she halted in her tracks once she realized a furry—and noisy—alien had gotten there first. Ms. Clawford must have sensed she had company because, amid her feeding frenzy, she stopped and stared, fixing those magnetic green eyes up at the dog. RBG tilted her head to the side, unsure of what to make of this strange baby fluff.

She let out a tiny rumble. RBG lay down, leaning on her elbows, and scooched closer.

Speaking out of the side of her mouth, Quinn whispered, "What exactly is going on in front of me?"

"Shush or you'll scare them," Aiden whispered back, riveted. Ned Carter shook his head and walked out, mumbling something about "What's the world coming to?" and "Never in my life . . ." followed by "Cats and dogs, coming together . . . what's next!" Officer Johnson's shoulders shook with her quiet laughter as she followed one of the criminalists into the other room.

Meanwhile, Cindy Clawford and RBG were nose to nose, sniffing each other out. The cat let out a more insistent growl, which Quinn guessed was a command, because her dog lay down on her side while Ms. Clawford, half the size of one of RBG's legs, pounced on her and proceeded to knead her middle like a lump of bread dough.

"Okay, you speak fluent feline—or at least you did when we were little," Quinn said. "Can you tell me what's going on?"

Daria snort laughed. "Isn't it obvious? She's claiming your dog!"

Quinn blinked.

"And she *likes* it," her cousin threw in. "Looks like RBG's got herself a new cat-baby, which makes *you* a brand-new grandma."

Quinn was still transitioning from a *me* to a *we*: no way was she ready to be a cat-nana. Aiden—the *former* love of her life— was laughing.

"What about Chad's father? Doesn't she go to next of kin?"

Aiden stopped laughing. "Babe, everyone growing up knew how he treated Chad—and that was his *son*. Imagine what he'd do to a defenseless animal."

"Fair point. So, option one is out."

Aiden draped his arm around her, cupping the curve of her shoulder in his hand while placing a soft kiss on her right temple. "Think of it this way: now RBG has company when you're out of the house."

Ugh. An excellent point.

Officer Johnson brisked back into the room, a soft padded pet carrier in hand. "Let me tell you something: Chad Frivole spared no expense when it came to this animal. This right here? It's Gucci. I didn't even know Gucci made cat bags. He even had a mini chaise longue made for her—her initials are embroidered in gold thread. And I don't mean gold-colored thread, Detective—I mean thread made of gold. That's bougie on a whole other level."

Shae handed over the carrier. "Good luck with that."

Quinn gazed down at the two animals. Between kneading RBG's fur and grooming herself, Ms. Clawford stopped long enough to note her audience and give a curt rumble in response, then proceeded back to her business.

Quinn squatted down, resting her weight on the balls of her feet. She eyed her dog. "You're sure about this?"

RBG licked Quinn's nose.

She let out a resigned sigh. "Fine, but this is on a trial basis only."

That got her a couple of blinks and her new kitty's version of a meow, which was more like a low-throttled growl. She would later read that Burmese cats don't really meow like other felines. But in that moment, Quinn didn't speak cat yet, so she didn't know what Ms. Clawford was trying to say. But it must have been positive, because when Quinn picked her up, she didn't swat her razor claws at any exposed appendage.

Quinn brought her close to her face. "You're going to be good?"

Chad's cat answered with a tuna-stink yawn.

"I'll take that as a yes." Quinn finagled her into the carrier. Between bonding with RBG and having a full belly, Ms. Clawford had no fight left in her—for now. Quinn zipped the bag and stood up.

"I'm going to be here for a while," Aiden let her know, "but I'll come over later with the cat supplies. And I'll bring sustenance worthy of a new cat mamma."

Quinn was surprised. "Are you allowed to do that?"

"Buy you dinner? I think that's in the Caine Family Rule Book: make sure you're fed, lest you turn into a scary gremlin."

She pretended to laugh. "Funny. I meant taking stuff away from a crime scene."

"He was murdered in his car, not his house. We'll seal it up for a while, but it's fine to take the cat's things for her."

"Excuse me. Excuse *me*! I will speak to whomever is responsible for this invasion of privacy!"

Everyone spun around. Standing with Officer Carter in the doorway was someone none of them recognized. Middle-aged. A spray-tan complexion with black, curly hair. The clincher was the purple suit. Purple silk, to be precise—like something Prince would wear, but this guy didn't have The Purple One's magic. He resembled an overdressed lounge act despite his suit looking like it was worth more than Quinn's entire wardrobe.

She noticed Aiden's back straighten. "And you are?"

The man tried to push himself forward, but Ned Carter grabbed him by the arm.

"Do you know who you're assaulting? I'll have your badge. Now, let go of me!"

Of course, Ned Carter checked first with Aiden, who gave a slight nod, meaning it was okay to let the guy go. Carter handed the man a set of gloves and booties. "Put these on first."

The newcomer eyed the baby-blue paper fabric set with its white elastic trim and sneered. "I did not buy this custom-made Brioni silk suit in my favorite shade of aubergine only to ruin the aesthetic with something hospital issued."

"This is a murder investigation, not a fashion show. You're lucky I haven't thrown you out. You either put those on or get out."

The prig rolled his eyes as he snatched the protective gear out of Ned's hand. "Fine." He covered his hands and feet. "I still need to know who's in charge here."

"That's me. I'm Detective Harrington. I'm still waiting to hear who *you* are."

The man dusted off his jacket where Ned had held him. "I'm Chad's manager, Halster Fitzsimmons the Third."

"Sounds fake," Quinn blurted out.

"Oh, it's real, young lady. It's a *family* name. My bloodline can be traced to twelfth-century England. The Earl of Pembroke himself personally rewarded my ancestors for bravery during the Anglo-Norman invasion." He refocused his attention on Aiden. "Listen, whatever Chad's done, I am sure there's a logical explanation. He never causes trouble." He peeked over Aiden's shoulder. "Chad? Wherever you are, don't you dare say anything until I can call my attorney. Sean Penn has her on retainer, she's that good!"

Aiden took a couple of steps forward. "Well, you're going to have to travel a bit to see him, because his body is at the morgue."

Halster Fitzsimmons paled. "His what?"

"Someone maneuvered a sackful of poisonous snakes into his car and rigged the doors so he couldn't escape," Aiden explained. "He sustained over thirty bites from seven snakes."

Quinn could tell by the expression on Mr. Fitzsimmons's face that the news wasn't sinking in.

"But we're in talks for another Broadway run. It's the part of a lifetime. We've got Julie Taymor directing!"

Daria cleared her throat. "Mr. Fitzsimmons, Chad made an announcement just last night that he was going to start a theater company here in Vienna."

"I don't know what he promised anyone around here, but believe me, his theater company was *never* going to happen."

Everyone in the room was quiet, not knowing how to respond.

"Are you . . . are you absolutely sure he's dead?"

"'Fraid so," Aiden answered. "I'm sorry for your loss."

"Chad is . . . well, *was* . . . my absolute favorite client. I had such plans for him. Did you know we were in talks for him to star in the movie version of his last show?"

Aiden gave Quinn a brief side-eye. "Uh, no. We didn't."

His manager scanned the room. "Don't misunderstand me. I cared for Chad. He was like a brother to me."

Daria crossed her arms in front of her. "Which brother—Cain or Abel?"

Quinn coughed to cover her laugh.

Mr. Fitzsimmons sniffed. "Who are you, and why are you here in my client's house?"

Daria lifted the cat carrier. "We were asked to collect and rehome your client's kitty cat. But since you two were so close, maybe you should take her?"

"Uh, no, I just got into a co-op in SoHo. *The* co-op. Very exclusive. No pets. Steve Martin lives there. So does Donna Karan."

Quinn turned to Aiden. "Guess that makes me a new cat mamma. We're out of here."

She grabbed the food bowls and the pet carrier and, followed by Daria and RBG, walked out of Chad's home. She left Cindy Clawford's monogrammed chaise longue behind because, though she might not know a lot about cats, she figured they were a lot like little kids—more interested in the box than the toy. The cat would soon find her preferred spots in Quinn's tiny farmhouse.

Chad's manager made sure to give them a wide berth as they passed. No love lost there.

As soon as they got outside, Daria commented, "Wow, that was weird."

"I know, right? That guy is a real piece of work."

Daria walked in step with Quinn. "If that's the kind of people Chad had to deal with, no wonder he wanted to come home so badly."

"Seriously."

Quinn opened the passenger door. As soon as RBG settled in, Quinn clipped her belt and placed the cat in the bag inside as well. Ms. Clawford was caterwauling like a captured banshee—until her dog rested her paw on top of the carrier, her nose against the netted side panel. Quinn turned to Daria. "Do you see what's happening right now?"

Her cousin offered a crooked grin. "Oh, I haven't missed a thing. It's hilarious. Seems your girl wanted a baby of her own—and now she's got one."

Quinn rolled her eyes.

"Should've let her mate with Rueger," Daria mused. "They would have had the most adorable pups."

"No, thanks. One dog's enough for me. Anyway, hop in. I'll drop you off on my way home."

Daria's hands were resting on her hips, a glazed stare leading nowhere special.

"That guy in there may be a big glitter bomb of pomposity, but no way would he kill off his meal ticket. I hate to say it, but I think the killer is someone from here—and she may have visited the abbey earlier today."

Quinn's knuckles whitened, her grip tightening around her keys. "What do you mean?"

Daria shared the impromptu quasi-confession she had overheard earlier. "Whoever she is, we can't assume she worked alone. Think about it: how long was Chad at Ms. Sarah's dog bakery—maybe fifteen, twenty minutes?"

"Yeah, about that." Quinn closed the passenger door of her truck. "If he had locked the car doors like he thought, then whoever broke in knew what they were doing. They had to break in, stow the snakes, and have time to jam both car doors—all without being seen."

"Well, we don't know if the killer was seen, or if there are cameras around that part of Church Street. Aiden would know."

"Don't count on him spilling anything," Quinn grumbled. "Except for asking us to come to retrieve Chad's familiar, Aid isn't going to let either of us near this case."

Daria grimaced. "I get it. But c'mon—that's quite a risk to take. Church Street's busy. Whoever broke in also needed time to sabotage the locks so he couldn't escape the car later."

The blood drained from Quinn's face. "Which is why, maybe, you send a friend inside to distract Chad long enough to get the work done."

"C'mon, Senya has a temper, but no way she's an accomplice to murder."

Quinn agreed. Senya was beautiful and smart and had a flair for drama, but her cousin was spot-on. No way would she kill Chad over being dumped fifteen years ago.

At least she hoped so.

"Perhaps Senya didn't think what she was doing would lead to his death. Maybe the person who did the actual dirty work only told her enough to make her think she was in on a prank, not a coup d'etat."

Daria sighed. "Or maybe it was Senya's plan all along. She's one of the top lawyers in the state. Who better to break the law than the person sworn to uphold it?"

Chapter Six

I had rather hear my dog bark at a crow, than a man swear he
loves me.
—Shakespeare's *Much Ado About Nothing*

"Welcome to Guinefort House's very first emotional support training class for dogs. I'm Sister Daria. You can
call me Sister D, if you're feeling sassy."

Her small funny, an attempt to break the ice, usually cracked
a smile. But there were so many people and dogs chattering away,
they missed her opening act.

"We should've worn our penguin outfits."

Sister Theresa was correct, and even though Sister Lucy wasn't
one for words, the expression on her face conveyed her agreement.

"I didn't want us to sweat off five pounds before lunch." Daria
swatted the gnats out of her eyes. "Well, considering this is a completely voluntary endeavor, I had thought they wouldn't need the
usual scare tactics."

"Ha! Rookie mistake." Sister Theresa surveyed the group.
"This bunch's soft. Need a firm hand."

"Corporal punishment is illegal. You're going to have to find new methods to scare people."

The corner of Sister Theresa's mouth twitched. "Surprised you've got this much spunk this early in the morning. Usually takes two cups to get a coherent sentence out of you."

Studying her shoes, Sister Lucy tittered. "She speaks the truth."

Daria gave a playful elbowing. "Well, good morning to you too. Glad you've come for the whole show."

"Happy to oblige." Sister Lucy perked up just enough for Daria to catch a glimmer of humor there. She was shy, but Sister Lucy appreciated smooth, dry wit.

And with that, she shoved the shiny whistle hanging around her neck into her mouth—and blew. Loud enough for the whole class to startle before going quiet.

"There's the stuff!" Sister Theresa cackled, slapping her thighs.

Daria took a step forward. "Good morning! Let's try this again. I am Sister Daria, and welcome to our first class on emotional support animal training. I assume you all are here because you actually *want* to be here and are looking for some additional emotional support from your beautiful dog babies."

"Let's be honest," Sister Theresa chimed in, "you want to be able to take Appletini or Maple Bottom, or whatever highfalutin names you're using these days, to places dogs really have no business going to, but hey, I'm seventy-eight. I've lived through the sixties, hair metal, and one too many Riverdance performances, so live and let live, I say."

One thing Daria could attest to: being part of this Order was never boring. "And with that, allow me to introduce Sister Theresa. Don't let her gruff manner and humor scare you."

"Actually, I've been told I can be quite charming. Inspire me, and you'll see it for yourselves."

The only person to ever have told Sister Theresa she was charming was Daria's cousin—last spring when she had been invited to dinner at the abbey. Daria loved Quinn like a sister, but yeesh, what a kiss-up.

Sister Daria clapped her hands together. "Okay, why don't we go around and—"

Cutting her off midsentence was a noisy flash of shimmery chrome and glass. A blue Mustang GT convertible skidded fast around the corner, barreling down their street and screeching to a halt in front of the abbey. Then a young woman popped out of the driver's side.

"Hold up! I'll be right there!" She slammed her door and ran to the other side of the car, retrieving the cutest English bulldog pup. Cradling her dog to her bosom like a newborn baby, she jogged over.

"So sorry I'm late! We're here! We're here!"

She went to the end of the line, placing her dog down on the grass like her pup was made of eggshells. "Okay, no more interruptions. Promise!"

Daria didn't mind her tardiness because she was too busy taking in the woman's navy-blue scrubs and grown-out roots. It was the same woman from a week ago, the one who had come to Sister Theresa a wreck over Chad Frivole's death.

Well, if she's the killer, she seems well over it now.

"No worries," Daria answered, trying to sound casual. "We were just about to go around the group and have y'all introduce yourselves and tell us what specifically compelled you to sign up for this class. Why don't you start?"

The woman's face brightened. "Oh, sure! Well, I'm Corri Rypka, and this precious girl is Queen E. Can you tell I'm kind of an Anglophile?"

Sure enough, the Queen was sporting a Union Jack collar with a rhinestone-encrusted tag in the shape of a crown. "Anyway, I've always been a dog lover, but because of my hours at the hospital, I've never felt right keeping one, but recently I got a new room-mate, and she works from home—and she adores dogs as much as I do, so here we are!"

"That's great," Daria offered. "And why this class?"

She hadn't planned on asking everyone why they had signed up, but Daria couldn't let the opportunity go by without at least trying to find out more about Corri's possible involvement in Chad's murder. Quinn might have promised not to poke around a new investigation, but Daria sure hadn't.

"Oh, right! Well, I'm a nurse practitioner ER nurse and I love my job, but it can be super stressful, so knowing I can come home to her, well, it's really helped me. I also love traveling, and I want Queen E to be able to go with me."

What were you expecting, a confession? For her to say, "Oh, yeah, after hooking up with my ex, who treated me like a heaping pile of donkey dung, me and my accomplice—probably Senya—devised a super-clever plan for murdering him; we should get extra credit for the snake handling—in broad daylight, no less"?

"That's great." Daria faked a smile while her attention went to the next student. "Now, what about you?"

The rest of the class rolled on without incident. Since there were so many students, Daria and her sisters worked up a sweat even without their weighty habits on. What surprised her most was that she had lived here her whole life and hadn't known any of her students before today. Either this town's population was going through a mighty growth spurt or more people were living under the radar than she realized.

"Yoo-hoo, Sister Daria! Telephone for you!"

It was her roommate, Sister Cecilia—or Sister Ceci, as she preferred—calling to her from the abbey entrance. Good timing, since class was over anyway.

"We'll tidy up," Sister Lucy offered. "Go take your call."

Before leaving, Daria noticed Sister Theresa making a beeline for Corri, who had stayed behind while everyone else was scattering back to their cars. All through class, her colleague hadn't shown any sign of even knowing Corri, but it was obvious Sister Theresa had a genuine fondness for the young woman. Daria couldn't help but wonder how they knew each other.

She walked into the house, closing the door behind her, surprised to find Sister Ceci talking on the phone. Ceci held up a finger, signaling Daria to wait. Usually her roommate was easy to read, but for the first time in, well, *ever*, Daria couldn't decipher her manner, except that someone was talking her ear off and making her hazel eyes grow wide as an owl's.

"Uh-huh . . . yes, absolutely. Okay, I'll tell her . . . I promise. Bye."

Sister Cecilia hung up the phone, and Daria was confused.

"What just happened?"

Ceci chewed the corner of her lip. "That was your aunt Adele. She said tonight is an emergency Caine family meeting."

Daria's stomach churned, a blooming sour taste coating the inside of her mouth. "Did she say what it was about?"

Her roommate scrunched her shoulders up to her earlobes. "She said she couldn't get into it over the phone."

"Wait a sec, my aunt called and then said she had to go? I don't understand."

"I got the impression that, while she was waiting for you to come to the phone, it started getting busy. It sounded like they were at the bookshop."

"Oh, okay."

"Who knows. Anyway, her exact words were 'make sure you tell my niece to come over.' Oh, and this was the most important part—she said, 'Don't forget to tell her to wear her habit, with the cross we gave her for confirmation. We're going to need all the reinforcements we can get.'"

Chapter Seven

> O Romeo, Romeo,
> wherefore art thou Romeo?
> Deny thy father and refuse thy name,
> Or if thou wilt not, be but sworn my love,
> And I'll no longer be a Capulet.
> —Shakespeare's *Romeo and Juliet*

Two strong, muscled arms wrapped around her from behind, pulling Quinn close, even though she was armed and dangerous. "Good thing I know it's you, or I'd be using this needle as a deadly weapon."

"I'll take my chances." Aiden rested his chin on her shoulder, peering down at her working hands. "I thought you just made a bunch of those."

He was talking about the small, handmade, recycled Moroccan leather notebooks Quinn designed and hand stitched especially for Prose & Scones. "I did. They sold out in two days." She pulled the thread through the middle of the pages, making a saddle stitch. "I thought the price point would've slowed the sales. They're not cheap."

"People around here know when they've found something special."

He gave her a feather-light kiss on the nape of her neck, Aiden's way of letting her know he was talking about more than notebooks. She wanted to bask in moments like these, allow the euphoric rush of everything Aiden wash over her. But there was no time, especially today.

"You can't hide back here forever."

Quinn let out a sardonic laugh. "Oh, really? Watch me."

He hugged her tight. "I hear you, babe, except you're forgetting one thing."

"What's that?"

Aiden released her. "Your brother needs you right now. They both do."

He was right, of course. Her stomach churned, making a loud, echoing grumbly sound. "Great, now I've got the collywobbles."

He let out a soft laugh. "Do I even want to know what that is?"

Quinn grabbed another restoration project she was working on, an English novel from the mid-nineteenth century. "It's an old word, meaning I've got butterflies in my stomach, but not the fluttery, romantic kind—the ones that usually accompany a trip to the bathroom."

"Difference noted. Thanks for the image."

She smirked. "You're welcome. I'm a giver. Anyway, as I was saying, I read it while repairing this book for the Freeman House. They want it fixed so they can display it for their Christmas exhibit in a few months. It's really quite lovely." She turned around to face him, book in hand. "See this laced-case binding? It's not the sturdiest of designs, but whoever bound this beauty was either French or was trained by the French, because they added this wide strip of vellum with an extra paper spine inlay. Only the French—and maybe the Germans—ever reinforced their work that way, at least during that time."

His eyes crinkled with his grin. "Lace-case bindings really do it for me too."

She narrowed her gaze, pretending to be annoyed. "You mock my bindings, but there's more to this book than meets the eye."

"Of course there is. Go on . . ."

She turned the pages in a slow rhythm. "What makes this book so special is how generations of women in this family wrote their impressions of the story in the margins as they read along. Some are even dated. This is going to be a great addition to the exhibit."

The Freeman House was one of Vienna's most adored historic landmarks, not just because they sold old-fashioned toys and candies but also because they curated unique exhibits highlighting local history, relating them to national events.

"Supposedly, the author had a secret love affair with a local woman, Elizabeth van Laer—with their whole courtship occurring over Christmas right here in Vienna. She rebuffed him for another, and he went back to England, never to marry. Isn't that heartbreaking?"

Aiden gave a patient smile. "It is."

"I actually read the whole novel, something I don't usually have time for. I couldn't put it down. It reads like a roller coaster ride: the slow build of getting to know each other, the rush of falling in love . . . and just when you think you're about to witness the most charming proposal, she turns him down. Doesn't even pause for the sake of decorum. And as she gives her reasons, you realize how utterly unreliable the narrator has been throughout their courtship. How one-sided the whole 'affair' turned out to be. Scary how men mistake basic kindness and friendship for affection. Isn't that an interesting take on a love story? So unusual for the era, if you ask me."

"It absolutely is." Aiden made his way toward the door. "You're also stalling."

Busted.

"Ugh, do we really have to go out there? We can bunk in here for days. I have a minifridge with snacks."

He didn't answer, which of course was his answer.

"I know, I know . . . I just can't believe my parents." She checked the time on her phone. "Let's get this over with." Quinn sucked in some air. "Are you sure you want to stay? Now's your time to bail on this—and all future—Caine weirdness."

He let out a soft laugh. "I'm going to chalk that comment up to stress."

"I'm just saying—"

"I know what you're saying. First, your brother's been my best friend since we were kids, so news flash, this isn't exactly my first Caine rodeo. Secondly, do you really think I'd leave my girlfriend alone to deal with this nonsense?"

"Yeah, but nothing like this." Quinn sighed, scanning the mounted corkboard containing her collection of enamel pins. The irony of the moment wasn't lost on her: Adele Caine had been the one to inspire her pin collecting, after seeing the late secretary of state Madeleine Albright's brooch collection at the Smithsonian years ago. Now Quinn had a modern version of her own: all of them quirky, most hilarious, at least to her. She needed extra reinforcements for the battle ahead.

"Ah, this is the one." She plucked it off the board and pinned it to her blouse with one of the rubber backings she kept in a clay pinch pot on the shelf, one she had made while at Louise Archer Elementary.

Aiden brushed her hair off her shoulder. "I want to see."

It was a troop of mushrooms bearing the saying *Let that shitake go.*

"That's perfect. If only wearing a pin was all it took to make everyone out there come to their senses."

She turned off the desk lamp.

Aiden opened the office door for her, and sure enough, two pairs of eyes were locked on hers, their furry necks craned back.

Quinn's hands went to her hips. "Well, hello to you too!"

It was RBG and Cindy Clawford, pressed together side by side, sitting on their haunches. Quinn was still learning to speak cat, but she interpreted her new kitty's grumbles to mean *Excuse me, but where is my dinner?*

RBG responded by sniffing her kitty's head before giving her ear a lick.

Quinn liked Cindy Clawford. She would probably fall in love with her before too long, but she recognized that ever since this adorable, tyrannical force of fur had come into their lives, RBG was a smitten kitten for this cat and focused most of her energies on her new friend.

They grew up so fast.

"Look at that, cats and dogs—supposed natural enemies—living together in peace and harmony," Quinn said.

Six heads spun in her direction.

Quinn met their steely gazes.

Her mother was the first to speak up. "That's a ridiculous comparison. You know we're happy they're getting married."

"So then why does it look like you two are attending a wake?"

Her parents, Adele and Finn Caine, were standing together by the register, her mamma leaning against her father, who was stiff as a post bean. Her aunt was behind the counter, pale as a sheet while sipping from a small glass of wine like it was a medicinal tonic. Uncle Jerry was all red in the face, unable to keep still as he wiped down the countertop over and over in tight, concentric motions, cleaning spots that weren't there.

Ironically, sitting near the history and religion sections were Bash and Rachel—and on her finger was an engagement ring, shining like a newborn star. Even though they were holding hands, Bash's whole body was tense. Silent fury. It was different for Rachel. She just kept taking slow, deep breaths, holding herself together by the barest of threads.

"You know, this *is* a happy occasion," Quinn blurted out. "It would be lovely if y'all could remember that."

"Our niece speaks truth, brother." Uncle Jerry tossed the rag he was using under the sink behind the bar. "Besides, don't you think it's time you realized your boy is a man—has been for a long while—and that man has never had a religious bone in his body?"

"This isn't about tallying up how many times someone goes to church, Jer," her dad interjected, turning his attention toward Bash and Rachel. "You know we love you both. We *are* happy that you're making this commitment to each other."

"Absolutely!" her mamma piped up. "Rachel, you're like family. I don't want you to misunderstand us. We just don't understand why Bash has to convert."

"I don't 'have' to do anything," her brother clarified. "I *want* to do this. Besides, I don't recall you having any reaction when Caroline married Raman last year—and he's a Buddhist. They don't even believe in God."

Caroline was their cousin through their mother's family line. The whole Caine crew in Virginia adored them, but having part of the family living in Northern California meant they didn't get to see each other much.

"Buddhism isn't the same thing," Adele countered. "It's more of a philosophy than a religion. She still considers herself a believer."

Cousin Caroline was a lot of things, but she was absolutely, positively *not* a believer. The only Trinity she came close to worshiping was the one from the Matrix franchise.

Bash shook his head. "You're making assumptions, not just about Caroline but about me as well."

Adele shooed his comment away. "You may not be as devoted as your father and I, but that doesn't mean you don't believe. Besides, what do you really know about Judaism? Reading a few books is one thing, but going through the process of conversion is quite another."

Bash opened his mouth, but Rachel got there first.

"Mr. and Mrs. Caine, with all due respect, Bash and I have been together on and off since I was sixteen. Haven't you noticed that my faith and culture are really important to me?"

"Well, of course we have. But you've always joined us for Christmas and Easter. You've even come to church with us. We thought in time . . ."

"That I'd leave my faith behind and join yours?"

The comment hung in the air like a low-lying thundercloud, the weight of it heavy and dark.

Bash's eyes scanned the others before landing on Quinn, questioning whether she'd known their parents felt this way, all without saying a word. She shook her head, because of course she hadn't known.

Aunt Johanna put down her wine. "Adele, Finn, it's not as if he's converting and moving to some kibbutz in the middle of the Negev desert. They'll be right here, and when they have their babies, they can come over to your home—or ours—and celebrate how we celebrate."

"Absolutely!" Rachel chimed in. "I'm not asking anybody to give up Christmas or Easter. We still want to be part of those celebrations—"

"As long as they're in our homes, not yours," Finn Caine mumbled before clearing his throat.

The store was officially closed, but a knock on the back door cut through the air.

It was Daria, waving.

"I'll get it," Aiden offered, walking across the store to unlock the door and let her in.

"Hey, everybody!" She was all smiles, and Quinn knew—right then and there—her cousin had no idea what she was walking into.

"What's going on? What's wrong?"

Rachel caught sight of Sister Daria in her habit, her big gold cross catching the light. "Seriously?"

Daria's hand went to her necklace. "What?"

Quinn's brother scoffed. "Which one of you arranged for this little show?"

The room fell silent.

Daria rocked back on her heels, as if her body could rewind time itself. "Can someone tell me what's going on?"

"I'll be happy to. Your spiritual calling is being used as a prop to make a point." Bash stood up, his hand still holding Rachel's. "Next time, maybe you want to ask a couple of questions before taking out the heavy artillery." He turned to his fiancée. "Can't tell you how sorry I am about all this. I had hoped this would be an impromptu engagement party."

Aiden stepped forward. "Man, don't leave. Nothing's going to get solved that way."

"This is true." Quinn had to think fast. "Listen, let Aid and I grab some takeout. No one can think straight on an empty stomach."

Cindy Clawford let out a couple of curt "meows," as if to remind them about the more important task of making sure she was fed. RBG let out a low bark, which must have meant *Cool it*, because two seconds later, her cat was kneading the dog's side, "making biscuits."

Bash and Rachel shared a glance, deciding. But Quinn knew her brother: the minute he took in his fiancée's tear-rimmed eyes, that was it. He was done.

Still, she had to try something.

"Uncle Jer, I think there's a couple of bottles of champagne in the back of the fridge. It's the good kind, by the way." Bash would be unreachable, but Quinn still had a chance with Rachel. "What do you say, Rach? I've been waiting for the two of you to get engaged since the first day Bash brought you home to meet us."

Rachel stood up, letting out a heavy sigh. "Me too, Quinn. But I think it's best we leave. Give everyone time to calm down."

As they walked toward the doors, Daria bolted in their direction, her hand reaching out to touch Bash's sleeve. "Hey, I didn't mean to—"

"Shh, I know you didn't." His expression gentled before his gaze hardened at his parents. "Never, in a million years, would I have thought you'd react this way."

Their dad's voice shook. "C'mon, son, don't do this."

Bash opened the front door, suddenly looking worn down. "That's the thing, Dad. We didn't—*you* did."

And with that, they left. Quinn watched them walking down the street, trying to wrap her head around what had just happened—and not being able to miss Rachel's head and shoulders bobbing up and down. She was crying in the curve of Bash's arm.

"He's wrong, you know," her father muttered, pretending to be absorbed in opening the register. "We all love Rachel. We don't have an issue with her being Jewish."

"We have always been welcoming," her mamma added.

"Yeah, Mom, just as long as Bash doesn't become one of them, right?"

"That's uncalled for, Quinn—and frankly, unfair. We're a family of strong faith. It's always been important to us, and so it's understandable we don't want to see your brother throw that away."

To her surprise, Aiden chimed in. "Finn, Bash only goes to church because it's his way of showing respect for you and Mrs. Caine—not because he has his own connection to it."

A vein popped out on Finn's forehead. "Are you telling me I don't know my own son?"

"What I'm telling you is that kids—even grown ones—do what they can to make their families happy, and going to church was the way Bash did that for you."

"It's true, Uncle Finn," Daria added, still fiddling with her cross. "Honestly, there was a time he wasn't even sure if he believed in God, so the fact that he's found a connection through Judaism is all good in my book."

Adele's hand went to her chest. "How can you say that? You're a woman of the cloth now! You know, he hasn't been back home very long. Who knows, in time maybe he would've felt that connection to God through our house."

"Aunt Adele, did you ever consider that becoming Jewish is part of God's plan for Bash? Out of all the women he's dated—and you know there were many—not one of them came close to his heart like Rachel has."

Adele's shoulders dropped. "We just wish . . ."

"We know what you wish," Quinn interrupted. "And I know you had no intention of insulting her, but you did. Big-time. And by hurting Rachel, you've hurt Bash—on what should've been the happiest day of their lives."

Daria adjusted her wimple. "I can't believe you had me wear . . . what were you thinking? Of course Rachel's going to think you have issues with her being Jewish."

Quinn's mom didn't seem so confident anymore. "I didn't mean it like that . . . I just didn't want him forgetting where he comes from."

Daria gave an *Oh, please* eye roll. "He was baptized and confirmed, Aunt Adele. He knows where he comes from."

Quinn snatched RBG's leash and the pet carrier from her office. Without a word, Aiden scooped up their new kitty and secured her inside before she had a chance to balk by using her death talons. Quinn clipped on RBG's leash and closed her office door.

Uncle Jerry smoothed the stray hairs on his head. "Where do you think you two are going?"

"Out. These two need sustenance."

"That's a good idea. I'm coming with," Daria added. "I need a ride back to the abbey anyway."

Adele's eyes rounded. "But what about dinner? I've got a lamb roast in the oven back home."

Since the first day Prose & Scones opened, the store had felt like an extension of home. In some ways, it was even better because the shop always smelled of books and coffee, two of Quinn's favorite vices. Any room devoted to books took on a sacred aura. Books had been both her escape and her salvation since she was old enough to read.

But having just borne witness to that family scene sullied the space for Quinn. She needed to get out. "I think it's safe to say we aren't joining you."

"Don't be silly. You've got to eat." Her dad gave her a pleading look that communicated, *Don't do this to your mother.*

"I'm not that hungry," Quinn lied. Her cat growled.

Aiden lifted the carrier up. "Don't worry, she wasn't talking for you. We know you're always up for eating."

They'd had Chad's kitten only a week, but already she was getting sturdier, stronger, all while she kept her diminutive stature. If the vet ever complained, Quinn was prepared to blame Aiden. He couldn't resist giving her treats.

"Don't you think you're being a little overdramatic?"

"No, Mom. I think y'all are being awful. I know that's not your intention, but it doesn't matter," Quinn voice shook as her gaze locked with hers, knowing this was the moment she no longer placed her parents on a pedestal, as a child often does. They were people. Just people: layered, fallible, and deeply flawed. Aiden laid his hand on the back of her neck, a light squeeze to show his support. Quinn took in a shoring breath. "I can't believe I'm saying this, because I've always been so proud to be your daughter . . . but after witnessing this whole thing, I'm . . . I'm . . ."

Finn Caine's voice rose, a tinge of a dare in his tone. "You're what?"

For a split second, she was about to falter, acquiesce the way a kid does in order to avoid punishment. A muscle memory reflex. But then, Quinn recalled the devastation in Rachel and Bash's expressions-and so, she lifted her chin. "I am sick to my stomach over what I observed here tonight. I'm wondering if I know you two at all, because the parents *I* knew wouldn't have been capable of such blatant, anti-Semitic crap. You owe Rachel and Bash a big apology, and until you do that, I'm not coming around either."

Chapter Eight

My words fly up, my thoughts remain below:
Words without thoughts never to heaven go.
—Shakespeare's *Hamlet*

The only place Sister Daria was self-conscious wearing her habit was at the Vienna Inn. Not because anyone there would give her hassle; she had grown up in that tavern. They made the best chili dogs in Northern Virginia, which—as far as Daria was concerned—were the only acceptable post-game eats allowed. Besides, the owner was a kind and generous man, sponsoring so many local sports teams he'd lost count, although the wood-paneled walls never forgot a one; their T-shirts and jerseys on the walls cozied up next to crayon drawings on paper place mats. If someone blindfolded her, Daria would still be able to find her way around, that's how well she knew her hometown inn because of how little it had changed through the years.

But *she* sure wasn't the same, and she hadn't been back since she had first taken the veil. Not because she'd lost her taste for chili dogs, but because her habit had become a different kind of veil. A chasm between her and the people she'd known all her life. Even the usually cantankerous day shift waitresses, once quick with a sarcastic jab, had been at a loss when they'd first caught sight of her in her penguin outfit. One of them had thought she was dressed for Halloween.

After her cousin and Aiden dropped off Quinn's pets, making sure they were both fed, the three of them had decided to grab drinks at the inn. Now they were parked by the side of the building, waiting on Daria.

"Give me a second." She maneuvered out of the heavy woolen tunic. She made sure to fold each piece of clothing—and there were several pieces—into neat squares and rectangles on the leather back seat so they wouldn't wrinkle.

Quinn watched from the sun visor mirror. "Do you always wear regular clothes under your habit?"

Great, another barb about her garb. Now she understood why Scottish men were so over being asked what they were—or weren't—wearing under their kilts.

"Actually, we're supposed to be naked underneath. Easier to feel the Holy Spirit breeze that way."

Quinn's jaw fell open. "Really?"

"Sweet Jesus, you're gullible."

Aiden unbuckled his seat belt and twisted her way. "Listen, as much as I enjoy the Quinn and Daria show, I'm starving, and there's a chili dog with my name on it."

With her Anglican rosary in one jeans pocket and her pocketknife in the other, Daria followed the two of them inside.

She realized the latter was a ridiculous—and unnecessary—accoutrement to be carrying in there. The inn might be a no-frills joint with a host of characters permanently affixed to their barstools, but the most dangerous thing that would ever be unleashed in there was a tongue-lashing. Still, she never went anywhere without both safeguards on her person. Just in case.

The place was packed. A local adult soccer league occupied a bunch of tables to the left—men and women covered in grass stains, sweat, and big grins. Holly Berry, the lady who had tried to rescue Chad out of his death trap of a car, was one of them. She still had a couple of mud smears down the side of her neck and a twig sticking out of her ponytail, but she didn't seem to care or notice. Considering the time of year, Daria surmised they'd either had their first practice or their opening game. Holly's eyes caught hers. She waved.

Toward the back, by the bathrooms, she spotted the Clink-n-Drink ladies, a variegated group of mom friends who had gotten their rhythmic moniker for their weekly happy hour habit from one of their daughters. Quinn knew them fairly well. In fact, they had directed Daria's cousin toward a clue in finding Tricia Pemberley's killer a few months back. Sarah—a member of the mom collective and owner of In the Doghouse—lifted her beer in a quick greeting. The others followed. Daria was feeling the Vienna love,

"Well, look-a-here. It's Duke and Duchess Cream Cheese, our town's new silky-smooth treat."

The comment was meant for Quinn and Aiden. Daria's head spun. "What the heck?"

The woman wasn't done yet. "Tell me, Quinn, how does it feel to have landed one of the most delicious bachelors around—the other one, of course, being that hot brother of yours?"

Daria's cousin was speechless, and Aiden glanced skyward, muttering, "Deliver me."

Daria made a tight fist inside her pocket. Even though the woman wasn't in her usual navy-blue scrubs, Daria recognized her from the dog class. Only now she'd finally had her roots done.

"Cut it out, Corri. Don't take your bad mood out on them. You're better than that." The obvious leader at Corri's table turned to the three of them. "Hey, Aid. Hi, Caine girls. Excuse her. We promise, the claws only come out when she's drinking."

Leave it to Ella Diaz to make peace in her own way. She and Corri were sitting across from each other, and next to them were Senya and Jenny. And judging by the collection of empty beer bottles on the four-top, they'd been having their own little party for a while.

Corri's hard outer shell melted faster than ice cream. "Ugh, ohmygawd, you're right. I'm an awful person, like, send me straight to the depths of hell, FedEx." She stopped to remove strands of her golden hair stuck on her mulberry lips. Her brows then came to a point. "Wait, you're from the puppy class?"

"Emotional support animal training, yes," Daria corrected.

Senya let out a snort laugh. "Wow, Corri, being a big ol' B to a nun's family member."

Quinn shooed away the concern. "Don't worry about it— already forgotten."

And Daria could tell by her cousin's expression that Quinn was really over it. Meanwhile, Daria kept repeating the Lord's Prayer on a loop in her head to loosen her fist while counting prayer beads in the other. Maybe Quinn was the one better suited for monastic life than she'd ever be.

Jenny gave them a wide smile, gathering up the empties. "Why don't you three sit next to us? It's probably the only other table available right now anyways."

"That's okay," Daria answered before thinking. "I mean, that's really nice of you, but we don't want to intrude."

Ella pretended to make a kerfuffle. "Uh, hello, it's the inn! Not like anyone can have a private conversation in here anyways. Besides, the place is packed. You'll never get another table before closing."

"She's right," Aiden said. "But it's your call, babe."

Quinn scanned the area. "Sounds good to me."

Jenny gave a quick nod before heading over to the recycling bins. Daria watched her as she took the time to peel the labels off each glass bottle so they'd be processed through the local recycling plant without any issues. Witnessing her take that kind of care impressed Daria. It made her wonder all the more why this Hufflepuff of a woman hung out with three Slytherins. "All about balance, my girl," her mother would tell her. "You don't pair sweet with sweet. It needs the sour, to even out the flavors on the tongue." Sister Daria concluded Jenny Kieval was most certainly the sweet amid the sour, the bitter, and the tangy. There was no other explanation.

The three of them took their seats. One of the longtime waitresses, Blanche, lumbered over. Daria glanced around, noticing she was the only old-timer on the floor. The rest of the wait staff appeared barely over drinking age. "What's with all the Bettys?"

Blanche sucked in her teeth. "You really haven't been in here in a while, have ya?"

"Not really."

Jenny came back and sat down. "I imagine being a nun in training keeps you busy."

Daria smiled. She didn't know Jenny well, but she liked her. *Wonder if she knows what her friends might be up to?*

Blanche scratched under her chin, giving a shrug. "Marty's still got most of my people on days but opted for some younger talent for the night shift. I'm only on because one of the chickadees needed a cover."

Marty was the latest owner of the inn, having purchased it twenty years ago from the Abraham family. The hand-over had been a seamless transition, mostly because he'd sworn not to change anything. The joint was old and dingy, with water-stained ceilings, but the beer was cheap and the food was decent. Daria couldn't help but find it ironic that the regulars had had a conniption when Marty needed to renovate some rotten beams but seemed completely at peace with the change in the late-shift waitstaff.

Blanche continued talking. "I don't blame him. They bring in the single dads and the frat boys, the latter being a real pain in my keister, but watching 'em get turned down by Barbie and Skipper is my new favorite reality show."

Ella scanned the guys at the bar, a *tsk* escaping her. "Unfortunately, bros and grandpas seem to be the only pickings around here tonight. Whose idea was it to come here again?"

"Oh, please, like Bazin's is any better?" Senya took a last pull from her beer. "Don't get me wrong, the food is off-the-charts, but half the men who skulk around there are married. Once some guy offered to pay for my drinks, and I swear I spotted a Blockbuster video card in his wallet. I almost choked on my martini olive."

Blanche was losing patience. "So what'll it be?"

"Two Guinnesses and a dressed dog with fries," Aiden said before eyeing Daria.

Being at the abbey for so long had made her lose her taste for beer or ale. The Reverend Mother adored red wine, and people always gifted her the good stuff.

"Actually, I'll just have a glass of Pinot Noir."

Blanche's gray brows shot up. "Bad news, Princess Grace, we have either white or red. Pick your color."

"Red, then," Daria answered, a little embarrassed. No one in her life had ever called her *princess*.

Blanche walked off, swearing to herself.

Senya pushed her lustrous dark-brown hair behind her ear, leaning forward. "So, what brings you three out tonight?"

Quinn shrugged. "No special reason. Just wanted to get some fresh air."

The four women shot each other looks.

"It must be bad. Because, honey, no one comes in here for"—Ella used her fingers to make air quotes—"'fresh air.'"

She was sharp; Daria had to give her credit. But no way was she spilling the tea on the extreme scene at the bookshop. *Thanks for the trauma, Aunt Adele and Uncle Finn.*

Blanche was back. "Booze up!"

"Thanks." Aiden made sure both she and Quinn got their drinks before he took his own.

Elbow on the table, Jenny swooned, letting the side of her head drop into the palm of her hand. "See? That's what I'm talking about, ladies. A man with manners. You, my friend, are a rare bird. A unicorn of your species. Let me ask you something: if I promise to pay my parking tickets, can I have a tiny swab of your DNA?"

Aiden eyed her over his beer.

Corri's eyes widened. "Jesus, Jenny, that's a weird ask, even for you."

"I don't think it's weird," she retorted.

Aiden cleared his throat. "Well, for one, I don't handle parking tickets."

"I knew that. I just forgot." Jenny leaned half her body in his direction. "I remember reading about your promotion online a year or so ago. The youngest detective in the history of Vienna. Impressive."

Quinn got close to Daria's ear. "I must have sniffed gas fumes on the way over and am currently hallucinating, because it looks like little miss scared-of-her-own-shadow is really feeling herself and is hitting on my boyfriend."

Daria almost sputtered out her wine. "Yep. Miss Wallflower's in full bloom, ready to pollinate."

She could tell Aiden had heard their exchange, because he was fighting a lip curl.

"Do I even want to know *why* you want my DNA?"

"To clone you, of course." Jenny turned to her friends. "Y'all know I could do it, too."

Ella and Senya stared for a beat before letting out a collective howl. Senya leaned across the table, speaking loudly over the din of customers. "We always know when our Jen-Jen's had enough to drink, because she starts talking about how she's going to clone her perfect man."

"I have a bachelor's degree in biology, a master's in chemistry, and another master's in secondary education." Jenny was slurring her words. "I can totally do it . . . or I can figure it out as I go."

Corri tossed both hands up. "You see? Now maybe you can understand why I gave Chad a second chance before he was murdered."

The whole table froze. In fact, the entirety of the Vienna Inn stopped space, time, and sound before getting back to their business. Corri's eyes turned into saucers as she slapped a hand across her mouth.

Aiden didn't miss a beat. "You went out with Chad Frivole the night before he was killed?"

Corri parted her fingers, still over her mouth, so she could speak. "Did I say that out loud?"

"Yes, you did. Now answer my question."

Daria almost gulped her wine down the wrong pipe. Again.

Meanwhile, Ella was looking like she was ready to slap the stupid out of her friend. "Girl, that man treated you like a pile of cat litter leftovers back in school, and you agreed to go out with him anyway? What were you thinking?"

Her eyes went cold and hot at the same time. "What? Miss Michelin Star never gets lonely? Chad may have been a dumpster fire, but that was years ago, and some of us have learned how to"—she pointed her finger in the middle of Ella's chest—"let. Stuff. Go."

Ella was unfazed. "Oh, please, I leave the forgiveness business to my priest and the parole boards."

"She's right, Cor. He was a narcissistic hot mess back in school, and he was until the day he died," Senya spat. "Didn't I tell you how I bumped into him right before he got killed?" She glanced over at the two cousins. "Ask those two! They were witnesses."

"It's true," Quinn answered. Daria was tempted to inform Corri that Chad had been making moves on her and her cousin moments before he was murdered, but she didn't have it in her to defame the dead.

"Okay, fine. He used to be a jerk, may he rest in peace." Corri crossed herself. "But Aiden, I swear I had nothing to do with it. Ask Sister Theresa. She knows all about it. If I'd murdered him, she—or Daria—would've come to you. I'm sure they tell each other everything."

"It's an abbey, Corri, not a sorority house," Daria reminded her. "And for the record, Sister Theresa never said a word to me. She kept your confidence."

Blanche interrupted. "Hey, I've got a chili dog and fries."

"That's me." Aiden reached for his plate. Before eating a bite, he grabbed a handful of fries and placed them on a smaller dish already on the table and slid it over to Quinn.

"Oh, you don't need to do that," she insisted. "These are yours."

He grabbed the ketchup, opened the top, and pounded on the back of the glass bottle, making the perfect pour. "I know we're still new, but let's not tell ourselves lies. It's only a matter of time before you'd be giving me that look. This here saves us the trouble."

Quinn pretended to glare. "Well, maybe this time I'm not hungry. That scene earlier today was enough to curb anyone's appetite."

Senya's sharp ears and mind didn't miss a thing. "Why, what happened earlier?"

Neither Daria nor Quinn knew what to say. Quinn reached over and swiped a fry from Aiden. "What? It tastes better off of your plate."

His body shook with silent laughter.

As much as they tried for the redirect, Senya wasn't letting the topic go. "What, is it bad? Is everyone okay?"

"Everything's fine," Quinn answered. "Just a family matter."

Daria said an extra thank-you prayer that her cousin wasn't sharing anymore. She'd been known in the past to spill the tea—not because she was a gossip but because she was just so open, without realizing that others might have an agenda. Daria hadn't even given herself enough time or the headspace to fully process what had happened earlier that evening.

Aiden refocused on Corri. "I'd like for you to come in to the station tomorrow and give a statement."

She looked flustered. "But I don't know anything!"

Aiden's expression gentled. "I understand, but you may know more than you realize."

"That's true," Senya added. "Listen, I'll go with you, if you want—as your friend *and* your lawyer."

Corri balked. "Why would I need a lawyer? I said I didn't *do* anything!"

Aiden sunk his teeth into the hot dog, emitting a happy murmur from his throat as he swallowed, followed by a barely audible sigh, like he had all the time in the world to enjoy his meal. Daria wondered if he really was as relaxed as he appeared or if he was just playing it that way to lure Corri in to coming in on her own. It was always difficult to tell with him, because Aiden was not an easy read. Except when he looked at Quinn. Even a blind man would be able to tell he was in deep with her.

For some reason, acknowledging that truth on a conscious level stung more than it should, especially for a woman two years into being a novitiate and preparing to make her final vows in less than a year. She was happy for Quinn. She knew down to the mushy pulp of her bones that she and Aiden were going to marry someday. Have children.

She took another big swallow of wine.

Just then, as the rest of the adult soccer team was leaving, Holly said her good-byes and then walked over to their tables. "Hi, guys! So nice to see you."

Everyone said hello. Corri stared at her ponytail. "You know you've got a branch sticking out of your hair."

Holly shrugged and laughed. "I'm going for a new look. Whadday'all think?"

That earned her a group chuckle.

"Want me to get it out of there for you?" Corri asked.

Holly waved her off. "Nah, I'll have a shower when I get home." She smiled at Quinn and Daria. "Listen, I just wanted to come over and congratulate the Caine crew on their happy news."

Quinn drew a blank for a second.

Daria piped up, "Wow, news travels fast. We just learned of it ourselves tonight. How did you hear?"

Jenny's head cocked to the side. "What are y'all talking about?"

Ella got up from her seat, credit card out. "I saw that too. Bash and Rachel got engaged. Rachel's family posted an unofficial announcement on Facebook."

Just then, a recording of the Star-Spangled Banner started to play. Everyone groaned before the bartender called out. "You know what the song means! You don't have to go home . . ."

"But you can't stay here!"

Seemed everyone knew the drill.

Hearing the national anthem at the end of the night was a Vienna Inn tradition, borrowed from a time when televisions had only a few network channels, all playing the anthem to let viewers know programming was done for the night.

"Dingdong, another bachelor's off the market," Corri grumbled. "This night stinks."

Even with Jenny having dumped a bunch of beer bottles earlier in the evening, there were still plenty of empties left. Holly's eyes surveyed the table. "Ladies, why don't I drive you home? And before you argue with me, it's my pleasure to do it."

All the women at the table shared a look before agreeing to go with her.

Aiden stood up with them. "Mrs. Berry, why don't I walk with you to your car?"

Jenny hiccupped. "See? Such a clone-worthy guy!"

Holly smiled. "That'd be great, Aiden. Thanks."

"Let me just take care of the bill."

Ella was back, stuffing her credit card and receipt back in her wallet. "Already done! Don't argue with me, Detective. It's no big deal."

Aiden might be a modern, liberated guy in a lot of ways, but Daria didn't need to date him to know he wasn't the type of man who was comfortable with anyone footing his bill.

"Can't have you paying for me, Ella."

Before she could argue, Aiden made a beeline over to the bar to pay their part of the bill.

She threw her hands up. "Why is he making such a big deal? It was a few drinks and a dog."

"He can't because you're a person of interest in the Frivole case. Doesn't look good, you paying for anything for him." Senya grimaced. "I let my guard down. That won't happen again. C'mon, girl, we're not waiting for him to walk us to the car."

Holly gave Quinn a quick hug. "Please give my best to your brother and Rachel?"

"Of course. Drive safe."

By the time Aiden had straightened out the bar bill and returned, Ella's group had left with Holly. The cousins and Aiden made their way outside toward their own car.

"Do you really think any of them had anything to do with Chad's murder?" Daria asked.

Aiden waited until the SUV was down Maple Avenue, way out of earshot. Hands on his hips, he fixed his gaze on the vehicle as it drove away. "It's never good for a cop to speculate on a case with civilians." He met her and Quinn's stares. "Even with those who are like family. Sorry, Daria, I know that's not what you want to hear."

She let out a sigh. "No, I get it. I don't like it, but I get it."

Something was working behind Quinn's gaze. "Either one of them murdered Chad and the others are covering for her, or they're all in it together. Except for Jenny, that is."

Daria chuckled. "Yeah, she wants to clone men, not kill them."

"Or maybe someone's been threatening Chad for a while."

Daria was on the same train of thought. "Enough for him to want to get out of New York for a while. Setting up Vienna's own Mean Girls would offer the perfect cover."

Chapter Nine

Some Cupid kills with arrows, some with traps.
—Shakespeare's *Much Ado About Nothing*

"Say what you will, but I'll take canines over little children any day."

Leave it to Sister Theresa to start a conversation in the middle: no explanation, no lead-in. Considering they had just finished a visit to Cunningham Elementary School armed with emotional support dogs, Daria knew she was referring to the pup-and-progeny meet-and-greet.

"As opposed to big children?" Daria teased.

Sister Theresa scoffed. "You mean teenagers? They're fine. At least they speak their minds and can smell people's bull poop from twenty paces."

Daria hoisted two mammoth-sized bags of dog food in each arm. Moments like these made her recall all the time she used to spend at the gym; meanwhile, her dog care regimen had her in the best shape of her life. She could've saved a ton of money in her youth by just hauling around big bags of puppy chow.

"I would think being an only child would've made you want lots of kids." Daria was speaking from experience, since she too was an only and used to dream of having at least four children.

As soon as they turned the corner into the kennel, the dogs went crazy, which was to be expected, because once those keen canines spotted the bags, they knew it was grub time.

Not much else was as loud as packs of dogs, especially when they were hungry. Daria threw down the bags, then took out her knife and cut into them before pouring out their contents into the awaiting bowls. She double-checked to make sure there was enough water too, although usually that was taken care of by whichever sisters had been assigned the early-morning shift, which entailed getting the dogs hydrated, letting them out, and scooping up the yard.

Sister Theresa wiped her forehead with the back of her sleeve. "I've always preferred the company of animals. My parents were the same. Maybe that's why we had eight times as many animals around than people. I don't think I saw another child until I was seven, when my mother's sister came to visit."

"Seven? I can't even imagine."

She chuckled. "She came to us—eight months pregnant, mind you—with her husband and five children."

Daria made a noise, clutching just below her navel. "Ugh. Hurts just thinking about it."

"I'll tell you something." Sister Theresa knelt to pet the dogs. "Watching my poor aunt juggling the diapers and feedings while my uncle kicked his feet up to watch the game—while yelling at her for not keeping the noise down—I swore I'd never marry or have kids."

Daria heard similar stories from older nuns all the time. They had grown up in households where they were supposed to get married and start breeding as soon as possible. Monastic life offered a respectable alternative, marrying Jesus instead of just another Joe. It made Daria wonder how many of them had truly felt called to this life and how many were just using the church as an escape hatch.

Was that what she was doing? It was a question the Reverend Mother posed every so often, and God forgive her, it would make her angry every time.

Daria could hear her mom's "When it stings, it rings true, gumdrop." Hadn't Daria used to say the same thing, back when she counseled in an office and her clients were human?

Ruff!

Daria glanced down: it was Rueger, her dog brother from another mother. She squatted to eye level and proceeded to scratch the folds of his neck. "Well, good morning to you too, buddy. Have a good lunch?"

He emitted an indecipherable sound between a groan and a moan as she continued scratching. Rueger and Daria were a lot alike in that they both didn't really want to deal with people until after their sustenance. Of course, Daria was responsible for scratching herself.

Sister Teresa offered a Cheshire cat grin. "Don't mean to interrupt you two, but we better get going."

Daria gave one last kiss to her boy. "Go on and play. I'll see you for supper."

He licked her nose before trotting off with the other dogs. Of course, Rueger didn't play as much as he surveyed and supervised. Daria watched as he patrolled the perimeter, keeping watch on his charges. They were mostly German shepherds, but there were also a few large-breed rescues in the mix. He was half German shepherd, half Rottweiler, his mamma having gotten knocked up by a wandering looker. No one could have predicted he'd grow into the alpha dog of Saint Guinefort's.

It had only been Daria's third day at the abbey when she was asked to assist in the birth. With a gentle hand, she had caressed the laboring dam throughout the night, her uneven breathing pushing her ribs against her skin. The dam delivered two, four, six pups. They thought she was done, but then the mamma howled and number seven slid out, his tiny, black-and-tan body slick with afterbirth. With eyes sealed shut, he wiggled back and forth while letting out a yawn almost as big as his body. Back then, he fit right in Daria's palm, her fingers able to curl over his furry little head.

The others had wanted to name him Lucky, but since he was the runt of the litter, Daria had insisted the boy needed a name with gravitas—"A name to build confidence!" she explained to the other sisters. Once he weaned, Daria sneaked Rueger liverwurst treats, a way to get some extra nutrition in him. Anything to encourage a growth spurt.

Daria would share Rueger's progress with the sisters over meals, not missing how they exchanged glances. "Don't get attached," they warned. Daria pooh-poohed their concerns, informing them she'd grown up with cats and chickens since she was old enough to walk. Sure, he was adorable gruffness on four paws, headbutting his way through his siblings to get to the food and human attention, but there were a lot of puppies coming and going through Guinefort House.

At least, that's what she kept telling herself.

She used to marvel at all the ways her people-y clients used to lie to themselves to avoid whatever truth they were running from, which made the irony that much richer when she exhibited the same tendencies herself.

Eight weeks later, Rueger had—somehow—broken out of his pen. The nuns stopped everything in a frantic search—through the kennel, all around the fence line, the woods bordering their property. Daria had never been so frightened. She hiked up her robes and traversed the creek behind the property. Shoes soaked. The water weighing her down as her heart sped up.

After no results, the sisters decided to stop at the house for bathroom breaks before heading into town. Sister Daria had gotten so worked up, she needed a minute to collect herself. She hauled her body like a bag of bricks up the stairs to her room—only to discover a lump under the covers of her bed, squirming and chewing on the end of her blanket. It was Rueger, who, with a head tilt and a happy bark, seemed to be asking her, *Where ya been?*

That was it. Daria was a goner.

The feeling was mutual, even if Rueger hadn't needed to endure the same emotional gymnastics as she. But that was one of the many beauties of dogs: they were infinitely patient when it came to the slowness and shortcomings of their human charges.

As Daria approached the chapel, a warm, comforting glow flowered open in the middle of her sternum. It was her God spot, the place where she felt—rather than heard—His voice. It was the only part of her corporal being she still trusted, for her heart was susceptible to lies and told her only what she wanted to hear, and her brain had become a skeptical, jaded grouch, as if she'd been broken up with a hundred times instead of just once. Maybe once was all she could take.

But her soul was still whole, thanks to Him. Praying Matins, Lauds, Prime, Terce, Sext, None, Vespers, and Compline through the day and evening gave her more than structure: being called to prayer granted her peace. Not a single note was ever bellowed in the proper key, which was why some of her sisters had resorted to wearing at least one spongy plug in their ears. Sister Daria didn't care. She reveled in the spirit of the hour, a respite for every living part of her.

The Reverend Mother closed her prayer book. "Children, before you return to your duties, we have a few pressing matters.

"I received a call from a young woman with a rather large dog food donation for us. Usually she'd leave it on the curb for pickup, but considering she says there are fifty bags, she thought it best to give us a call to coordinate the delivery."

Sister Ceci piped in. "We'll need Quinn Caine's truck."

"I've already called her. Sister Daria? Your cousin will be here any minute. Do you mind helping her today?"

"Of course not, Rev Mo. Happy to help."

The others tittered, getting a kick out of the Reverend Mother's nickname. Judging by the abbess's sliver of a smile, Daria surmised she didn't mind.

Daria hadn't fibbed when she said she was happy to be of assistance, because fifty bags, depending on their size, could feed their dogs for months. If her emotional support animal certification program took off the way she hoped, that would mean their Order could build an extra kennel and storage structure on their land. She emitted a happy sigh.

The horn honked. She'd know the sound of Quinn's gold Ford F-150 truck anywhere.

"Guess that's my cue."

Daria double-checked her pockets under her tunic, feeling Sister Theresa's gaze boring into the top of her head.

She glanced up. "What?"

"If you're going to be loading supplies like a donkey, best to leave your tunic and wimple here—asking for heatstroke otherwise."

"Careful, or I might start to think you love me or something."

Sister Theresa snorted. "Don't get mushy, girl. If you pass out, that's time off our schedule tending to a hot flower."

Daria knew better: Sister Theresa cared about her. They all did. She peeled off the extra layers.

Sister Ceci thrust both arms forward. "Gimme! I'll bring them to our room."

Daria handed them over. "Thanks."

As soon as Sister Daria walked out of the chapel, the humidity hit her square in the face. The early-morning chill had burnt off, and although it was already late September, their small section of the mid-Atlantic region hadn't yet gotten the fall memo. In fact, the only autumnal color to be found was Quinn's truck, painted a particularly glaring shade of gold—which she had named Golda because she appreciated both literal and metaphorical titles.

Daria was about to open the passenger door when a familiar howl sounded and a furry black blur barreled across the yard. He might have been a big boy, weighing in at 140 pounds, but Rueger was light on his feet when it came to something he wanted.

And what he wanted was to ride side by side with his best girl, RBG.

He had a heck of a running start, so he was able to leap right into the back, skidding to a halt against the inside panel. Even though RBG was wearing a safety harness, she managed to reach over and lick the side of his face as a reward.

Quinn rolled down her window. "Well, well . . . who knew dogs could fly!"

Daria lifted herself on her toes to peek inside the truck. "Is there going to be enough room for fifty bags plus these two?"

"Probably not." Quinn put the truck in park, removed an extra harness from her glove box, and got out. "But who cares? We'll make multiple trips."

"Cool." Daria hopped into the cab of the truck while Quinn managed to finagle Rueger into the safety harness. Her cousin hopped back in and drove down Vale Road.

"Fancy seeing you so soon."

Daria checked on the dogs through the cab window. They were in their own little world. "I know. So who's the big donor?"

Quinn's two front teeth sank into her bottom lip. "You'll never guess. I'll give you three tries."

"Seriously?" Daria pretended to knock her head against the window. "You know I loathe guessing with the heat of a thousand suns. Just tell me."

Quinn turned on her blinker, rolling to a stop. "Okay, fine, it's Ella Diaz. We're going to meet her at her new restaurant."

Now Daria was confused. "Why would Ella Diaz have fifty bags of dog food, especially at her restaurant?"

"I know, weird, right? She'd been a VIP guest at some charity auction last year"—Quinn paused to turn onto Lawyers Road— "and between the noise and forgetting to wear her contacts, she ended up being the winning bid for a lifetime supply of dog food."

"Oh, come on now."

Quinn turned left onto Church Street. "She thought they were auctioning off a lifetime supply of Rachael Ray's new dishes but ended up with Rachael Ray's Nutrish. Guess she has her own dog food brand. Who knew?"

Daria tittered. "Huh. I stand corrected."

"I'm thinking, with this new bounty, I may need to direct future curbside donations to some other rescues. Supposedly, Ella's going to be getting fifty bags every year for the rest of her life."

They drove by Prose & Scones, and Daria noticed her cousin didn't bother slowing down. She didn't even glimpse in the shop's direction.

"When was the last time you went to work?"

Quinn slowed for some pedestrians to cross, keeping her eyes glued straight ahead. "I work every day. I just happen to be working from home right now. I didn't want to get behind on orders."

"I meant when was the last time you spoke to your parents?"

Quinn tightened her grip on the steering wheel. "I'll talk to them when they make things right with Bash and Rach." Quinn's phone beeped. "Do me a favor and see who that is?"

Daria picked up the phone from the console. "Let me guess, same password?"

Quinn made a face. "Actually, no. Aiden got on me about that the other day—"

"He's right."

Quinn rolled her eyes. "Whatever. Anyway, so now it's the same password, but add 571."

Using the cell phone's area code wasn't much of a stretch, securitywise, but no way was Daria going to irk Quinn further. She entered the code.

"Wow, this is a coincidence. It's Bash. He says he hasn't heard from your folks yet, but he heard around town that they've been seeking counseling—therapy, not pastoral."

Quinn let out a relieved sigh. "Well, that's a good start. They've got a long way to go, though, that's for sure."

"And I thought I was the only one to hold a grudge in the family." Daria glanced over. "Hey, you all right?"

Quinn kept her eyes on the road. "This debacle with my parents has really thrown me off."

Daria rested her hand on her forearm. "Well, of course it has."

"But that's not the only thing," her cousin went on. "There's you too."

She took her hand back. "Me?"

Quinn nodded. "It's like you have this image of yourself as this hard-as-nails woman—and I'm not saying you're not a badass, because you are—but what's the harm in acknowledging your softer side? I mean, you're the one in social work, so I'd think you'd know by now that being vulnerable is a strength, not a weakness."

Speaking of *When it stings, it rings true*? Well, Daria had apparently just dived headfirst into a metaphorical pool of jellyfish.

"I love you," Quinn reminded Daria.

"Me too. And I know you're right."

Quinn reached over and squeezed her hand.

They were now at the other end of Church Street, which was still part of Vienna, but not the charming or historic section. Quinn hit the blinker before turning right into the parking lot of an underwhelming strip mall. The zigzag-shaped building was stucco, painted the color of mud, with signage straight off a seventies font board. Daria couldn't even remember the last time she had visited this area of town. Not that it was run-down or blighted. There were businesses here: a well-appointed consignment shop for children's clothing, a place to buy and sell rare coins and collectibles, and Big Planet Comics, which was the place to go if you were a DC Comics fan. For reasons Daria didn't know or hadn't ever really thought about, the east section of Vienna was well maintained but hadn't received the extra PR attention of the northwest part of town.

Until now.

After parking the truck and releasing the dogs from their harnesses, Quinn and Sister Daria were able to take in the near completion of a new neighborhood gem, even if it was still covered in dust.

"Welcome to Clarity!"

There was Ella Diaz walking toward them, her hair swept up in a perfectly imperfect messy bun with a smile gleaming bright enough for a toothpaste ad. Even in simple leggings, steel-toed boots, and a tank top, the woman was a stunner.

Daria waved. "Hi, Clarity. I'm Cranky, and this here's Credulous."

Quinn play-smacked her arm. "This place is looking great."

Ella glanced behind her, as if she needed to double-check the restaurant's progress for herself. "It's coming along, although it might kill me in the process. You're here to pick up the dog food?"

Daria grinned. "Yep. You have no idea how helpful this donation is for our Order. Big dogs equal big appetites."

Ella eyed Golda. "Quinn, you're going to have to pull your truck around back. I have the donations on pallets there."

"Oh, okay." Quinn signaled RBG to follow—which meant Rueger also tagged along for the short ride.

Daria shielded her eyes from the sun. "Mind if I use your bathroom?"

"Sure thing, jelly bean." Ella motioned her toward the restaurant.

Daria followed her across the parking lot. "How'd you pick your restaurant name, by the way?"

"Well, when I was trying to choose what kind of cuisine I was going to feature for this next place, I started to feel boxed in, ya know? Like why should I have to narrow all my culinary experiences down to a singular choice?"

Try living a vow of poverty with six other nuns. Talk about limiting one's choices, Daria thought.

"Anyway, I was getting myself all worked up"—Ella opened the door for Daria—"until it hit me: 'Ella? Since when have you ever followed the rules? No reason to start now.' So forget picking just one region or flavor profile. I'm going to cook what I want, when I want. It was a real moment of clarity . . . hence the name."

Daria's eyes adjusted to being inside, taking in all the changes. "Whoa, this place . . . you got rid of the dirt-colored stucco and popcorn ceilings."

Ella's chest swelled with pride. "Isn't it looking great? Been a real pain in the ass, but I want it the way I want it."

"I'll never get how popcorn ceilings were ever a thing." Daria craned her head back. "I mean, who thought walls the texture of goose-bumpy chicken skin was a compelling aesthetic?"

A deep voice came from behind them. "Well, your arrival automatically improves the aesthetic all on its own. Ella, introduce me to your beautiful friend."

Daria turned around, not really expecting anything, which was why catching sight of him was especially unanticipated: a man tan and tall with black, silken hair in a temple cut like the Vikings used to wear—shaved on both sides of the head with the middle and back of the crown grown long and braided at the nape. He had eyes like a wolf, piercing amber set on her, with a glint of mischief and something else unexpected: warmth.

Something in her stomach flipped, and everyone grew quiet. Could they hear her heart beating outside her chest?

Ella must have sensed the rising tension. "Don't mind my brother. He looks like a marauder off a pirate ship, but I swear, he was raised with manners. He was just dropped on his head many times as a child. Makes him say whatever thought comes to mind, like a gumball machine."

"Don't mind her; she's just jealous because our mother loves me more." He held out his hand. "Hi, I'm Lucas."

Ella rolled her eyes.

Daria placed her hand in his, a zap of electricity startling them. She pulled it back.

"Whoa. Uh, hi. I'm Eliza . . . uh, I mean, Daria. Sister Daria."

His smile faded. "Wait, you're a nun?"

For the first time in years, her heart sank. "Yeah, well, sort of. I take my final vows in about a year. But it's not official yet."

I'm babbling. Why am I babbling? And why are my hands sweating?

I need to get out of here.

"Uh, where's the bathroom?"

"Oh, sure." Ella pointed to the back of the restaurant. "Go straight down. Make a right. It'll be the first door on the left."

"Thanks." Daria kept her focus on the other side of the restaurant, willing herself not to give Lucas another glance, because no way did she need to deal with all that sexy funny charm in such a tall drink of water.

She opened the bathroom door, turned on the light, and twisted the lock on. There was a bare toilet on an unfinished concrete floor. A small pedestal sink was perched under a cracked mirror. Guess Ella hadn't gotten around to renovating this part of the restaurant yet. Daria did her business, then washed her hands, leaving them under the cold water before splashing her face.

"Sweet Jesus, what is the matter with me?" Her reflection didn't answer. "Daria? Remember, he's just a guy. A gorgeous one, but just a guy."

The Reverend Mother's voice played back in her mind: "Remember, my dear girl, the Devil is clever. He doesn't pop into your life wearing horns and a tail. He will test you where you're weakest—and he'll be charming beyond measure while doing it."

She let out a sigh of relief. *That's all Lucas Diaz is—a temptation from the Devil himself. A test of my sincerity and veracity of purpose.* Frankly, Daria was embarrassed for herself. She wasn't some schoolgirl still mooning over Team Jacob from Twilight. She was a grown woman who was devoting her life in the service of God, not to be enslaved by endorphin rushes in the shape of a modern-day Latin Viking king. She dried her hands on her jeans, since there weren't any paper towels around. She chose to ignore the phantom press of his warm palm in hers.

Quinn must have lost patience, because she leaned on her horn, but she ended it with a friendlier "Shave and a Haircut" rhythm. Daria heard Ella's hurried footsteps go by, followed by Lucas's sauntering ones. She was just about to join them when she noticed the sound of hissing and rattling.

Was it the fluorescents?

She gazed up, and while the lights pulsed, she didn't think it was the same sound. Daria turned off the light, just in case, standing still in the dark. Listening.

Another honk of Quinn's horn. She was probably annoyed Daria wasn't helping. But Daria couldn't deal with that yet, because the hissing was loud—and it sounded like it was coming from the other side of the wall.

Sister Daria exited the bathroom, glancing down the hall, which led to a closed door. There was a warm, white glow peeking from behind the door reading *Staff Only*. Quickly, Daria got to the door and, wrapping her shirt around her hand, tried opening it.

The knob twisted, but the door wouldn't budge. Even worse, when she jiggled the handle, the hissing kicked up a notch.

"This is ridiculous," she muttered, taking out her phone and pocketknife. She slid the screen and pushed for the flashlight mode. Then, perching the phone between her chin and upper chest, she directed the light into the lock. It was too small and thin for her knife alone, so she reached for one of the bobby pins in her hair and slid it into place.

"Like butter," she whispered.

"Ah, the zipping method—a favorite of lock pickers for years. Good call."

The sound of Lucas's voice startled her, making her drop the phone and her knife.

"What are you doing here?"

He walked over. "I think that's my question, not yours."

"Jesus, I didn't even hear you."

He was standing over her now. "Jesus is many things, but I think being your wingman in a break-in isn't one of them."

She retrieved her knife and phone. "I just needed to see what was making all that noise."

"Are you sure you're a nun? Because you're not like any sister of the cloth I've ever met."

Dude, you have no idea. "Why aren't you more upset you found me picking your sister's lock?"

He brushed past her and, without needing a light, felt around the lock and retrieved her bobby pin. "Here, you forgot this."

But instead of handing it over, he pried its metal arms open and, with a feather-light touch against her forehead, scooped her hair out of her eyes and slid it in place.

"You didn't answer my question."

"I'm not upset because we're not open yet, so if you were trying to rob the place, you'd be the worst thief ever, because there's no cash."

She scrunched her face. "Oh, please, even at my most delinquent, I never stole anything. Well, outside my own family, that is. And I was more *borrowing* the car than *stealing* it."

"I bet that's a story. I'll have to hear it another time." He was trying not to laugh. "And to finish answering your question, you're Bash Caine's cousin, which means you're your own unique flavor of interesting, but definitely no thief." He wiggled the handle while giving it a good push. The door opened right away.

"It wasn't locked, *tentadora*. It just sticks."

She ignored his use of the Spanish word for temptress and walked right in.

And lined up against the wall, with white heat lamps, were three terrariums of rattlesnakes.

Sister Daria crossed herself. "Jesus, Mary, and Joseph, Ella Diaz keeps *snakes?*"

"What's going on? What are you doing in here?"

· It was Ella, with Quinn peeking over her shoulder—and coming down the hall were Jenny, Corri, and Senya. What were they doing here?

"I heard the hissing and rattling and other echoes of death while in the bathroom!" Daria explained. "Maybe you can enlighten everyone as to why you're keeping *live snakes* in a restaurant?"

Lucas was flummoxed. "It means they're fresh. How else is my sister supposed to offer authentic snake tacos on her menu?"

"Exactly!" Ella huffed.

"Snake tacos?" Quinn paled. "Is that a thing?"

"Yes, that's a *thing*," Ella groused. "It's a traditional recipe, from Santiago de Anaya." She read the blank expressions on most everyone's faces. "For the Muestra Gastronómica? It's an annual food festival in Mexico. Don't even think of accusing me of cultural appropriation, by the way. We are one-quarter Otomí—our maternal grandmother was born in the hills of the Valle del Mezquital.

"Now that I've answered your question—which I did *not* have to do—explain to me what you're doing back here? Even if you heard them, that was still none of your business."

Quinn cleared her throat. "Do you not understand how beyond awful the optics are right now?"

"What . . . because of Chad? Oh, please. If I was the killer, it would've been really, really dumb to keep these snake babies out in plain sight."

Ella's friends gave each other a quick glance. "I'm guessing this means you can't sneak out for a quick lunch, Ells?"

She swerved around. "Sorry, Corri, but I'm too busy being accused of murder!"

Lucas's soft smile was gone. "My sister had nothing to do with Chad's death, bad optics or not."

Senya cut in. "Oh, so I see how it is: automatically the brown girl did it? For your information, indigenous cuisine from the Americas uses rattlesnake, jicama, ant larvae, corn smut—"

Quinn's eyes rounded. "Corn smut?"

"It's called huitlacoche, and it's an edible fungus. Quite delicious, actually." Lucas turned to Senya. "I appreciate you defending my sister, but aren't your parents from former Yugoslavia?"

Senya's eyes narrowed. "Hey, I'm on *your* side, remember?"

Quinn took out her phone. "Listen, everyone, the best way to clear all this up is to call the police."

Ella was having none of it. "No way; I'm already behind schedule. They're going to shut me down before I even open!"

"No, go ahead—call the police," Senya insisted. "I'm Ella's lawyer, and I cannot *wait* to file the biggest discrimination lawsuit in the history of Fairfax County. Oooh! How's *this* for a sound bite: 'America's Fave Town Hates Brown. Loses Millions.'"

Chapter Ten

Weaving spiders, come not here;
Hence, you long legged spinners, hence!
Beetles black, approach not here;
Worm nor snail, do no offense.
—Shakespeare's *A Midsummer Night's Dream*

"Once again, Detective Harrington, I don't care one flappity flip about the 'optics.'" Senya was only a few feet away, and yet she was still loud. "Everyone here knows Ella Diaz did not murder Chad Frivole with rattlesnakes."

Before Quinn had had a chance to fish her phone out of her back pocket, Ella had already called the cops herself, and in less than ten minutes, it seemed half the Vienna Police Department was now in her restaurant.

Tapping her Manolo stiletto toe, Senya was already cooking up a conniption as the investigative team walked through the double doors. "Oh, sure, come on down and waste taxpayers' money searching my client's place of business. Knock yourselves out."

A Midsummer Night's Scheme

To say Senya Petrova had a flair for drama was a major undersell. Captain of her high school debate team, she'd developed a reputation for being able to argue with anyone, about anything. People who knew her were relieved she used that mouth and brain for the greater good; she'd gone to law school and had earned the highest conviction rate as a county prosecutor. Everyone had thought a run for public office was the next, natural step, but she'd surprised friends and neighbors when she hung her own shingle instead—as a criminal defense attorney—before the age of thirty. Being parked right outside Washington, DC, meant she had plenty of business.

Of course, Aiden had arrived with his team—all business and none too pleased his girlfriend was, again, somehow at a potential crime scene. To his credit, despite the cheek tic at the sight of her, he kept it professional. "I'm going to need you all to exit the viper room so my team can investigate."

"Of course, let's move it," Ella ordered. "The sooner we get this done, the quicker I can get the crew back to work."

Meanwhile, Officers Shae Johnson and Ned Carter pulled them all aside, one by one, for the interview portion of the impromptu program.

Corri gave one last glance at the reptiles, making an *ick* face. "Uh, no. Couldn't pay me to touch them."

Ella snickered. "And you wonder why you never get a second date."

Quinn covered her mouth, a feeble attempt to not laugh.

"Stop that! This is serious." Senya hit the record button on her phone, pointing it toward the officers. "I'll save you all the trouble: Ella has nothing to hide, and neither do I. Interview over."

"Noted." Officer Carter scribbled in his pad. "Of course, that means Miss Diaz will be the only one here deemed uncooperative."

Jenny chewed on the edge of her thumb. "Quinn, please tell me Aiden isn't going to assume Ella did anything wrong?"

"He's a professional," Quinn promised. "He's always telling me to let the evidence unfold and have it speak for itself."

Senya's temper was contagious, because now Ella was riled up. "I've told you, the snakes are going to be taco meat. I value them too much to use them as assassins."

Shae Johnson signaled a member of the team. "Cool, cool . . . so you won't mind having our criminalists fingerprint you. All of you?"

Jenny nodded. "Absolutely. Go ahead."

"Uh, absolutely *not*," Senya ordered. "Not unless Shae and her crew have a court order."

"But we have nothing to hide!" Jenny insisted.

"It sets a bad precedent, handing yourself over as evidence for just showing up somewhere for lunch. Speaking of which, I'm starving."

Jenny glanced at her phone, and her face paled. "I have to get back to school. My class starts in ten minutes! I'm barely going to make it if I leave now."

"Well, if you let us fingerprint you, we can send you on your way," Officer Johnson told her.

Senya stepped forward, shaking her head back and forth. "No, no, no, no. That is unacceptable."

Jenny now had tears in her eyes. "I don't want to miss class. It looks so unprofessional."

"I have to get back to the hospital too," Corri informed them, noticing her friend's obvious stink eye. "You're one of my best friends, Senya, but I'm not going to feel bad for needing to get back to work. I don't have the time—nor your income—to stand on principles." She thrust her hands forward. "Go ahead, take my fingerprints so I can get out of here."

"Me too!" Jenny mimicked.

Senya threw her hands up. "You are free to leave *now*. They can't hold you, you know."

"So I should wait until they get a warrant and show up at my school? Those kids look up to me! No way; that can't happen. Let's get this done now."

Aiden signaled for one of the criminalists to come over. "Bring your kit, Prue. We'll see if their prints match the ones we found on Chad's car."

Senya rummaged through her purse. "I see you're not refuting their fears, Detective. That's not going to look good in court." She started dictating into her phone. "It's twelve oh three PM on September seventeenth. Note that Detective Aiden Harrington of the Vienna Police is holding my client, Ella Diaz, and innocent bystanders, Corri Rypka and Jenny Kieval, for questioning and to provide fingerprints for possible links to the murder of Chad Frivole."

If the spitfire counsel was getting under Aiden's skin, he didn't let on. He wet his pen on the tip of his tongue before jotting down another note. "You do realize they can leave as soon as we secure the scene. That's standard police procedure, Senya."

"Guilt or innocence, the optics are bad. Really, really bad."

"The same can be said for your client. Like it or not, Ella has a roomful of rattlesnakes in her new restaurant. She also comes from a family of car enthusiasts. She grew up in Frankie's Garage, formerly run by her father and uncle and now owned by her brother. Bet she'd know how to rig a locking mechanism on car doors, and if not, he would."

Lucas muttered something in Spanish under his breath before asking, "Am I being accused of something?"

Prue secured the latch on her kit. She had taken everyone's prints via a portable scanner, no ink required. "All done, Detective."

The criminalists were still going at it. "We're waiting for the herpetologist to arrive."

Aiden turned his attention back to the rest of the awaiting potential suspects. "You are all free to go, but if you could stay for just another few minutes, I'll have my officers escort you back to your school and hospital themselves. No red lights getting in your way."

Corri shrugged. "I'm good to wait. I just texted my supervisor and told her what's up. She'll be fine."

Jenny, who was normally a tad high-strung, was now almost apoplectic. "Well, *some* of us aren't buddy-buddy with our bosses, because that would be way weird for me. I guess I could call Ash and let her know what's going on, have her explain. Although I don't know how I'm supposed to explain how I went out for lunch and am running late because of a murder investigation that has nothing to do with either me or my friends!"

Her crew took Jenny's reaction in stride. "Wait a second. I know all your friends," Ella asserted. "Who's Ash?"

"I meant Ashley Anderson, the guidance counselor. She's awesome, but you, Detective Harrington?" she fumed. "Not so cloneworthy anymore."

From his expression, it was obvious Aiden wasn't going to touch that one. "We'll be done in a few minutes. Then we'll get you back. Ella? I would like you to come in for questioning. Obviously, Senya should accompany as your attorney."

Senya glanced through her schedule. "Let me have a little time to confer with my client."

Ella's breath was uneven, like she couldn't get the air fully into her lungs. "This can't be real."

Lucas enveloped her in a hug. *"No has hecho nada malo. Está bien."*

She nodded into his chest. "I'm going to have to delay the opening."

He shushed her as he kissed the top of her head, rubbing up and down her back. "Bet you my Triumph you'll get a crap ton of publicity and be booked solid for the rest of the year."

Daria chimed in. "Maybe consider taking snake tacos off the menu? Just saying, it might be too soon."

Quinn was relieved her cousin said something, so she didn't have to. It took big brass ones to still want to serve a cause of death as a grand opening special.

Either Ella was the most authentic person alive, dedicated to doing things her way no matter how it looked, or she was a brazen psychopath, salivating over the chance to serve her accomplices on a plate.

Aiden's phone rang. He glanced at the number on the phone, his brows going up. "Harrington," he answered. He stepped away from the group.

Ella glared. "For your information, I've had these snakes for months—way before someone decided to use a bunch of vipers as deadly weapons. I need them for their meat, not their venom."

Quinn could tell by the look on Daria's face that she wasn't buying it.

"Who else knew about them? That you were raising rattlers for their meat?"

Ella's body jerked. "I don't know. The construction crew, for sure. That's why I kept them in the back room. Not that they needed any reminding. Trust me, they stayed far away."

"Maybe they did, but what about others?" Daria pointed toward the door. "You have no warning sign, and yeah, the door sticks, but it wasn't locked. Anyone could've gotten in there."

"Exactly. When was the last time you counted them?" Quinn asked. "Have they had any babies? If so, have they all been accounted for?"

Awareness swept through Lucas's expression. "You're wondering if someone else snagged some, knowing my sister had them readily available." He squeezed his sister's shoulder. "Someone may be trying to set you up."

Ella shook her head. "No one's taken any of my snakes, although several died in transit to me. But since then—nothing."

Well, there goes that theory, Quinn thought. "Did the ones who survived hatch any new babies?"

"They're called snakelets," Jenny corrected. "Rhymes with bracelets." She clocked everyone's expression. "What? I used to volunteer at the National Zoo. I led their Lifecycles of the Smooth and Scaly program for years. Such fun!"

Aiden came back to the huddle, his eyes locked on Quinn. "You won't believe who that was . . ."

He didn't give her a chance to ask.

"That was your brother. First thing, he and Rachel are fine. Apparently, someone broke into their new apartment."

Quinn pressed a hand to her stomach. "What the heck happened?"

"Nothing taken, but they found poisonous spiders in their bed. We're talking brown recluses, black widows . . . who knows what else. Dozens of them."

"Well, can't blame that on me!" Ella balked, shuddering. "Ugh, I hate spiders."

Daria paled. "That can't be a coincidence. Was someone looking to harm Bash or Rachel?"

"Maybe both?" Senya scrunched her face, rubbing up and down her arms. "Can you imagine? I'd burn that mattress straightaway."

"That's beyond awful. Thank God they're both okay." Jenny took out her car keys from her purse. "But I really have to get back to school."

"Yeah, that's fine." Aiden whistled to catch Officer Carter's attention. "Escort Ms. Kieval back to Madison and Ms.—"

Corri interrupted. "I don't need an escort. As long as I leave now, I'm cool."

Aiden gave a brief nod. "Thank you for cooperating today."

"I need to get the kibble back to the Abbey. Quinn?" Daria tugged at her sleeve.

Quinn held Aiden's eyes. "Yeah. It's okay we're taking off?"

Aiden was busy with his team, comparing notes. He glanced up. "I'll see you later. After I'm done here, I'm headed over to their place."

The cousins thanked Ella again for the donation, but she was too busy being consoled by her brother to notice.

Daria clipped the dogs into their harnesses, both charges less than thrilled to be sharing truck bed space with food they couldn't rip into. As soon as she hopped into the cab and slammed the passenger door, Quinn released the brake and stepped on the gas.

"What the heck? I haven't even gotten my belt on!"

"Well, buckle up, because I'm not sitting back and letting someone come after my family."

Daria cleared her throat. "You mean *our* family. Are you thinking the person who killed Chad is the same one that—"

"I don't know, but like you said, it's too bizarre to be a coincidence: first a car full of snakes and now a bed filled with spiders? It's like a really twisted version of the ten plagues."

Her cousin eyed the road. "Yeah, well, this traffic isn't going to divide like the Red Sea, so maybe slow your roll?"

Quinn scoffed. "Someone is coming after my family. Scratch that: *our* family. And it's going to take more than a couple of Camrys to stop me."

Chapter Eleven

The tempter or the tempted, who sins most?
—Shakespeare's *Measure for Measure*

Sister Daria wiped her face and forehead with the front of her T-shirt. She was dripping sweat, having had to move the dog food from the curb to the shed herself. Quinn was gone.

The plan had been to unload the truck fast and head over to Bash and Rachel's apartment together. But Quinn took one look at the storage shed behind Guinefort House and went pale.

"What's the matter?"

Quinn bent over, her hands on her knees. Breathing hard. "I think I'm going to pass out."

"Sit down and put your head between your legs."

Quinn eyed her.

"Just trust me," Daria insisted. "It works."

Her cousin did as she was told while Daria stroked her hand and back, ignoring the cold sweat. Using her soothing, social worker voice, she reminded Quinn she was safe.

"What triggered you?"

Quinn raised her head and pointed at the storage shed.

Daria hadn't realized it was the same make and model as the one the killer had locked Quinn in during her kidnapping. She hadn't been stuck in there for long, but Daria figured trauma didn't come with a minimum time requirement. She tried getting her cousin to call someone: Aiden. Her parents. A therapist at the Women's Center.

Quinn wouldn't have it.

At least Daria had convinced her to leave RBG behind for the rest of the day and night for a doggy sleepover. She knew Quinn was planning on spending the night with Aiden, so at least Daria could breathe easy that she wouldn't be alone tonight. Watching RBG play with Rueger in the field, galivanting and cavorting around, helped the day regain a bit of levity.

She called Aiden anyway, letting him know what had happened.

Daria might be a licensed social worker, but Quinn wasn't her client and she felt not a scintilla of remorse for telling Aiden the details. As soon as she was done with the load, she was going to call her aunt and uncle too—this mini feud be damned.

Sister Ceci stood next to the pile. "I think this load's bigger than I am!"

"She's right." Sister Theresa patted the top of the stack. "And this is only half the donation, right?"

Daria nodded. "I could only get half of it in Quinn's truck. I would've gone back for the rest . . ."

"If it weren't for the snakes at the restaurant." Reverend Mother shook her head while crossing herself. "Dear Lord in

Heaven, what's next—locusts? Boils? It's like living through the Passover."

"Give me a second to change and I'll help you with the rest," Sister Ceci offered.

"That would be really awesome." Daria smiled, relieved to not have to do it all by herself.

"A laudable gesture, but perhaps an unnecessary one." The Reverend Mother motioned toward the street.

The most tricked-out truck Daria had ever seen had slowed down and was parking right in front of the abbey. On the side panel it read *Frankie's Garage* in a bold, retro-folkloric font with swirls of colors around it in the shape of a car. The *G* in garage had a mohawk along the upper curve of the letter. Lucas waved hi to Daria and her sisters.

Sister Theresa let out a low whistle. "It looks like Santa found my Christmas wish list from 1966. Better late than never."

Sister Ceci fanned herself with both hands.

He walked around to the back of the truck. "Where do you want me to put these?"

Daria waved back. "Hold on a sec!" She turned to her roommate. "That's Lucas Diaz. He's our donor's brother. Why don't you direct him to the kennel storage? The outside storage shed's all full. I'm going to hop into the shower."

The Reverend Mother emitted a sound from the back of her throat, which was never a good sign. "Sister Daria, why don't *you* direct Mr. Diaz where to go? No need for someone else to finish what you've started. You've done a wonderful job today. When you're done, you can shower."

"Yes, Reverend Mother," she responded. She knew it made sense, but that didn't mean Daria hadn't hoped to put some yardage between her and Lucas.

"Come, let us return to our duties. Our sister is more than capable of handling things here," the Reverend Mother added while shooing the others along. She walked over to Lucas, who had two bags hoisted on each shoulder. As soon as he realized the head of the Order was approaching, he offered a megawatt smile, placing the bags down so he could shake her hand.

Sister Daria had no choice but to join them.

"I want to thank you for bringing over the rest of the donation to us, Lucas."

"For you? Anything."

Daria regarded their easygoing demeanor. "Do you two know each other?"

"Oh my, yes! I've known Lucas for years. He comes around to help us with the occasional handyman job. Although I haven't needed to call for a couple of years because you did such commendable work the last time."

Lucas shrugged off the compliment. "Oh, that reminds me . . . I may have a 2014 GMC Sierra 1500 for you by the end of the month. It's in good shape, only fifty thousand miles on it. My cousin Alicia's getting herself a new one, and I convinced her to donate it for the tax write-off—and to help her soul. She was a hellion when we were kids."

"That would be wonderful," the Reverend Mother mused, "but I wouldn't want to step on Father Anthony's toes."

Father Anthony was the priest at Saint Mark's. *Must be Lucas's church*, Daria surmised.

"Nah, I already got him a truck, a car, and a van. Trust me, he's good."

The Reverend Mother clapped her hands together. "Excellent! Then yes, we'd be so appreciative. It would certainly give Quinn Caine a break in picking up donations."

"Speaking of which." Lucas picked up the dog food bags, balancing them on his shoulders. "Where you want these?"

"Sister Daria will show you," she told him.

Before she turned back toward the chapel, Daria could've sworn she saw a little sparkle in the Reverend Mother's eye. What the heck was that about?

"You going to show me the way or just stand there torturing me?"

Daria coughed. "If you've been over here as much as the Reverend Mother alluded, then I'm thinking you already know the way." She went over to his truck and grabbed a couple of bags. "By the way, flirting with me is a waste of my time and your energy."

He let out a soft laugh. "There's always time for flirting."

Gawd! Even with Daria using one of the bags to shield her view of him as she walked, she could just tell he had on one of those self-satisfied grins.

"Well, then don't waste *my* time, okay? I'm sure you drive women crazy. They'll be a much more receptive audience."

"I don't care about what other women think. I would, however, like to get to know *you* better."

Nope. We are not going there. No way. No how.

"There's not much to know. I've only traveled a little. I'm a social worker slash nun-in-training, and I love dogs. There ya go. End of story. Now let's focus on work, okay?"

Still using the bag as a shield, Daria led the way to the kennel storage unit, already left unlocked by one of the other sisters. Daria flipped the light switch and glanced inside. "Not much room, but enough for the rest of the food in your flatbed."

He tossed the bags down. "Where are you keeping the rest of it?"

"In a garden shed on the back of the property."

Lucas frowned. "That may be a problem. Show me."

Usually she did not do well with such a bossy tone, but for some reason, it didn't bother her coming from Lucas. Maybe because he had taken the hint and had stopped asking her questions about herself. Maybe perhaps underneath the Viking-styled hair and classic Mesoamerican good looks was not just a guy but a man, the rare kind who invested even more in his community than he did his braiding technique.

"This way," she told him, walking over to the shed. Now, every time she saw it, Daria was reminded of Quinn's reaction. She took out the key and opened it for him. "I'm guessing this shed came in since you were last here?"

He nodded, wiping his forehead with the back of his hand. "Yeah. I mean, it's fine for what it's intended for, but not for this. See how there are those slits of light coming through the metal panels?"

She peeked her head in to see. "Yep."

"Right, well, that's exactly how mice and rats and whatnot are going to get in. They'll eat through those bags in no time. This shed's okay for some garden tools but definitely no good for food storage."

"We're a small Order, and we're running out of room around here. If it's okay with Sister Ceci, I guess I could keep the rest in our room?"

Lucas's expression went soft. "Nah, don't do that. I've got you. Let me transfer all this food from the shed into the kennel unit, and I'll take what I have in my truck back to my garage. I'll store it there until I can get you a new concrete storage unit built."

Daria chewed the corner of her lip. "There's no way we have the budget for a whole building right now. Maybe in a year, if we're lucky."

"It's not a problem. I can get the materials and labor donated. My cousin Lupe is in construction. It's a simple structure. She and I will knock it out in no time."

She gazed up at him. Daria couldn't deny it: she liked them tall. She squinted while shielding the sun with her hand. "Exactly how many cousins do you have, Lucas Diaz?"

He cracked up. "You're kidding, right? We're Catholic. I have eleven cousins, and those are just the ones who live around here, although most of them are in Herndon."

Tires screeched against the asphalt. Flashes of bright chrome and electric blue singed Daria's retinas. She'd know that car anywhere.

"Corri Rypka," she muttered under her breath.

Lucas turned. "What is she doing here? Didn't she say she had a shift at the hospital?"

Daria knew Corri was itching to speak with Sister Theresa, probably about her role in Chad Frivole's murder. Guess a guilty conscience was enough reason to call in sick for the rest of the day. But no way was she going to say anything to Lucas. He might be a good man, but that didn't mean she was going to trust him.

But she couldn't help but wonder: what if Corri was there to confess?

Corri got out of the car, and the second she spotted Daria and Lucas, she frowned. She dashed into the abbey as if the bottoms of her shoes were on fire.

Lucas went right back to work, muttering, "Not my circus, not my monkeys," and Daria silently marveled at how he made those heavy sacks of dog food look like slumber party pillows.

"Uh, hey, are you good handling this on your own? I need to check on something."

"Yeah, go do your thing. I've got these."

Walking inside, she was able to view straight through the house. Corri was seated across from Sister Theresa, head in hand. Daria didn't know if it was a sin to eavesdrop, but she had spent her young life asking for forgiveness instead of permission. And the only way to hear what was going on was to linger in the kitchen.

She tiptoed in, immediately reaching for a couple of glasses and a large carafe of iced tea in order to give the illusion of purpose. Someone before her had propped the kitchen window open, an attempt to capture anything resembling a breeze inside the house. Daria couldn't have picked a better setup: she had a front-row seat to Corri's possible confessional.

"It's bad enough she wasn't really upset when Chad died," Corri was saying, "but now she's acting like it's the end of the world that she has to come in and talk to the police, that her precious restaurant is on hold because it's a potential frickin' crime scene!"

For once, Sister Theresa was at a loss for a snappy retort. She had her elbows dug into her knees as she leaned over, almost head-to-head with Corri.

"I would think Senya, as an officer of the court, would be encouraging Ella, as her client, to act remorseful. But instead, their energies are feeding off each other. I'm telling you, it's not healthy. Senya keeps insisting that Ella being suspect number one is a civil rights violation, but it's really hard to see that when, I don't know, she's kept a stockade of snakes on her property, like they're her familiars or something."

Sister Theresa let out a weary sigh. "Ella is one of your best friends. Do you really have such little faith in her?"

Corri sank back into her chair. Well, as much as anyone could relax in a galvanized metal garden seat. "I sound like such a bi . . . I mean, I sound terrible, don't I?"

The sister didn't answer. Again, Daria was stunned over her restraint: very un-Theresa-like.

Corri's voice shook. "You know, before he was killed, he bought treats for my dog baby. He was going to come over later that night so I could make him my pierogies. You've had them, so you know they're the bomb."

Sister Theresa offered a small encouragement. "Indeed. If you hadn't become a nurse, I would've encouraged you to become a chef."

Corri scoffed. "Yeah, well, *that* was never going to happen. Anytime I'd even hint at being interested, she'd go off on me, saying, 'I'm the one who's going to Le Cordon Bleu. Not you. It's my destiny, not yours.' Ugh, I got so sick of hearing that when we were younger."

"You're your own person, Corri. If you really wanted to go to culinary school, you could have gone. I would've made sure of it."

Corri stared off, fixated on a couple of squirrels scampering up and around an oak tree.

Sister Theresa touched her hand to bring her back. "I know you love being a nurse. So what is really troubling you?"

"The date we had the night before? It was magical. He took me to dinner in the city. Then we had champagne on the footsteps of the Lincoln Memorial. He said he remembered back in high school how I'd always wanted to do that—and he wanted to make my wish come true."

Sister Theresa reached into the pocket of her tunic, pulling out a clean tissue for her. "That's a beautiful memory."

Corri took the tissue, blotting under her eyes so she didn't smear her makeup. "Thanks. But it was more than that for me. He apologized for everything he did. Writing my number on men's bathroom walls all around town. Telling his buddies I gave him an STD just to make sure none of them would ever want to ask me out.

"You know, when he bumped into Senya at the dog place, he could barely recall what he had done to her back in school—but he remembered everything he did to me. When he came back, he called me first thing to tell me how sorry he was. That's why I agreed to go out with him. You should've seen Senya's face when I told her. She's always run hot, but I'll tell you, Sister, that day, something went ice-cold behind her eyes after that."

A low whisper tickled Daria's right ear. "And I thought you were surprising me with some tea—not listening for some."

She shushed him over her shoulder.

"Well, at least make it look real," he chuckled, removing the glasses from her hands and pouring iced tea for two.

But it was too late. The sound of their commotion had drifted from the kitchen into the backyard.

Corri stood up, clutching her purse tight to her front. She made brief eye contact with them through the kitchen window. "Uh, yeah, I've gotta go anyway."

Sister Theresa followed, gesturing toward the sliding glass door. "I'll walk you out."

Corri slid the door open, walking through. In a nervous gesture, she ran her fingers through both sides of her hair, like a comb. "Sorry I didn't say hi before. I just really needed to talk to my—to Sister T."

Daria just knew she was hiding something. Actually, many things. "I thought you had to be at the hospital?"

Corri let out a huff. "My boss sent me home. Said I was too shook-up to work today. Can you blame me? I still can't believe Chad is dead! Now I'll never know what could have been."

Lucas grimaced. "Are you sure you're all right to drive? Thought you were going to take a hedge out, the way you flew in here."

Her shoulders relaxed, loosening the Vulcan death grip she had on her purse.

"Yeah, I'm fine. Thanks for asking, though." Corri's eyes traveled the length of him. "It's really good to see you, Lucas."

"You too, Corri. Say hi to Justin for me."

Justin was her little brother. An innocuous response. Friendly. Neighborly. Totally expected between two families that had grown up together.

A muscle in Daria's left eyelid start to twitch.

Corri tilted her head, gazing up at him through long giraffe lashes. "You know, we should hang out sometime. There's this cool ax-throwing place opening. How fun would that be?"

Wow, did she just ask him out? Right in front of her and Sister Theresa? Not one, but two nuns? Well, one nun and a baby penguin, but still.

Sister Theresa rolled her eyes. Meanwhile, Daria wanted to rip Corri's throat out. Take the hussy's esophagus as a trophy, then play jump rope with it for the rest of the day before throwing it in the garbage.

Note to self: double my prayer load and bathe in holy water later.

"Appreciate the invitation, Cor, but thinking about ax throwing after there's been a murder just doesn't do it for me. Besides, in the little spare time I've got, Sister Daria and I are going to be doing a bunch of projects around here. Help get this place in good shape. Thanks, though."

Corri's mouth puckered like she had given mouth-to-mouth to a lemon. But then she seemed to remember that she had an audience and swapped the bitter for something more saccharine sweet.

"Oh, no problem. I totally get it. I mean, Chad died from snakebites, not axes, but I guess I see your point." She pierced

Daria with a visual dagger. "It's really good he's here to help you now, because one day Lucas will be married with kids and won't be able to give you and this place a second thought. Not even on Sundays, since, you know, he's Catholic."

Man, if Daria weren't a novitiate, she would sideswipe the spit out of Corri's mouth. But nope, she wasn't going to be that girl anymore. Just as the Reverend Mother had taught her: it was crucial to have more than just a hammer in her emotional toolbox.

"We appreciate him. Lucas is a giver in a world full of takers." Daria turned to him. "Thanks again, by the way."

Something she couldn't quite decipher flared behind his gaze. "For you . . . and the Order? Anytime."

"Well then! Corri, I'm sure you have somewhere to be." Sister Theresa practically pushed her toward the front door. "Sister Daria, why don't you head for chapel? I believe you're behind on some much-needed prayers."

Chapter Twelve

If you prick us, do we not bleed? If you tickle us, do we not laugh?
If you poison us, do we not die? And if you wrong us, shall we
not revenge?
—Shakespeare's *The Merchant of Venice*

"Forget a wedding registry at Crate & Barrel. Just have them send money straight to my therapist. Because now we *both* have arachnophobia."

Even with a blanket over her shoulders, Rachel couldn't stop shivering. Aiden noticed the concern on everyone's faces.

"She'll be okay. It's the adrenaline," he told them.

Rachel's mother, Jeanie Slingbaum, didn't seem convinced. "Are you sure you weren't bitten? Maybe we should go into the bathroom so I can do a thorough check."

"I wasn't bitten. I didn't get close enough. I. Am. F-I-N-E—fine."

Rachel had her knees curled up under her chin, hugging her legs close. Her mom was on her left and her father was pacing the floor like an expectant dad from the fifties. Bash was on her right, also white as a sheet, his eyes darting over to her dad.

"Phil, I need you to stop wearing a groove in the floor. This place's a rental."

He stopped pacing, but Rachel's dad was too worked up to sit down. "Well, from now until your house reno's done, you and my daughter will be staying with us. We have plenty of room, a state-of-the-art alarm system. I have cameras everywhere. No way anyone's going to break in without getting caught. Plus we both work from home. We're around all the time."

Bash rubbed his forehead, as if willing the furrows to smooth under his touch. "That could be a long time. We just approved the plans. We're talking at least six months, maybe even a year."

Mrs. Slingbaum's face brightened. "Even better if you ask me! How convenient would that be for us while we're planning the wedding?"

Rachel and Bash shot each other a look.

The teakettle started whistling, but not like any other kind Quinn had ever heard.

"Wait a sec, is your kettle actually whistling 'Tea for Two'?"

"Isn't it fabulous?" Mrs. Slingbaum fawned. "I found it through one of those SkyMall catalogs and I couldn't resist! I don't know if I told you, but when our Rachie was a little girl, she loved to throw tea parties. Real ones—not pretend. Of course, I would only let her use iced tea instead of hot, but still . . ." She drifted off, staring at her daughter. Tears welled up. "If something had happened to you."

Rachel reached for her hand. "But it didn't. I'm good. I swear."

Quinn took the kettle off the burner. "Who wants some tea? It looks like there's plenty of my mom's blend here."

Almost everyone raised a hand. Because even if everyone was still upset with Quinn's parents, they knew Adele Caine had the most epic homemade tea blends.

Aiden cleared his throat. "Speaking of your folks, have you called them? Let them know what happened?"

Bash scoffed. "Not yet, but that's mostly because *I'm* still not sure what happened here."

Even though he had a notepad in hand, Aiden called over Officer Johnson, who had obviously been off duty before this. She was wearing a sleeveless, formfitting dress in the most flattering shade of orange, which made her gorgeous ebony skin and tawny eyes glow with their own warmth and energy. The gold heels and dangly earrings made it even more obvious the attempted murder–by–spider bite had interrupted plans for a date night later.

"I'm going to have Shae run down what we know so far," Aiden told the group as Quinn handed mugs of tea around the table.

Rachel gave an awkward smile. "I'm sorry we got in the way of your date. You look amazing."

Shae waved off the concern. "I got dressed early." She flipped through the pages of her notebook.

Mrs. Slingbaum thumped her hand over her heart and sighed. "Ah, brings back such memories. Our girl used to change her clothes five times before going on a date with Bash."

"Ohmygawd, Mom!"

Quinn tried not to laugh. Seemed Rachel wasn't immune to regressing to her teenage self when she was around her mom, like anybody else.

Shae turned her attention to Aiden. "Everly should be here any minute with a change for me."

Aiden gave a chin lift. "Good. Go ahead and continue your investigation."

She nodded. "All right, just to confirm, you two came home together?"

"Yeah." Bash rubbed his eyes with the heels of his palms. "We were going to have a meeting with our architect to go over some changes we wanted to make, but I had forgotten some papers at home, so we came by to get them."

Shae checked her notes. "And what happened next?"

Rachel took a sip of her tea. "Ooh, that's really good."

"Yep, my mom makes the best tea—and the worst future mother-in-law."

Quinn balked. "Bash!"

Shae spoke up. "Let's not get distracted. This investigation is too important."

Rachel threaded her hair behind her ear. "While Bash was getting the papers together, I went in to use the bathroom."

Shae jotted down a note. "The primary bathroom?"

"Yes."

Bash was losing patience—and his manners. "Does it really matter where she went to the bathroom, Shae?"

"It's a good thing I *did* use that bathroom; otherwise I, your future wife, might not have noticed someone had messed with our bed!"

Bash wasn't the only one on edge.

"She's right, you know." Shae glanced up from her notes. "Your bedroom faces east and has only one window. At night, it would've been a lot harder to notice anything off."

The truth of her words hit the mark. Quinn could tell from her brother's ashen expression. "Duly noted."

Officer Johnson kept her expression stoic. "And what happened then?"

Rachel let out a shaky breath. "I left the bathroom, and I noticed my pillow looked . . . I don't know what the right term would be . . . frumpled? And there were small lumps under the coverlet.

"I know this is going to make me sound anal, but I keep our bed very tidy. I like to walk in at the end of the day and have it look like it came off a showroom floor. One glance and I knew something was off."

"All right, so you sensed your bed had been tampered with," Shae recapped. "Had you noticed anything else off in the room or the rest of the apartment?"

"I hadn't, but then again I hadn't been in our bedroom since early this morning."

Bash rubbed a hand over his face. "There certainly wasn't anything touched in the rest of our place."

"The window shade!"

Shae's brows went up. "What about it?"

Rachel eyed the window. "Bash always keeps the shade down. The buildings on this street are close together—and our bedroom faces this other guy's bedroom window."

Bash grumbled. "Yeah, I don't need anyone getting a free peep show of my fiancée. I always keep the shade down."

"I noticed it wasn't," Rachel continued. "And I remember thinking, *Wow, that's weird*, but again, I brushed it off, thinking maybe Bash had heard something outside and yanked the shade up, forgetting to put it back down.

"Anyway, I'm by our bed and I see something move. I throw the covers back—and there's a bunch of spiders crawling everywhere. I screamed at the top of my lungs."

"Scared me to death. For the rest of my life, I never want anything to elicit that sound from you."

"Bear-Bear," she whispered, hopping out of her chair and coming over to surround him in an enveloping hug. Bash held her tight, burying his face in her hair.

One of the criminalists called out. "Officer Johnson? You have a visitor downstairs. Everly Fine?"

The sound of Everly's name provoked the first slight smile from Shae that day. She glanced over at Aiden. "Detective?"

"You continue your work, Officer." Aiden's eyes scanned the room, looking over the criminalists, the forensic entomologist, and other police officers in the apartment. He called one of the officers to go down and collect Shae's clothes. "When you make detective someday soon and you're in charge of an investigation, you do not leave in the middle of questioning or a debriefing. Send someone else."

Another member of the team walked over.

"Detective? Officer Johnson? The bug guy got all the spiders. Did a triple sweep. We dusted for fingerprints. Only Ms. Slingbaum's and Mr. Caine's showed up. The perp was probably wearing gloves. We did retrieve a couple of long, dark-brown hairs, though—we'll test them. The perp definitely came in through the bedroom window, because whoever it was left a partial footprint right outside the window. Our team is now dusting the fire escape outside. We're hoping to recover a full print. Oh, and one last thing: the mechanism on the window was intact."

Quinn placed her teacup down on the counter. "What does that mean?"

Aiden frowned. "It means the window wasn't locked. Easy, direct access."

Bash cursed under his breath. "Yeah, that lock hasn't worked right since we moved in. The landlord's been dragging his feet, but this is on me. I should've just fixed it myself." He turned to Mr. Slingbaum. "I let you down."

For the first time all evening, something tempered in Rachel's dad's countenance. "You're four floors up, son, and you've been in this place, what, two weeks? It's not like either of you have enemies to worry about."

Mrs. Slingbaum paled. "Until now."

Someone handed a neatly folded stack of clothes, with more practical shoes on top, over to Officer Johnson. She excused herself to go change.

Aiden took over. "I didn't want to say anything until we had a chance to fully examine it, but whoever rigged your bed with spiders left something else—something meant for you, Rachel."

He motioned for a member of his investigative team to bring over what they'd found.

As soon as Quinn spotted what was in the evidence bag, her vision blurred and the floor beneath her feet crumbled. She grabbed the kitchen counter, blinking hard to clear the fog.

In her boyfriend's hand was a small, hand-stitched leather notebook with gold embossed scales of justice on the cover.

"That's my notebook." Quinn's voice was hoarse.

Officer Johnson walked back into the room while putting on latex gloves, now wearing her uniform. Aiden handed the evidence over, and Shae fanned through the pages. "This notebook belongs to you?"

"Yes, I mean, no, not exactly." Quinn blew some stray hair out of her eyes. "What I mean is, I made it. It's a limited-edition notebook we sell exclusively at the shop."

Aiden gaze locked on the boa constrictor hold she had on the counter. "You all right?"

She took in a deep breath through her nose and out her mouth, a grounding technique she'd learned from a therapist years ago. "Yeah, I'm totally fine. It was just, I don't know, jarring to see something I made at a crime scene. May I see it? Up close?"

Aiden turned his attention to Officer Johnson. "You're the co-lead on this investigation. It's your call."

Shae paused for a few seconds before snagging a pair of latex gloves, handing them over.

"Even with those on, please be careful. Don't put any undue pressure on it. We don't want the pages to rip or the ink to smear. It's already been dusted for prints, so you don't have to worry about that."

Aiden tapped his pen against his notebook. "Any results?"

Shae shook her head. "They were smart. They must've wiped it down before they wrote a word."

With gloves on and practiced care, Quinn perused the contents. "It's hard to reconcile such ugly words with such distinctive, elegant handwriting."

"It's the same handwriting found on the note," Shae informed her.

Quinn stopped. "Wait, the one found in the bag in Chad's car?"

Those tawny eyes steeled. "Exact same."

Quinn couldn't help but shudder.

The writing was graphic, with the names and dates of Bash's hookups through college, as if a shadow had been following him. Watching from a safe distance. Taking notes. For *years*.

How does evil walk beside us, so close, yet remain undetected? Quinn wondered.

Her brother seemed to have a penchant for expressing his affections outdoors: under football bleachers, in wooded areas along walking paths, even once in the alley by the bookshop. Bash had given this creep a front-row seat to his sex life—along with knowledge his sister would've been perfectly content going the rest of her life without.

Officer Johnson studied Quinn while she reviewed the notes. "Would your parents be able to tell us who bought this particular book?"

Quinn handed the notebook back. "I mean, sure, if they paid with a credit card. I made sure we had different SKUs for each design, so I would know which ones were selling the most. But if they paid with cash, you're out of luck."

Officer Johnson looked up. "Unless your parents or a staff member happen to remember the customer who bought it?"

"It's worth asking them," Bash interjected. "My dad's useless when it comes to remembering names and faces, but our mom? She knows everyone and is sharp as a tack."

"So is the manager, Leah," Quinn checked the date on her phone. "She should be over there now."

Officer Johnson scribbled another note. "Not you?"

Quinn really didn't want to air family business with a third of the Vienna Police Department in the room, but she'd learned from dating a detective that it was always better to offer the whole truth in an investigation.

"I haven't been to the shop in a little while. We've had a temporary falling-out."

She removed her gloves. "What about?"

Rachel straightened in her chair. "It was nothing related to what happened here tonight."

The room grew silent, with everyone glancing at each other, waiting to see who would say what next.

Mrs. Slingbaum rolled her eyes. "This is ridiculous—if you won't tell them, I will." She readjusted herself in her chair. "Rachel and Bash got engaged recently."

"Congratulations," Shae answered.

At the same time, they all said, "Thank you."

Mrs. Slingbaum went on. "Bash's parents—Adele and Finn— really didn't react well to the news that Bash plans on converting before the wedding. The whole situation was handled badly—by both parties."

Bash's body jerked. "Wait, what?"

"Mom, are you kidding me? How can you say that?"

Arms crossed, hip leaning against the kitchen countertop, Phil Slingbaum joined in.

"Because we would have had the same reaction if the circumstances were the other way around," he let them know. "What did you expect, Sebastian, that they were going to say 'Mazel tov' and throw you a bar mitzvah?"

Mrs. Slingbaum patted her daughter's hand. "You didn't help yourselves either by telling them about your engagement *and* Sebastian's conversion all at the same time."

Rachel's mouth hung open. "I can't believe you are actually *defending* them."

Her mother raised her chin. "You didn't answer my question. If it was the other way around and it was *you* who had to break the news to your father and me that you were becoming a Christian, would you have handled it the same way?"

Rachel's gaze went down to her shoes.

"That's what I thought." Her mother relaxed her shoulders. "I'm not saying Adele and Finn don't have some soul searching to do. It's heartbreaking to discover people you hold in such high regard harbor such lowly, unexamined prejudices. But I *do* know they're never going to find their way with you two isolating yourselves from them."

Officer Johnson cleared her throat. "Not to interrupt, but uh . . ." She stalled, thumbing through the notebook again. "I need to ask you two about the contents off this notebook."

Bash moved his chair closer to Rachel's. "Shoot."

She held the book to the light. "It appears this journal was written with you, Rachel, as the intended audience. The perp apologizes to you for the spiders, hoping your 'snake of a fiancé' is the one 'caught in their web.' They also write how sorry they were to have to 'unleash sorrow and fury to last a lifetime, but it's better you know before you seal your fate with"—she cleared her throat—"a womanizer who mounts anything in a short skirt."

Rachel swallowed, and Quinn's eyes darted to see if she was still holding her brother's hand. She was. "Go on, Shae. Everyone knows Bash had a, um . . . colorful past while we weren't together."

"Whoever this person is? They've written through most of this book with examples—some of them quite descriptive—of Sebastian's various liaisons. This person has names, dates, and places. He, she, or they have been following you for years."

Rachel and her mother exchanged a look. "May I see a list of those dates?" Rachel asked.

Bash turned to his fiancée. "I'm more than willing to give you and the police a detailed timeline. I've never cheated, Rach. Never even thought about it—and I spent most of the time we were apart trying to run from the truth: that breaking up with you was the single most stupid mistake of my life." He eyed Rachel's parents. "Phil? Jeanie? I know this looks bad, but I swear I didn't betray your daughter. I wouldn't."

Mrs. Slingbaum's mouth pursed. "You're right, it doesn't look good."

"Right now, we're more concerned with someone out there having enough vitriol for you to want to kill you—and having Rachel caught in those cross hairs," Mr. Slingbaum groused.

"We're going to get a transcript of the notebook for you to review—both of you—to determine not only its veracity but whether or not you can surmise some suspects based on the information they left," Aiden offered.

"It's obvious it's someone who attended UVA." Quinn took a sip of her tea, now ice-cold. She dumped it down the sink. "And it's probably a student, most likely someone local, since the observations move from Charlottesville to Vienna. I didn't get to read every entry, but I don't recall seeing any accounts based in his time in grad school or from Colorado or California or any of his other temporary stations.

"Whoever compiled this info had to be keeping a record of my brother's, for lack of a better phrase, 'shenanigans' somewhere else, because this notebook was made and sold within the last few weeks. Maybe . . . just maybe . . . they kept their original records?"

Shae placed the notebook back into the evidence bag, zipping it up. "You'd make a really good detective."

Aiden beamed. "I tell her that all the time."

"My parents would kill you if that ever happened," Bash told his best friend. "They're still ticked off at me for being a firefighter."

Aiden tucked his notes in the inside pocket of his jacket. "I suggest you two pack your bags and plan on staying at a hotel or your parents' place. Because like it or not, we've got a potential serial killer out there, and you, Bash, have got a target on your back."

Chapter Thirteen

Hell is empty and all the devils are here.
—Shakespeare's *The Tempest*

"Well, hey there, stranger! I was starting to think it was something I said."

The moment Quinn walked back into Prose & Scones was surreal.

Bittersweet. A little on edge. But with Leah's ebullient greeting, she let out a held breath, and the sound of her jaw clicking inside her head stopped.

"How could've it have been something you said?" Quinn reassured her. "You're a delight!"

Leah batted her lashes. "This is true. It's great to see you."

Quinn's gaze went from left to right, scanning the shop.

Leah leaned over the counter, a hand cupped around her mouth in a whisper. "They're not in today, if that's what you're worried about?"

"What?"

"You're looking for your folks, right?"

Quinn blushed. "Uh, yeah. I was."

A wave of relief collided with another of disappointment. As much as she wasn't in the mood for rehashing what had happened during Rachel and Bash's engagement night, she had to admit, she missed them. "Did they tell you what happened?"

Leah was about to answer when a customer approached the register with a load of books heavy enough to qualify them for their own professional weightlifting class.

Leah's eyes rounded. "Mr. Morrissey! Another stack already? I thought it would've taken you months, with all the books you bought last time."

The middle-aged gentleman slid his book pile onto the counter. "Ha! Not likely. I'm telling you, send your televisions into exile, my dear. Ever since we got rid of ours, I've perused teems of superb reads." His lopsided grin curved right as he patted the top of the stack, like he was showing affection to a child for a job well done.

Leah tittered as she started to scan his purchases. "Well, God bless Bill Morrissey. You're certainly keeping us in business."

He wasn't the only one. Adele and Finn Caine might not be in the shop, but almost everybody else in town seemed to be there. Usually the sight of so many patrons would've pleased Quinn, but she knew the police were close behind. They'd want to interview the staff, look over shop receipts, maybe even talk to the customers. Anything it took to determine who might have bought one of the leather journals. Quinn wanted the same thing; she just wished there didn't have to be an audience while they conducted police business.

She'd put a lot of love into those handmade notebooks. While the covers and styles were unique, Quinn had made sure they all had her favorite Tomoe River Japanese paper, known for its cottony velvet feel and durability. Nothing grabbed the ink better. Some had been sewn with a whimsical bow stitch, others with a triangle stab binding. The thought of one of her book babies being used to malign her brother so that Rachel would leave him—all while stashing poisonous spiders in their bed? Uh, no . . . whoever it was had to be stopped.

Leah interrupted her fugue state with a snap of her fingers. "Quinn! Your face and ears are all red. Are you okay?"

She shook off her ire. "Yeah, all good. Listen, I need your help searching for the proverbial needle in a haystack. I know we're swamped—"

An adorable human with tattoos and Bantu knots sauntered over. "I can help you. Finding what doesn't want to be found is one of my jams."

"Oh, this is perfect," Leah chimed in. "You haven't had a chance to meet our latest addition. We hired them while you've been, uh, working from home and such. Quinn? Meet Sol—pronouns are they/them."

Quinn gave the first genuine smile she'd had in her all day. "It would be a huge help, but are you sure?" She looked around. The crowd was still abuzz. "Don't get me wrong, I'd love it. I just don't want to get in the way of your work."

Sol replied with an impish grin. "I have found, in my young years, there's different types of busy." They pointed to the far side of the shop. "See those parents over there in the children's book section? They've combined a weekly playdate with finding the latest books and toys their kiddos are into. It may only be September, but I made sure to have a Halloween display at the ready. I can tell the witchy finger puppets are a hit. It helps that those witches are just cool and not scary, as they should be for kiddos." Sol made a one-eighty upper-body twist while keeping their legs locked, pointing to the other side of the store. "And over there by the front, we have our people absorbed in the wellness slash self-help section. I have found they want plenty of space to do their browsing. If they need or want assistance, trust me, they will let us know. The same is true for those into crafts or gardening. The customers who like to get their gab on usually reside in fiction, especially speculative and YA, or in the best seller sections. They are passionate about their books with a capital P and come here to connect with their fellow tribespeople. I get that on a cellular level."

"You speak truth, oh wise one." Quinn peeked around, just to double-check. Sol was right: everybody—for the moment—was in their own little Shangri-la. "Okay, so I need to see if we can find a particular customer, someone who bought one of the new handmade leather journals we've been selling."

Leah's fingers danced across the register keys, clicking to their own rhythm. "Well, each one is unique, so that shouldn't be too difficult to find. Plus they haven't been for sale long, so we don't have to dig too far back." She squinted while biting the corner of her bottom lip. "Annnd . . . voilà!"

Quinn felt her pulse quicken, thrilled she'd be able to point Aiden's team in the right direction—which was fortunate, since a police car had just pulled into a parking spot right in front of the store.

All handmade book sales flashed across the register's screen.

"Isn't technology amazing?" Leah mused.

Sol peered over the frames of their glasses, reading the entries. "Which one are you looking for?"

"Oh yeah, that would help. It's the one with the scales on the cover and a simple saddle stitch binding. I was going for a Libra minimalist vibe. Or if someone wanted a gift for someone in law enforcement. The justice scales are versatile that way."

The three of them perused the purchase entries. Quinn heard two car doors open, then slam shut.

Sol let out a low whistle. "Whoa, you've sold a lot of them. How did you have time to do all of these? There must be thirty, forty of them sold."

"Thanks."

Three tiny bells rang.

Sol was still going. "Sun with noble binding, pressed flowers with secret Belgium binding, music notes with a pierced accordion binding. I see what you did there. Nice."

But Quinn wasn't in the headspace to receive compliments. Officers Shae Johnson and Ned Carter walked in, making a beeline for the shop counter.

"Long time no see."

Ned Carter removed his police cap, giving a brief nod. "Quinn."

"You know why we're here." Leave it to Shae Johnson to get right to business.

Leah's mouth gaped. "Is Quinn in some kind of trouble?"

"She's been here, with us!" Sol maneuvered themself in front of Quinn, arms crossed, chin raised. "Consider us her ironclad alibi."

Officers Carter and Johnson shared a look between them, and whatever magic book spell the customers were under before was now broken. All eyes were on them.

"Why are you here for Quinn?" Bill Morrissey insisted.

"No way she's done anything that needs the cops," Maxie, one of the baristas from Caffe Amour, interjected. "Uh, no offense, guys."

"People! Quinn Caine is *not* in trouble." Officer Carter was just loud enough so everyone could hear him. "She's assisting in a police matter. So y'all settle down. Mind your business."

Everyone murmured to themselves and went back to browsing. One of the advantages of living in suburbia: most everyone found comfort and solace by following the rules.

Leah hit a key so that the screen went back to the main page. "Before I show you anything, I need to ask if you have a warrant."

"Do they need a warrant?"

Leah gave her best OMG face, which was turning hot pink. "Quinn! Didn't you take AP government? Search and seizures are covered in the fourth amendment!"

Now Quinn was embarrassed.

"It's fine," Ned Carter answered, handing over paperwork. "Yes, Mrs. Grover, we have a warrant."

Quinn perused the document. "Everything looks like it's in order."

"The ink barely had time to dry," Leah mused.

Keeping her voice down, Quinn whispered, "Leah, we may have a serial killer in our town. They've done their part. Now let's do ours." She turned to the officers. "Sol, Leah, and I were just going through the sales." She patted Sol's shoulder. "Appreciate the solidarity, by the way. I need you to move, though; I can't see the screen."

"Oh! Right!" Sol jumped out of the way.

Leah's finger was on the monitor, a marker for where to read. "All right, so we're looking for justice scales, correct?"

Quinn nodded. "Yep."

Leah dragged her finger down. "Ah! Here it is!" She highlighted the entry and clicked return. "Well, isn't that just craptastic." She glanced up at the officers. "Whoever it was, they paid cash. So I can't tell you who it was."

Shae sighed. "Guess that would've been too easy."

"Excuse me?" a customer interjected. "Can someone ring me up?"

"I can"—Sol slid away from the group—"but let me take you to the other register."

The elderly customer cradled his books—both on World War II history—against his chest as he fished deep in his trouser pocket with the other, pulling out a small, square piece of paper. "This still good?" He handed it over to Sol.

Their face lit up. "Yes, it is." Holding the little paper by the top two corners, they waved it back and forth. "He's a member."

It took a second before Quinn understood. "Sol, you're a genius!"

Before she even had a chance to explain, Leah was already on it, highlighting the purchase entry. "Officers, as Sol just reminded us, even if someone pays cash, customers who are members still have their purchases credited to their accounts. That way they can earn points towards future discounts, like the gentleman at the other register showed us. That's the standard ten-dollars-off coupon they receive."

"Good." Officer Johnson turned the monitor closer to her and Officer Carter. "Fire it up, and let's see what comes up."

Leah nodded, and Quinn knew her heart was probably beating just as loud as hers.

She hit the return key. A new page pixelated across the screen with a list of all the books the member had purchased over the last several months:

Rattlesnake Recipes for the Zombie Apocalypse, by Laura Sommers

Rattlesnake Pet Guide, by Dr. Xan Xeo

The Native Mexican Kitchen: A Journey Into Cuisine, Culture, and Mezcal, by Rachel Glueck and Noel Morales

How to Get Away With Murder: Solve Puzzles to See If You Can Commit the Perfect Crime, by Brain Games

Leah swallowed. "The member is . . . Ella Diaz."

"Right." Shae shoved her notebook in her back pocket. "I'm going to need a copy."

Leah hit the print button. "I'll go get it. The printer is in Quinn's office."

Meanwhile, Quinn stared into nothingness, her brain unable to absorb the idea that Ella Diaz had wanted to hurt, possibly kill, her brother. She'd most likely murdered Chad Frivole with snakes she'd raised herself. Assassin familiars. "That is so messed up."

"What does Aiden always say?" Shae reminded her. "Follow the evidence and let it speak for itself."

Leah came back with the print copy requested and handed it over. "What's going to happen now?"

Officer Carter opened the shop door. "We're going to bring Ella Diaz in for questioning at the station. She's our lead suspect."

Chapter Fourteen

To weep is to make less the depth of grief.
—Shakespeare's *Henry VI*

"Well, if this ain't the most highfalutin high-cotton funeral I've ever seen."

"Did you see the swans in that little pond? I heard they were flown in special just for this!"

"Forget the swan lake show. Did you see the spread they're setting up back at the main building? I heard his manager flew in five Gs' worth of corned beef and pastrami from some New York deli named after cats."

"It's Katz's Deli, you idiot: K-A-T-Z apostrophe S. They cure their meat for four weeks!"

Sister Daria, Quinn, and Aiden were doing everything in their power not to bust out laughing with all the talk swirling around them at Chad Frivole's funeral. Daria had come by to say hello before rejoining her sisters on the other side of the grave site.

"Of course it would be more interesting where you two are hanging out."

Quinn's head tilted. "What do you mean?"

"Because no one's going to smack-talk around a bunch of nuns, that's what I mean." Daria lowered her voice. "By the way, how are Bash and Rach doing?"

Quinn had called her late the other night to clue her in on the horrific ordeal the two had endured. Usually she would've been chastised for receiving a call so late, but when the Reverend Mother heard what had happened, she crossed herself and had everyone get on their knees, right in the middle of the living room, to pray for her cousin and his fiancée's safety.

"They're all right, although I think Rachel's going a little stir-crazy. Between her dad giving his entire security system an upgrade rivaling the Pentagon to Bash taking time off work just to follow her around and watch *her* work, she's over it."

Daria gave herself a good scratch under her wimple, because while she might adore horror movies, she now got the itchies at the mere mention of spiders. "Remember when we were kids and we spent a week over the summer watching that Arachnophobe Beware Movie Marathon at the old theater on Maple, where the Spokes bike shop is now?"

Quinn's face lit up. "Heck yeah I do! I miss being able to walk to a movie theater. That was awesome."

Daria was a huge B movie horror fan—the cheesier, the better. "Those were classic kitsch, Aid. We're talking *The Incredible Shrinking Man*, *Possum*, *The Mist*—and my personal favorite, with *the* William Shatner—"

"The King of Kitsch himself," Quinn added.

"—in *Kingdom of the Spiders*. That one was especially fabulous because they used real tarantulas."

The sound of someone weeping stopped their chitchat. It was Chad's manager, walking toward the grave site, where three chairs awaited, facing the crowd of mourners. He had eschewed the purple suit for a more somber, traditional choice, but Daria noticed he had still color-coordinated his handkerchief with his tie—both in a muted sage green.

Quinn's brows furrowed; her mouth quirked to the side. "I know everyone mourns in their own way, but how is it that the last time we saw this guy, he hardly demonstrated a reaction to hearing Chad was murdered—and now he's inconsolable?"

The question was barely out of Daria's cousin's mouth when Ms. Jennifer—part of the Clink-n-Drink Ladies—swung around. "No kidding, he's a mess!"

Daria had always liked the Clink-n-Drink gals, especially Ms. Jennifer. "Where's the rest of your crew?"

"On their way. And they better appreciate me holding these seats, because everyone keeps giving me dirty looks when I tell them they're saved."

Mr. Fitzsimmons, Chad's manager, took one of the seats by the open grave, taking out a new handkerchief so he could blow his nose. Right behind him was Dennis Frivole, Chad's father, who plodded heavily toward the front—head down, muttering to himself. He took the chair on the other end, grunting almost the whole time.

The Lord himself couldn't have picked two more polar-opposite men if He'd tried.

Ms. Jennifer tightened the tie in front of her outfit—a classic Diane von Furstenberg wrap dress. Daria didn't know bubkes about clothes, and usually didn't care, but even she knew that dress was vintage coolness. She ran a hand down her plain tunic, wondering how many other women had worn this piece before her, curious if the wool blend had passed down to her because her predecessor had died or harbored doubts and left the Order.

"Hey, Jen! We're here! So sorry, a meeting with my agent ran longer than I expected."

It was Ms. Carina, another Clink-n-Drinker—also an up-and-coming mystery author. She might be rushed, her blonde hair disheveled, but it worked for her. So did the all-black wardrobe with red lipstick. She dressed that way even when there wasn't a funeral.

"I got a call from Sarah—she can't make it. She has to cover someone's shift at the dog shop. And Withers said—"

"Let me guess," Jennifer interrupted. "One of her kids has a volleyball game or a scrimmage?"

"Nope! Don't say it! I'm here; I just decided to come in my own car," Withers cut in, taking one of the seats. "I might not have known Chad, but I can be here and support the people who are mourning him." Then she proceeded to stick her tongue out. It was like watching crack-the-whip banter between Clairee and Ouiser from *Steel Magnolias*.

Daria and Quinn exchanged a glance while Aiden focused skyward again, mumbling "Deliver me" under his breath.

That's when the three friends remembered they had a mini audience. Carina shushed the other two. "We're spooking the young'uns. I promise, we're only playing."

Jennifer gave a real grin this time. "Exactly! That's just how we do."

Withers's head was still on what they were talking about before. "By the way, not to gossip further, but I heard Lisa McDevitt is Chad's lawyer."

"She's awesome," Carina piped in. "She's my lawyer too."

"Right, well, not that I heard this from her, because she'd never divulge, but I *did* catch from a bunch of others that Lisa read Chad's will a couple of days ago—along with a personal letter to his manager about how much he credited the man for his career. Supposedly Halster Fitzsimmons had no idea Chad looked up to him like a father figure—enough to leave him a considerable sum of money."

"Well, that explains it." Quinn sighed, shaking her head. "The change in attitude, I mean. The tears down the left are from guilt and the tears on the right from gratitude."

"Everyone, please take your seats." A handsome, chubby young man spoke into the microphone. "We're going to get started in a few minutes."

Daria glanced back at where the nuns were seated. "I've got to go sit with my Order, but I'll see you two around."

Quinn grabbed Daria's sleeve. "Oh, hey! I forgot to tell you . . . guess who got an invite to Rachel's parents' place tomorrow?"

"Your whole side of the Caine family tree?"

Quinn nodded.

Aiden chimed in. "I think they're trying to mend fences."

"Well, after Rachel's mom schooled us, I'm hoping my brother is ready to make amends."

Daria hoped so too. "Is he still planning on converting?"

"Oh, yeah, he's genuinely into it." Aiden stopped to take the programs from one of the passing ushers, keeping one and handing the rest over. "Uh, is it just me, or do all the ushers—"

"Eerily resemble Chad? That's an affirmative." Quinn took her copy and passed the rest to her cousin. "You don't think Mr. Fitzsimmons hired models just to usher, do you?"

Daria fanned herself with her program. "Who knows? Probably. Maybe doppelgängers pair well with deli and swans?"

Sister Lucy whistled for her.

"Okay, I have to go now, for reals. Later."

As Daria walked to the other side of the grave, she scanned the crowd to take note of who was there. Droves of School of Rock musicians and staff; almost the entire faculty of James Madison High School, including science teacher Jenny Kieval. Daria was surprised she wasn't sitting with her crew—until she realized Corri was seated with the Inova Hospital medical team who had tried to save Chad's life. Senya was seated far away from both factions. Was there a division within their ranks?

She recognized a couple of celebrities. No one over-the-top famous like George Clooney or Elizabeth Banks, but definitely faces she'd seen in commercials and soap operas. Not one of Chad's fellow cast members from his last Broadway show had made the trip.

That said, front and center was Chad's manager, tears streaming down, his whole body shaking with grief. All the while, Chad's father appeared to be using every ounce of willpower to keep himself upright. Daria didn't need to breathe his air to know it reeked of booze. He was wearing a suit two sizes too small, probably worn last in more sober days. His hair was washed and combed, but he still could've used a haircut and a shave. She heard the people around her, including some of her own sisters, whispering the same observations.

Meanwhile, Mr. Frivole was staring at his shoes. That's what Daria noticed—that and how his chest rose and fell slowly, each breath laboring under the weight of all that had happened and what could now never be. Daria had to look away; his pain was too hard to witness.

If any of the women in her Order had noticed what she had, they weren't saying; they were too focused on him showing up to his son's funeral inebriated. It made her wish she could switch her seat. With her program in hand, she stayed with her Order. But for the first time in two years, Daria was embarrassed to be with them.

"Hello, everyone, thank you for coming out today. I'm Dexter Thorton, Chad's best friend. He wasn't very religious, so he asked me, via the reading of his will, if I wouldn't mind leading the service today." The young man was back at the mic. He stopped, letting out an aching sigh. "I don't know what he was thinking, but I'm going to do my best."

He brushed his thick red hair out of his eyes, then, resting his hands on either side of the lectern, dropped his shoulders. "I must say, Chad has a sense of humor, even in death. Because the last time I've done anything even remotely religious was when I played the saboteur Friar Lawrence in an off-off-off-Broadway rendition of *Romeo and Juliet*—and we all know what a turd heel that guy turns out to be."

Everyone in the audience let go of some nervous chuckles. Daria felt a hulking presence take the seat next to her, the only one available.

"What did I miss?"

It was Lucas Diaz. In a suit, a well-fitting one. And he smelled like sandalwood and bad decisions.

"Shh!" Daria kept her focus straight ahead. "What are you doing here, anyway?"

He kept his voice low. "I'm here to represent the Diaz family."

Now Daria was curious, enough to meet Lucas's gaze. "How is your sister doing?"

He stared, something working behind his eyes. "You're the first person to ask how she is. Everyone has already decided she's guilty of murder. I know it doesn't look good, but I know my sister: no way she did this."

Daria couldn't help herself; she took his hand in hers. "You've never wavered in your belief. That must mean a great deal to her."

He shrugged. "She's more pissed at the world to have time to feel anything else. Things are moving, anyway. My sources tell me that Senya's now a suspect too. The police think she was purposefully stalling Chad inside the dog treat shop while my sister tossed in the snakes and rigged the car doors."

"What do you mean, your 'sources'? You own a garage, not a detective agency."

"I'm in a service industry, *guapa*, which means people talk to me and around me, all the time." He squeezed her hand. "I know it doesn't look good—the snakes, her knowing her way around a car because of growing up in garages, the notebook—but I don't care about any of that. No way did my sister hurt anyone."

Daria wanted to believe him.

When he had committed to building her Order a climate-controlled storage unit, free of charge, she had initially thought he was doing it as an excuse to spend more time with her. There was no denying there was a heated vibe between them. She had even asked around, wondering how she'd been raised in the same town as this Cheshire cat character without ever meeting him. The answer had been simple: his parents had divorced when he was in middle school, and he'd lived two years in Vienna, Virginia, then two years wherever his mother—a colonel in the U.S. military—was stationed, going back and forth until he finished high school. A rough gig for a kid, if you asked Daria.

But after hearing how he was always helping people, she'd realized she'd been wrong. An invisible weight had lifted off her shoulders at the same time something in her stomach sank.

"You're a good man, Lucas Diaz."

The corner of his mouth curled up. "You're just figuring that out, Elizabeth?"

Hearing her old name on his tongue made her blush. "I don't go by that name anymore."

His gaze studied her expression. "Shame. Suits you."

She didn't know how to respond, a rarity for any Caine woman. She took her hand back and rubbed her palms across the skirt of her habit, noticing all of a sudden how sweaty they had gotten. She wished she could air out under her arms as well.

"I . . . I don't have a lot of experience being around men—that is, men not related to me."

His eyes went from playful to kind—merciful, even, as his eyes moved to her mouth. "Do I make you nervous?"

Sister Theresa tapped her leg. "You two do realize we're at a funeral?"

"Sorry," she mouthed, turning her attention back to the dais, letting Lucas's question lie dormant.

"Now, don't worry," Dexter went on, "like any properly trained thespian, I prepared for my role. In this case, that means I went online and registered for that Universal Life minister kit. My irrational rationale: if I can marry people, then I can send them off to the pearly gates.

"You know, we met on our first day of acting class. I was just an overweight, terrified kid from Mansfield, Ohio, still scared of girls and pinching myself that I'd gotten into Julliard in the first place. I was sweating so much the professor stopped class to ask if I needed an IV drip before I passed out from dehydration."

His humor earned him some chortles.

"He's not that funny," Lucas whispered. "People are just grateful no one's up there sharing what a jackwagon Chad could be."

The irony was, he was correct—yet again—but no way was Daria engaging further. She just shushed him and pretended to not be interested in what he had to say.

"Out of everyone there, including the most beautiful people I'd ever seen in real life, Chad was the one who came up to me after class and asked if I wanted to run some lines with him. And that was it, best friends from then on.

"Back then, we didn't appreciate what a gift it was, to meet close friends so easily. When you leave college, the business of keeping a roof over your head the size of a postage stamp takes over, the grind of landing acting jobs that actually pay becomes your focus. But Chad and I never lost touch—and he never struggled to get work. Yes, for the record, it was infuriating.

"For those of you who remember, Chad played Dr. Andrew Tennyson III—the wealthy brain surgeon on *As the Tide Turns*—before becoming a model and spokesperson for Ralph Lauren. Believe it or not, I had to convince him to take that job! As handsome as he was, Chad didn't want to just be known for his looks. He wanted to be known as an actor's actor—the kind other actors admired. What he really wanted—more than anything—was to be in the theater. You see, it was Chad's first love, which means I can understand why he wanted his legacy to remain here too."

The mention of Chad's legacy made his father's face go beet red, his expression a simmering rage. That's when Daria heard two voices she knew well.

"Oh, wow, he looks like he's ready to blow a gasket."

Sitting in front of her was Leah Grover, Prose & Scones' social media manager, loud-whispering to her husband, Ryan.

He let out a low whistle. "Whoa, no kidding. He's not even trying to hide it."

"I heard Chad didn't leave him much in the will."

Ryan turned his head. "Now how would you know that?"

She snorted. "Oh, please, everyone won't shut up about it."

Meanwhile, any nerves Dexter had been feeling earlier in his eulogy had burnt off.

"But I will always remember the Chad that had my back. I can't begin to tell you how many times he'd take me to dinner, trying to convince me he needed the company and wasn't just making sure a starving actor was eating—or insisting I stay with him when I couldn't afford rent. He's the one who got me my first national commercial, which led me to my first reputable agent. He's saved my life . . . all the more reason why I can't believe his is over."

"See? Proves my point." Lucas crossed his legs at the ankles, leaning back farther in his chair. "People are complicated. It takes time to really know someone. Most people have more layers than an onion."

She couldn't help but grin. "Nice *Shrek* reference."

"Thank you." He pretended to tip an imaginary hat. "Chad could be a piece of work, but he had goodness in him. But you knew that already, right? You work to see the goodness in everyone."

"I suppose I do."

They locked eyes.

"You, Elizabeth Caine, now Sister Daria of Saint Guinefort's Order, are a good woman."

"No, I'm not," she said, without thinking. "I'm weak. I can help others, but I run away from my own problems."

Where had that piece of truth serum come from?

He shrugged. "So, now you recognize it, you have the power to change it."

"Shh!"

That warning came from Sister Ceci—who never shushed anybody. Daria shrunk into her seat, embarrassed.

Dexter removed some tissues from his jacket pocket, wiping his eyes and shoring himself up with a couple of deep breaths. "Chad loved growing up here. He regaled me with stories of singing at School of Rock gigs, especially in front of the Lincoln Memorial, of playing Tevye in his high school production of *Fiddler on the Roof . . .*"

Chad's manager pretended to clear his throat—and he was loud.

"I guess that's my cue that I'm taking up too much time," Dexter said, taking another tissue to wipe the sweat off his neck and face. "I'd like to introduce a man who meant a lot to Chad, the one who made a Vienna kid's dream of performing on Broadway come true."

Meanwhile, Lucas had more to say. "Hey, so I spoke with the Reverend Mother earlier, and after this, she said you can come with me to get what we need."

"What are you talking about?"

"Forgive her, Lord, for how quickly she forgets," he whispered toward the heavens, his hand on his heart as if she had wounded him. "You're going to help my cousin and me get that storage shed built for you so I don't have to keep a thousand pounds of dog food at my garage."

Oh, *that*.

"What do you need me for? I know nothing about construction."

He let out a soft laugh. "Well then, *pollito*, guess you're gonna learn."

Her skin began to burn. "Excuse me, but did you just call me a little chicken?"

"Perfect for you—you squawk and cluck like a chicken who's terrified the sky is falling just because the weather changes."

That was it. God forgive her, but she hated Lucas Diaz right then. Because she had the feeling he wasn't really talking about the weather. And Lord forgive her again because, for the first time in, well, ever, she was royally ticked off at the Reverend Mother— for constantly throwing them together.

She also wished this funeral was over already.

"Now I will admit," Mr. Fitzsimmons began, "when Chad told me he wanted to come home for a while in order to join forces with the Vienna Theater Company and build a state-of-the-art production company in the middle of suburbia, no offense, but I didn't get it. Not only did I not understand, I flew down here with the specific purpose of trying to talk him out of it. But now, I understand."

Leah barely bothered to whisper this time. "Bet that trust fund helped make things real clear real fast." Everyone seated around her murmured their agreement.

"I'm proud to announce that it was my protégé Chad Frivole's last wish that I stay here and head up this glorious effort—and to announce our ambitious plan to open the Miriam Frivole Center for Theater Arts in two years' time."

The second Chad's mother's name left Mr. Fitzsimmons's mouth, Chad's father jumped up and kicked his chair off the small dais, making everyone gasp.

"*That's* where all my son's money is going? A big box for boys to wear tights and play make-believe? I'm suing you," he yelled, swaying toward the lectern. "If you grant the permits, I'm suing you." He pointed to the mayor. "I'm even suing that pretty blonde lawyer of his for doing all his dirty work! Where is sh-she?" He stuttered and swayed. "Hey, blondie! Come show yourself!" He stopped, spotting Lisa McDevitt close to the front. "You! I bet you're the one who talked my boy into this!"

And then, before anyone could stop him, he lunged straight at her—falling right into Chad's open grave.

"Oh my gawd!"

"I can't unsee that!"

"Someone stop him! He's trying to open the casket!"

Corri jumped up from her seat. "This is all my fault! I'm—I'm so sorry everyone, but I can't watch the man I love being so disrespected!" She grabbed her purse and worked her way through the crowd. She had huge black sunglasses on, Jackie Onassis style, but everyone could see she was crying.

"Excuse me, I need to get to my friend!" It was Jenny, leaving the cluster of her fellow teachers and running after Corri. "Wait up! You shouldn't drive when you're this upset!"

Lucas leaned toward Daria's Order. "Sisters, I think this is our cue to leave. It's not safe here for you."

Daria couldn't agree fast enough. "Let's get out of here."

"Good call, young man." Sister Theresa stood up. "Have her back before Vespers. Sisters? Breakfast at Amphora is on me."

Quinn speed-walked over. "Hey, can I grab a ride with you two? Aiden's going in to retrieve Mr. Frivole. Don't worry, he called for backup."

"Yeah, no worries. Should I go over and help?" Lucas asked.

Quinn shook her head. "Uh, no, definitely not. You do not want a piece of that hot mess."

Sure enough, Aiden had dashed over, hopped in the hole, and retrieved Mr. Frivole from his son's grave. Even with him being drunk and flailing his fists around, Aiden didn't even break a sweat subduing Chad's dad. Someone else had retrieved the chair he'd kicked over.

"Now, you can either sit here and calm down, or I put the cuffs on you in front of the whole town, and that's what everyone will remember." Aiden still had a tight hold on the man. Chad's father's shoulders drooped as he nodded, resigned to cooperate. Once Quinn witnessed the scene calming down, she said she was ready to go.

The three of them walked toward Lucas's truck. "Am I dropping you off at your place or the bookstore?"

Quinn worried the corner of her lip, eyeing Daria.

"What?"

Quinn looked over her shoulder and around. "Did you see how Corri yelled that Chad's murder was her fault?"

Daria muttered, "Hard to miss."

"Listen, this may be our only chance to find out if or how those women are responsible not only for Chad's death but for the attempted murder of my brother."

"I'd like the chance to clear my sister's name," Lucas said. "I refuse to believe Ella had anything to do with this, but I wouldn't put it past some of those so-called friends of hers."

Quinn's phone beeped. She checked for a message. "That's Aiden. He's going to put Chad's father in holding until he dries out, and he's having his team investigate local rehabs. Assuming he'll go."

"Well, that's something, I guess." Daria folded the funeral program and stuck it in her pocket under her tunic. She surveyed the grave site, noticing that most of the people had left.

Lucas leaned against the side of his truck, arms still crossed, the wheels in his brain almost visible to her naked eye. "Chad Frivole was, what, thirty-two, maybe thirty-three years old?"

Daria shrugged. "I think so. I'm not sure. Why?"

He scratched the side of his jaw. "How many young, single guys do you know who have a will?"

Quinn and Daria looked blankly at each other.

"Exactly." He went on with his theory. "Chad's in New York. No wife. No significant other. No kids. The only relative he really loved has been dead since *he* was a kid . . . I would think the last thing he'd be thinking about is his own death."

"And he still drew up a will." Daria continued his thought. "You don't do that unless . . ."

"Unless you have a reason to think you might die." Quinn finished her cousin's sentence.

The three of them let that soak in.

Lucas blew out a frustrated breath. "Well, if someone was threatening him long enough for him to draw up a will, that means the possible killer had contact with Chad before he came back to Vienna. No way that's my sister. She's a man-eater, for sure, but she's no killer. You need to know, my only reason for going along with all this is to make sure Ella is no longer a suspect."

"I respect that." Quinn shoved her hands in her pants pockets. "My motivation is keeping my brother and Rachel safe."

Chapter Fifteen

They whose guilt within their bosom lies, imagine every eye
beholds their blame.
—Shakespeare's *The Rape of Lucrece*

The three unlikely musketeers ended up finding Corri in the
first spot they checked, thanks to Daria.

"Well, you were right. There's Corri's car," Lucas mused as he
parked behind her. "I'd know that cold blue steel Ford anywhere."

Quinn opened the passenger door. "And just in case there's
another blue Ford Mustang in town, that license plate is a dead
giveaway. Everyone knows Corri's a huge Anglophile."

Vanity plates were cheap in the state of Virginia, so it was
common for residents to add an extra slice of personality to their
vehicles. Corri's license plate frame had tiny Union Jacks peppered
all around—and her license plate read *UK-LVR*.

Lucas shut his door. "Looks like she didn't come alone." Parked
on the street in front of Corri's car was a 2010 Honda Civic. "It's
that teacher's car."

Quinn peered over Corri's ride to the parked car in front of hers. Like most Hondas, Jenny's car might have started off nondescript, but she had added her personality all over it. Her whole life was on the back of her bumper: a sticker proclaiming *Proud to be a James Madison High School Teacher*, another spelling *TEACHER* with periodic table symbols, Gandalf from *Lord of the Rings* commanding *YOU. SHALL. NOT. PASS!* The last one made Quinn snort-laugh: *I Believe in Dragons, Unicorns, Good Men, and other Fantasy Creatures.*

"Well, at least she's consistent." Quinn didn't want to waste any more time. "Let's go in. I have a feeling Corri's ready to talk. If Ella is truly innocent, she's the key to finding out. Maybe we can influence Jenny to put pressure on her?"

Daria nodded. "Agreed. Jenny's the conscience of the group."

The three of them walked into Saint Guinefort House, looking straight ahead, and found Corri seated in the back with Sister Theresa. Jenny had her arm around her friend and was trying to console her. Daria didn't even hesitate to barrel down the main hallway, Quinn and Lucas in tow, and slid the glass door open, surprising all three of the women.

Sister Theresa started. "You scared the wits out of me!"

Quinn closed the sliding door behind them. "Sorry about that, Sister, but we really needed to speak with Corri, and Daria said she'd be here."

"Because she's *always* here," her cousin quipped. "What's the deal with you two, anyways?"

Corri lifted her head out of her hands, mascara streaming black down her face. Jenny hugged her friend closer to her thin frame. "This is not a good time, ladies." Her gaze turned to slits. "Lucas, why are you here?"

"A better question is why your girl lost her ever-lovin' mind, yelling in front of everyone that his death was her fault?"

Daria huffed. "Why don't we let Corri talk for herself? And maybe Quinn can smooth the way for her when the police arrive here, which—in my calculations—may be any minute."

Corri wiped the black streaks off her face. "But I didn't kill him! He told me on our date that he'd been diagnosed with a heart condition. Hypertrophic cardiomyopathy. Doing eight shows a week was what was going to kill him. That's one of the reasons why he changed his life and moved down here."

"I don't understand." Daria sat down next to Sister Theresa. "Why would you think you killed him?"

Her tears kept coming as she wiped them with the sleeve of her blouse. "Because when the four of us had breakfast the next morning, I was talking about our date, and Senya and Ella were giving me a hard time. They couldn't understand why I'd give him a second chance after everything he put us through. I told them about his diagnosis, but not to be gossipy. Just so they could understand what he'd been going through, ya know?"

Jenny sighed, taking her arm off her friend's shoulder. "Corri's got a heart of gold. She's the sweetest person I know, so I got it. I understood. But Ella and Senya, not so much." She nudged Corri. "Tell them the rest."

"At first, they berated me pretty good, telling me I was all kinds of an idiot. But then, I don't know, something came over Senya's face. When I asked her what was up, she laughed, saying it served him right, that someone should give him a good scare. Teach him a lesson he really wouldn't forget."

The veins In Lucas's temples bulged. "And what did Ella say?"

Corri looked to Jenny, who gave a slight nod, encouraging her to go on. She was just about to answer when a swarm of cops came from around the house, surrounding the huddle on both sides.

"Corri Rypka, we'd like you to come in for questioning."

Sister Theresa stood up. "Is she being arrested?"

Officer Shae Johnson came through the sea of blue. "And who are you to her, Sister?"

Theresa pursed her mouth. "I offer her religious counsel. That's all you need to know."

The officer *tsk*ed, taking a step forward. "She's being brought in for questioning as a person of interest—and you're lucky you're not also at this point, Sister, especially since Ms. Rypka—who is not Anglican, nor a member of Christ Church Fellowship—seems to visit you no less than twice a week for the last seven weeks. Basically, ever since Chad Frivole moved back to town."

"She's done nothing wrong, seeking my counsel."

"Not wrong," Shae continued, "just unusual—especially since, no offense, you're not exactly known as a people person. Of course, we can do this the hard way—and I get a subpoena to arrest Corri Rypka for being an accessory to first-degree murder and another subpoena to search her apartment and your abbey for any evidence."

"Please! Leave her and the abbey alone," Corri cried. "She's done nothing but be good to me—and that's because . . . that's because Sister Theresa is my aunt."

Chapter Sixteen

I am a Jew. Hath not a Jew eyes? Hath not a Jew hands, organs,
dimensions, senses, affections, passions; fed with the same food,
hurt with the same weapons, subject to the same diseases, heal'd
by the same means, warm'd and cool'd by the same winter and
summer, as a Christian is?
—Shakespeare's *The Merchant of Venice*

Aiden held up two ties. "Which one?"

Quinn dabbed a touch of shimmering blush to each
cheek, twisting her torso in her vanity chair to get a better look.
"Either matches. But I like the blue one better—brings out the
gray in your eyes."

He tossed the green tie aside and began knotting the blue one
around his neck. "All right, so then what happened?"

Quinn filled him in on finding Corri and Jenny at Saint
Guinefort's and learning Corri was Sister Theresa's niece—but
why was the sister being so evasive? She also related that Corri
had volunteered to go in for questioning. She could tell from his

expression that he knew everything she was sharing but was letting her tell her version of what happened.

"You know, I thought you were going to cancel tonight, with having to interview Corri and all."

He straightened the knot. "If she'd been uncooperative, that would have been true. But Corri was more than happy to share everything she knew. Jenny too—although she was really just confirming everything Corri had said. They were also able to offer some gaps to our working timeline."

Quinn opened her clutch—another book transformed into a charming handheld purse thanks to the lovely Melissa, the artist behind Viva Las Vixens. She placed her phone and lip gloss inside, admiring how the federal-blue satin lining complemented the book purse cover of *Mastering the Art of French Cooking* by Julia Child. Quinn knew Rachel's parents were avid cooks and had recently taken up French cooking lessons at Culinaria Cooking School, and the purse was a quiet tribute to them, since they were hosting tonight's dinner.

From one of the drawers of her antique vanity, Quinn pulled out another accessory to wear on her Peter Pan collar for the evening: an enamel rolling pin with the phrase *Roll with it* written in cursive. If Queen Elizabeth II and former secretary of state Madeleine Albright could signal their views via estate jewelry, so could she.

"We better get going, or we'll be late."

Quinn slipped her feet into her heels as she walked toward the front door, grabbing a bouquet of fresh flowers and a box of French macarons. Cindy Clawford and RBG, meanwhile, were poised and ready next to Aiden.

"What's this?" she asked.

Aiden bent over to give each of them a proper scratch. "We'll be back soon. Mom and Dad have to play peacekeepers."

RBG licked his hand, and Cindy grumbled before strutting back over to her pillow. It seemed she was more interested in keeping her dog mamma company than actually going outside for an adventure.

Aiden opened the door. "Any chance we can forgo the family dinner drama for something less ulcer inducing?"

"Ha! You wish, Detective. You had your chance to bail on the Caine drama. You're in for the long haul now . . ."

*　*　*

Quinn waltzed in, took one look around, and couldn't help but ask, "What are you doing here?"

Daria placed her glass of wine down. "Well, isn't that a fine *How do you do*, cousin? I was *invited*—a bit last minute, but invited nonetheless."

"That's my fault." Rachel half raised her hand. "When Mom told me to invite the Caines, I was only thinking of immediate family, but she meant everyone. My bad."

Mrs. Slingbaum came out of the kitchen. "Well, it's all fixed now. What can I get for you two?"

Quinn scanned the room: Aunt Johanna had wine; so did Daria. Her uncle Jerry had a Scotch neat nestled in his palm. "Oh, I'll have a glass of whatever's open."

"Nothing for me," Aiden told her. "We're in the middle of a case. I need to stay sharp."

"Seltzer, then? Something else?"

Bash, meanwhile, couldn't sit still. "I can't believe my parents are late."

"They're not late," said Mrs. Slingbaum. "I told them to come at six thirty to give you two a chance to calm down, get a drink or two in you."

Bash stopped pacing. "Oh, well, now I feel like an ass."

Mr. Slingbaum handed him a beer and clinked the bottles. "Son, have a seat. You're making everyone nervous."

Bash plopped into the love seat next to his bride-to-be, taking her hand in his. He kissed her knuckles. "You okay?"

"Here you go." Mrs. Slingbaum handed Aiden and Quinn their drinks. "Please, sit. Relax."

Quinn did as she was told, but Aiden perused the perimeter of the room, taking note of the books and the art collection. "Is this an original Harvey Dinnerstein?"

"It is." Rachel's father grinned. "You've got a good eye, Detective."

"Call me Aiden."

"Why is no one eating the chopped liver?"

Rachel gave her mom a look. "Mom, I told you, these are WASPs; chopped liver is going to scare them off."

"It's Break Fast, Rachie. You serve chopped liver, bagels and cream cheese, blintzes and a kugel. We made two for tonight. Don't hide who you are—or where you come from."

Dr. Caine's face brightened. "Are we having breakfast for dinner? I love brinner, but Jo-Jo never lets me have it."

Daria's mom frowned. "That's because your cholesterol's a thousand and five! How much breakfast meat can one man eat?"

Bash tried holding back a cackle but failed. "No, Uncle Jerry—not breakfast, Break Fast, as in Breaking the Fast for Yom Kippur."

The lines between his eyes deepened. "Is that the holiday with the apples and honey?"

"No, Jerry, that's Rosh Hashanah, the Jewish New Year," Aunt Johanna piped in. "See? I know my holidays. And I'm going to try this liver. I bet it's delicious."

"You'd be right." Mrs. Slingbaum seemed satisfied someone was finally eating it.

Aunt Johanna put some of the chopped liver on a thin cracker, then popped it in her mouth. "That is absolutely scrumptious! You must give me the recipe for it."

She turned to Rachel. "See? What did I tell you?"

Meanwhile, Daria's father was still trying to winnow down the holiday list. "Oh, I know! It's the one with the trees?"

"For heaven's sakes, Dad, Yom Kippur is the Day of Atonement," Sister Daria informed him, downing the rest of the wine in her glass. "Rosh Hashanah celebrates the Jewish New Year, and then for the next ten days, Jewish people work on righting any wrongs they committed, culminating in Yom Kippur. It's like confession, but more condensed. Get it?"

Everyone stopped and stared at Daria.

"What? I was a religious studies major at Georgetown."

Just then the doorbell rang, and Rachel startled, almost spilling her wine. She offered a weak smile. "I guess I'm more nervous than I realized."

Her father patted her shoulder. "Don't be nervous."

"Really? You just said that to me."

"What?" he asked.

She rolled her eyes, exasperated. "Dad, isn't it true that, when I was a kid, you were the one who taught me that Albert Einstein said, 'The definition of insanity is doing the same thing over and over again and expecting different results'?"

"That's true."

"So then, explain to me why you always tell me not to be nervous when I'm anxious and expect that's going to help me calm down."

Uncle Jerry cough-laughed before giving his chest a wallop. "She got you there, Phil. Never tell a woman to calm down, even if that woman's your daughter. Rookie mistake."

Meanwhile, Mrs. Slingbaum opened the door. "Adele! Finn! Come in."

They offered tentative smiles. "Thanks for inviting us, Jeanie." Adele handed her a bouquet of peonies. "I heard it's the custom to bring flowers when you're invited over for Shabbat dinner or for Passover—and I remembered peonies are your favorite."

"They are—and you're right!"

Finn held out a box. "We also brought you some homemade baklava."

"Thanks, very thoughtful of you."

Adele and Finn, holding hands, walked in, their eyes fixed on Bash and Rachel. The awkwardness ate up the oxygen in the room.

Mr. Slingbaum invited them to sit down, then procured them some liquid courage.

Everyone took sips from their cups. Strained smiles. Darting eyes.

Rachel's father let out an exasperated groan. "All right, I'll be the one to start. I don't want this to be a whole drawn-out conversation. We've been fasting all day, and that means we're famished. Trust me, you don't want to aggravate Jeanie when she hasn't eaten. It isn't pretty."

"Jerry's the same way. It gets ugly, let me tell you," Daria's mother muttered.

"Okay, Adele . . . Finn . . . you said on the phone you wanted to start?"

Mrs. Caine took in an unsteady breath. "Yes, thank you for being so gracious and having us over. It means a lot to Finn and I. First of all, we want to apologize to you both for reacting the way we did. Just to be clear, we are thrilled you're getting married. We love you, Rachel. But our reaction to Bash's decision to convert to Judaism was inelegant."

Finn Caine coughed into his hand. "We were in shock, not that that's an excuse. We knew you ordered some books on Judaism, but we'd never discussed your interest. Frankly, after talking with our new therapist, we realize we haven't discussed faith or God with you in years."

"We just assumed you felt the same as we did," Adele added.

Bash swirled the bourbon in his glass. "In fairness to you both, it was brought to our attention that I could've done a better job letting you know where I was at, not sprung it on you two seconds after we announced our engagement. I apologize for that."

Adele sighed. "I would like to think we would have taken it better, but your father and I have been learning a lot about ourselves. As I said, we've been seeing a therapist.

"Through our work with her, a couple of issues surfaced for us. The first, you know, is our love for our faith. It sustains us, it's a comfort to us . . . it's the backbone of who we are. Without Christ, I honestly don't know where we'd be as individuals or as a family.

"So to hear that the God of our house wasn't Bash's North Star—for lack of a better phrase—well, it shook us. Badly. And we handled that . . . badly."

Adele Caine stopped to take a sip of her wine. "The second piece was remembering, when we were growing up, how the few Jewish children at my school would be teased, taunted even. The idea of our future grandchildren having to go through that . . . that's another part of where our reaction stemmed from. I know that was a long time ago, but the memory is fresh."

"That still goes on, you know," Rachel informed them. "I was bullied for being a Jew all through my school years."

"You were?" Adele's mouth parted. "I thought such ugliness was a thing of the past. Why didn't you ever say anything?"

Rachel tossed her hands up, exasperated. "Because that's been my reality for as long as I can remember. Northern Virginia is better than most places, but it's not perfect. People made comments about my 'Jew nose.' They said me wanting to be a lawyer was the perfect career for me because I was Jewish. Some of the kids involved in Young Life would try to convert me, asking if I wanted to make up for the sins of my people for killing Jesus. It didn't happen all the time, but it happened. And honestly, compared to my South Asian and Black friends, I felt guilty complaining. I still have white privilege that they didn't. Once Bash and I started dating in our sophomore year, no one dared say anything to me. He was the popular golden boy back then."

"Babe, I'm still golden," her brother teased.

Adele and Finn looked as if they'd been hit in the chest.

"And you got to relive those horrible memories on the night of your engagement," Quinn's dad said, his voice hoarse from emotion. Adele took his hand. "If you could find a way to forgive us, I promise you and your parents, Rachel, we will spend the rest of our lives making sure you feel welcomed and loved. And son?"

"Yeah, Dad?"

"We support your conversion—and we would love to be part of it, in whatever way you want."

Quinn felt the tears coming. Whatever tension Bash was holding on to evaporated.

"That's good to know, because about that bar mitzvah you mentioned . . ." Bash teased.

Everyone laughed, expelling sighs of relief, except Aunt Johanna, whose focus was back on the chopped liver.

Rachel finished her wine. "Listen, there's a reason why no one wants to talk politics or religion. I know this won't be a one-and-done conversation. Let's just promise to keep talking and remember we all love each other and trust we'll figure it out?"

Quinn butted in. "Mom and Dad, keep going to counseling. It's working."

"Babe." Aiden brought her in for a one-arm hug, trying to hold back laughter. "That's supposed to be the stuff you keep to yourself."

She shrugged.

"Okay, enough talking," Mrs. Slingbaum insisted. "Let's eat!"

Chapter Seventeen

The web of our life is of a mingled yarn, good and ill together.
—Shakespeare's *All's Well That Ends Well*

"Good gawd, Quinnie! What on earth are you burning?"

Quinn blew the aromatic tendrils away from her dad. "Relax, it's just dried rosemary and lavender from Mom's garden. I'm using it to energetically clear the space."

His glasses hung from the tip of his aquiline nose, eyes boring over their silver rims. "Can't we just get Daria to say a blessing or something?" He waved his hand back and forth. "Never mind, I'm getting some air."

Sol called after him. "You should be proud of your daughter! Lavender is calming, and rosemary protects the space from negative forces." They stopped talking when they noticed Mr. Caine shaking his head as he opened the door and stormed across the parking lot toward the Pure Pasty Vienna Shop.

Quinn kept waving the smoking herbs around. "Don't mind him. He'll either get their traditional beef pasty or go for their digestive biscuits. He's an emotional eater when he's aggravated."

"To each his, her, or their own." Sol grabbed the middle-grade bookshelf and pushed it off to the side. Almost all the shelving at Prose & Scones was on wheels so it could be maneuvered when more space was needed. For example, tonight's party.

"Your father has always had an overactive olfactory system." Her mother whizzed by with bunches of gorgeous autumnal flower in her arms. "His nose has prevented me from wearing perfume for over thirty-three years." She laid the flowers out across the bar, glass vases already lined up. "In my opinion, the shop smells divine. What could be better than the scent of flowers, herbs, and books fresh off the press? Leah, come help me with these?"

"Absolutely! But fair warning, I have no idea how to arrange flowers."

Adele Caine grabbed two pairs of shears from her gardening apron pocket, handing one set over. "Well then, it's time you learned. Saddle up!"

Under her breath, Quinn told Sol, "I burnt the herbs to clear any negative juju that may have been lingering from the last time we all got together in honor of their engagement, not to scent the air for ambience."

"Oh, I know. Respect that you didn't burn white sage. By the way, the shop looks rad."

Quinn completely agreed. The night of the Slingbaums' Break Fast dinner slash healing circle was when they had all decided the couple deserved a do-over. The Caine family had insisted on throwing them a proper engagement party at Prose & Scones.

In one week's time, the bookshop crew had hired a caterer, invited all the guests, drafted an engagement announcement for the *Washington Post*, and arranged for the decor. Quinn's mom, being an avid gardener, oversaw the flowers, which she was well on top of, with Leah's assistance. It had been up to Quinn to procure pictures of Rachel and Bash through the years, then have reproductions made and put on display around the store. The two of them had attended their share of homecomings and proms together, photos of which she placed in the entertainment section. Every other year at the high school baseball team banquet, they'd been allowed to bring a date, so those photos were perched in the sports section. And as soon as Bash had a car, the two of them had taken day trips to West Virginia, Maryland, DC, and lower parts of Virginia. Those framed memories ended up in the travel section.

Ryan, Leah's husband, perused the shop's Spotify. "Ah, sweet! You made a playlist for tonight."

"Well, of course Quinn did, silly." Leah had been a quick study and was putting the finishing touches on the flower arrangements. "If the shop had an official DJ, she'd be it. Well, go ahead, handsome, hit play!"

He complied with his bride's instructions. Music gamboled through the mini speakers. The minute Leah placed the last vase of flowers down, Ryan grabbed her by the hand as she walked by. "Dance with me, gorgeous." He twirled her around, her red curls bouncing in time to the beat of Stevie Wonder's "For Once in My Life." Her laughter filled the air.

"Ah, young love," Adele Caine tittered before giving her daughter a sympathetic smile. "I'm sorry Aiden can't make it to the party tonight. I know you must be disappointed."

"I am, but I get it."

Quinn's mother studied her expression.

"Stop using your mamma bear superpowers. I'm a grown-up, and there will be other celebrations." Quinn gave her a pointed look. "As long as there's an active investigation for a serial killer in our town, someone who wants Bash dead, I'm more than good with Aiden and his team doing what they need to do."

Adele Caine's mood sobered. "Yes, yes, of course you're right." She sighed. "Let's finish up."

Several hours later, the shop was shoulder to shoulder with their closest family and friends celebrating love and commitment and the upcoming marriage of two of their favorite people. Quinn had managed to get home and clean up just in time and was enjoying the party from the sidelines.

Daria came over and bumped shoulders with her. "Why so glum? The party is a hit! You definitely exorcised whatever negative vibes may have lingered from before."

"Is that a professional opinion?" Quinn joked, before taking a second glance and noticing her cousin looked, well, a little fancy, especially for a nun. "Excuse me, are you wearing makeup? And a new dress?"

Her cousin gave her the stink eye. "Tinted ChapStick does not count as makeup, and the dress is one of mine. I was getting ready at my folks' house, and they still had some of my old clothes."

Quinn sniffed Daria's hair. "You smell ready good too."

"What? Like I don't usually?"

Quinn chuckled. "I didn't say that. You smell like the old you—jasmine and sandalwood."

Her cousin didn't reply and pretended to be really focused on the crowd.

"Let me guess," Quinn went on, "your parents just happened to have your old favorite shampoo and conditioner at their house too."

"Yes, is that a sin or something?"

Quinn was having a little too much fun, but they always teased like sisters.

She was just about to apologize when she noticed Daria wasn't staring at the crowd in a glazed, aimless manner; her eyes were pinned on a certain mohawked business owner, who from the looks of it was making a beeline toward her cousin. Or at least trying to.

Realtor bombshell Trina Pemberley had blocked his path, trying her darndest to capture his attention. Hair flipping. Touching his arm. Giggling in a way you just knew was fake. Daria noticed Quinn watching her.

"They would be a good match, wouldn't they?" Quinn knew her cousin almost as well as she knew herself. But she'd play along, going at Daria's pace.

"What makes you say that?" Daria grumbled.

"Well, they're both single. Trina's been through a lot. I mean, her twin was murdered. It must be like losing your other half."

Quinn eyed where Trina and Lucas were standing and bit her bottom lip to keep from smiling. "You're right. She has been through the wringer, but I don't think he has a scintilla of interest in her."

Daria glanced down at her dress. "This old thing has seen better days."

"Hey." Quinn touched her upper arm. "You would look amazing in a burlap bag—which, for the record, isn't far off from your novitiate uniform."

Daria bumped her shoulder with her cousin's, holding back a laugh. "Facts. But stop it." She met Quinn's eye. "I'm being ridiculous, aren't I?"

"Nope. Not even a little bit."

Daria wiped the tint off her lips with a cocktail napkin. "Yes, I am. I'm supposed to be taking my final vows as a *nun*. What am I doing, getting dressed up for a guy who would probably dump me as soon as he got bored, or when his mother denounced him for not marrying a Latina? Or some other reason out of my control."

Quinn took her into a tight bear hug. "Listen to me," she loud-whispered in her ear. "You are enough, exactly as you are. You are magnificent. No one gets to make you feel less than. You hear me?"

Daria squeezed her back before talking into her ear. "I hear you. I love you. I have one question."

This is it, Quinn thought. *This is the beginning of her healing, for real.* "Ask me anything."

"Why is there some weird guy with a video camera staring at us?"

"What?" Quinn started before she spun around. Standing inside the shop by the front door was, indeed, a weird guy with a video camera. But now he wasn't staring at them. His eyes were darting around.

"Hey, why are you two in the corner?"

It was Lucas, in a suit with no tie, having finally extricated himself from Trina.

When neither Quinn nor Daria responded, he followed the direction of their gaze. "Who the hell is that?"

Daria patted the pocket of her dress. "We're about to find out."

The cousins kept the stranger in their sights, with Lucas by their side. As soon as the cam man realized the Caines plus one were heading over, he visibly swallowed.

"Hi there, I'm sorry. This is a private event," Quinn informed him, offering a polite smile. "The shop will be open at ten tomorrow morning."

"Right. Yeah, I s-see that," he stammered. "Is Detective Harrington here?"

Quinn stilled. Something was off about this guy. "What? Why are you asking?"

He shrugged. "Oh, well, I assumed he'd be here. He's your boyfriend, right?"

Now the off feeling turned into a body shiver, the really bad kind.

Lucas stepped forward. "You need to explain who you are and what you want. Now."

Quinn grabbed her phone out of her bra, the only safe place she had to keep it. "I'm calling the detective right now."

Aiden picked up on the first ring. "Babe, what's wrong?"

He knew her so well, he was attuned to the fact that she'd call during the party only if something was amiss.

"There's a guy here, with a video camera—"

"Tell him it's Doug . . . Doug Heffernagle." He tried peering around the three of them. "Is Rachel here? I don't see her around anymore. Not that I could blame her, with the break-in and all."

Lucas blocked his way. "Nope. You don't get even a glimpse of her." He pointed to the camera, nostrils flaring. "If you have video of Rachel on there or any other women, I swear on the Holy Virgin herself, I will mess you up and take myself to jail to celebrate. You hear me, man?"

Doug was white as a sheet. "Oh dear God, n-no. I would never disrespect her like that. She's an angel. So good. So, so pretty . . ."

Quinn hung up the phone. "He's on his way."

It was evident Doug hadn't heard a word. He seemed desperate to see Rachel.

Daria snapped her fingers in front of his face. "Focus, Dougie."

"Right! Um, maybe it would be better to show you what I've filmed somewhere private?"

Quinn motioned to the courtyard off to the side of the shop. "Over here."

The rest of them followed her outside and closed the door to the party just as Aiden's SUV pulled up.

Daria let out a low whistle. "Wow, that was fast."

"Yeah, well, he was close by," Quinn explained. "But even still . . ."

In a half second, Aiden was out of the vehicle, slamming the door, and barreling toward the group.

"Why are you here?" he groused in Doug's direction.

Cam man opened the video's viewfinder. "I heard your suspect's out on bail, and—"

Aiden interrupted. "No, I mean why are you here and not at the station?"

Doug averted his gaze. "Oh, uh, well, the shop is just down the street from my apartment. I thought you'd be here, for the party, and—"

"And you thought you could talk to me and get close to Rachel Slingbaum at the same time. Right?"

Seemed Dougie didn't have an answer for that.

Aiden cursed under his breath. "Show me what you've got, and maybe I won't arrest you for trespassing."

"Right, okay." He turned on the video camera. "Now, I know this looks bad, me having a video camera in my bedroom, but you're going to be glad I did when you see the footage I got."

Aiden and Quinn exchanged a look before all of them lasered in on the screen. The screen started off blurred, then found its focus: a woman was climbing stairs halfway up the fire escape of Bash and Rachel's building, her back toward the camera. She was wearing gloves, a jogging suit at least three sizes too big for her, and a baseball cap over long brown hair—blue at the tips—gathered at the nape of her neck in a ponytail. She kept her head down, the bill of her cap blocking view of her face. She also had a fanny pack on with a large Ziploc bag hanging by a carabiner clip.

"You can't really see them, because I was shooting through a dirty window and a screen," Dough narrated, "but in person, you could see something was moving around in that bag. Who knew it'd end up being a bunch of spiders?"

They watched as the woman in the video climbed off the fire escape onto the hanging ladder by Rachel and Bash's bedroom window. She was able to open the window with ease. The perp tossed the bag of spiders with the fanny pack, which seemed to have something rectangular stuffed tight inside the middle of it, taking up most of the room.

Probably the journal, Quinn thought.

They watched as the woman crawled through the window, the whole scene taking under ten minutes. Quinn glanced at the bottom corner of the video: the time stamp read 7:50 AM. The tape went to black. Doug hit the stop button.

"I didn't stay to see how long she was in there," Doug explained. "I had to get to work."

Quinn couldn't resist asking. "What kind of work do you do?"

"I own an adult entertainment store."

"Yeah, that tracks," Lucas scoffed.

Aiden ran his hand over his face. "Why am I just seeing this now? You come to the station every couple of weeks, and the one time you actually have information crucial to an ongoing investigation, you sit on it."

"Aw, c'mon, man, you know why. It looks real bad." He inserted a portable USB drive into his camera, downloading the content before handing it to Aiden. "But when I heard Ella Diaz was released, I knew I needed to come forward. I know she's still a person of interest, but she needs to pay for what she tried to do. What if Rachel had gotten hurt?"

Lucas barked out a laugh. "I hate to burst your bubble, but the woman on that tape is absolutely not my sister. She may have long hair like her, and whoever she is, she took the time to dye the tips blue, but that's not her."

Doug walked a few steps back, almost tripping over the patio chairs. "Ah, crap, you're her brother?"

Lucas ignored him, his gaze on Aiden. "Tell me you can see that's not her. The build's all wrong. She's trying to hide it with the baggy clothes, but there's no meat on her, plus whoever she is has tiny feet. Ella would kill me for saying so, but hers are huge. Wears a size ten and a half. We used to call her Bigfoot growing up."

Quinn shared a look with Daria and mouthed, "Is it Senya?"

"Maybe," she mouthed back.

Aiden caught the exchange but let it go for the time being. "I'm going to bring the drive back to the station, but for reasons I can't go into, I'm going to ask each of you to keep quiet. There's a lot up in the air, and I don't want word out yet."

Lucas balked. "What, so I'm supposed to let everyone think Ella's a criminal?"

Aiden's countenance remained. "I need twenty-four hours."

Hands on his hips and cursing in Spanish, Lucas let everyone know he didn't like it. "And you won't take her into custody again?"

"I can't promise anything," Aiden told him straight. "But I am asking you to trust me to do my job."

Lucas and Aiden held each other's gazes, locked in some strange silent-man-code exchange. Finally, he gave the detective a nod and chin lift.

"Thanks, man." Aiden held out his hand, which Lucas shook.

"Guess I'll get out of everyone's hair!"

Aiden blocked Doug's attempted exit. "Not so fast. I need you to come down to the station for a few more questions."

"Am I under arrest?" he asked, looking like he was ready to throw up.

Aiden's brow arched. "As of this moment? No. But don't push me."

Leah opened the shop's front door, eyes pinned on her. "Quinn! You're missing the whole party. Get in here!"

"Be right there," she promised. "Aiden, are we good to go?"

"Yes. Don't wait up for me. It's going to be a long night."

The three of them walked back in, her cousin and Lucas just ahead of her. Quinn watched them for a few seconds. They weren't touching but still close together. He kept his hands in his pockets but leaned in to hear every word Daria had to say, his besotted expression giving him away to anyone paying attention.

Meanwhile, the party was winding down. The catering staff had started cleaning up, but Quinn decided to help anyway. Anything to keep busy.

They had only invited people they loved, and the shop was still a wreck. Half-full plastic cups on the shelves. Crinkled-up napkins shoved behind the register. She filled a garbage bag in no time. Quinn was about to bring it outside when her father stopped her by placing his hand on her shoulder.

"Everything okay, Dad?"

He took the trash out of her hand. "I've got it."

"Oh, it's no trouble. I'm happy to—"

"You did an incredible job here tonight, honey. This party healed wounds your mother and I made. I thank you for that."

Her shoulders relaxed as she glanced over at her brother and his bride-to-be on the other side of the room. They were in a huddle with the moms, laughing and finishing up the last of the champagne.

"Thanks, Dad. Yeah, I'm just going to check on something for a client. I'm supposed to drop off that special order for the Freeman House."

Both his graying brows shot up. "The book for the Christmas exhibition? But it's only the first week of October."

"I know, I know. But it's Susan Fay asking. Who can say no to her?"

Susan Fay managed the Freeman House, both the storefront and its historical exhibits, tying Vienna's storied past in with current happenings in politics and culture. She was the quintessential New Yorker Italian mom: if she liked you, she loved you, which meant you got all she had to give. Watch out if you got on her bad side, though. "I have a list, all up in here," she'd often say, tapping her temple with her forefinger. "You don't want on this list, capisce?"

Finn grinned. "It's true. She a captivating woman."

"Also a woman who knows what she wants, and I'm guessing she asked for the book to be brought in early so she can have time to formulate the exhibit the way she wants."

"Oh, Susan wasn't the one who brought that in," her father corrected her. "She arranged it, but it was someone else . . . I think the great-granddaughter of the original owner."

"Do you remember who?"

Finn straightened his spine and stared off, the wheels on the bus going round and round. "Humph, I can't remember. I'm sure your mother can, but don't bother her now." He smiled in his wife's direction. "Let her soak in the frivolity."

On that note, Quinn went into her office, none too pleased to find someone had used her work space to store extra catering supplies. Stepping over bottles of wine, Quinn finagled herself to her desk, where the reconstructed novel laid. Thankfully, no one at the party realized the book was worth a pretty penny for the history it held alone, never mind the work she had done on it. She berated herself for not locking the tome away before the party. But then again, she'd had no idea her office was going to double as a party storage space.

"You are coming home with me," she said, realizing that speaking to her books wasn't a good sign of her sanity and probably meant it was time to go. Quinn placed the book in one of her literary tote bags along with some archival paper and such so she could wrap it properly.

Not until she arrived home, after walking RBG and settling in for the night, did she take one last look at the book. Sitting up in bed, she used her thumb to fan through the pages. The original work order slid out, the handwriting on the receipt now one she recognized. Distinctive. Tight loops with sharp edges. Lots of pressure; she was surprised the pen hadn't punctured the paper.

It was the same handwriting found in much of the novel's margin commentary.

A chill went through Quinn. It was the same handwriting found on the note left on the scene of Chad Frivole's accident. The exact same handwriting scrawled in the journal Quinn had made.

Her hands shook as she skimmed the work order receipt. Her pet babies must have sensed she was tweaked, because Cindy Clawford rubbed her head against Quinn's leg while RBG licked her foot. But she didn't notice because she was blinking hard, trying to get her eyes to focus.

"C'mon, c'mon . . ."

Finally, her vision cleared: the name of Chad's killer, the woman who had stalked her brother—and God knows how many others—was right in front of Quinn.

Chapter Eighteen

In nature's infinite book of secrecy, a little I can read.
—Shakespeare's *Anthony and Cleopatra*

Daria had her hands on her knees, trying to catch her breath. "Who would've thought? Concrete's a lot harder to lift than dog food."

Corri spread the mortar across the concrete. "Oh, please, if someone would've told me I'd be spending my much-needed, rarely-to-be-had day off building a glorified shed at an abbey, I'd have said stop sniffing glue and let me drive you to rehab."

"What a lovely image. Thank you for that." Sister Theresa shook her head while inspecting their work. "In spite of my niece's warped sense of humor, her work is impeccable. No lumps, no mortar spillage. Good job."

Daria stood up, looking back and forth between them. "Switching topics, and I know this is none of my business—"

Sister Theresa cackled. "An auspicious start."

She ignored her elder's reaction. "Why the secrecy, you two? I just don't understand. I thought you were an only child."

"Yes, about that," the sister answered with a shrug. "I lied."

Daria scratched her forehead. "I surmised that, thanks. The question is, why?"

Corri tossed the trowel into the mortar bucket on an exasperated breath. "No, it's a fair question. The long and short of it is that my mom—her sister—is a piece of work."

"Nadine never did like to share," Sister Theresa groused, grabbing the trowel and finishing up the edge her niece had started. "Even when we were kids. Can't begin to count how many times she tried to off me on the farm."

Daria swallowed. "Your sister tried to *kill* you?"

"Called them accidents, but everyone knew better—even my parents—but they lied to themselves. I get it. Who wants to believe their firstborn is a malignant narcissist with psychopathic tendencies? I left the minute I graduated high school. Joined my first Order. Changed my name. It wasn't safe for me back there." She stopped working and glanced up at Daria, contrition in her gaze. "Everything else I've told you was the truth. I don't like lying; makes me gassy—"

Corri piped in. "My mom doesn't know Sister Theresa is here in the DC area. She also thinks I'm a traveling nurse and I'm never in one place for too long." She sighed. "Look, all I have to do is see her for Mother's Day and Thanksgiving—so she has photos for her Christmas card—and she's placated. If she knew I had a relationship with my aunt?"

"Kaboom, thar she blows!" Sister Theresa sounded.

Lucas pulled up in his truck, his cousin Lupe following behind in hers.

Daria tried for the casual wave, all while her heart pumped almost loud enough to hear. She channeled her turmoil by lifting another concrete block and hoisting it onto the last one, just freshly mortared by her construction companions.

Lupe walked up, beaming in Lucas's direction. "*Primo*, you never told me how strong these sisters are. You should come work for my crew!" She offered her hand, which Daria shook. "You must be Eliza—I mean Sister Daria."

"Strong grip. Thanks so much for donating your time and that of your crew—oh, and the supplies, of course. It means the world to me and my Order."

Lupe paused, wearing a blank expression, before giving her cousin a sly grin. "*Me gusta*, Sister. Although you should know—"

Lucas stopped her right there. "Hey, why don't you three take a break and allow the professionals to do what they do." He whistled toward his cousin's crew and said something in rapid-fire Spanish.

What's that about?

They were about to unload the rest of the supplies when a gold F-150 barreled down Vale Road. Quinn's ride. Daria knew something was very wrong just by the way she drove down the street.

Lupe elbowed her cousin. "I'm going to get to work. I'll leave you to it."

Corri snapped her fingers in front of her face. "Daria? Hello?"

Quinn screeched to a halt and hopped out of her truck.

Daria worried the corner of her lip. "Something's up."

Quinn ran over to where they stood. "Oh, thank God you're here!"

Daria grabbed her hand. It was clammy, but she didn't let go. "Do you need to go inside? Talk privately?"

Quinn shook her head. Her eyes were bloodshot, like she hadn't slept. "I'll explain how I know later. Aiden and the police have already been informed. I've been at the station all night. They've probably got her in custody already."

"Wait a sec. Got who into custody?"

Quinn's hand went to her chest as she tried to catch her breath. "Jenny Kieval killed Chad Frivole and tried to kill my brother."

Daria snort-laughed. "That's a good one."

"I'm not joking. It's Jenny. I found a work order she submitted, her handwriting all over it with her signature. It was a perfect match for the note in the snake bag, as well as from the notebook left at Bash and Rachel's."

Even though standing still, Daria felt as though she would lose her footing. Corri smacked a hand over her mouth as if she was going to be sick.

Daria leaned her weight against a stack of concrete bricks. "This isn't real. This can't be happening."

Corri checked her phone. "And you're saying Jenny's already been arrested?"

Quinn shook her head. "I don't know. I mean, I assumed that's what the police were up to after I left the station. I came home to walk RBG, feed the pets, then came over here. Why?"

Corri showed her phone. "Then why did I just get a text from Jenny telling me she's missing me at the weekend thing but thinking of leaving because Senya and Ella are acting weird and leaving her out? Plus she's got a headache."

Quinn's mouth gaped.

Daria squinted to read Jenny's text. "So what do we do?"

Corri fished through her purse and pulled out her keys. "Quinn needs to call Aiden and get them over to Senya's place before she leaves, and we need to go over to Jenny's. See if we can find anything to help the police."

"Don't you think you should leave the evidence gathering to the police to handle?" Sister Theresa *tsk*ed. "You'll compromise potential evidence."

Quinn swallowed. "But what if, while the police are looking for Jenny, she's already laid another trap for my brother? Or for someone else?"

Sister Theresa kicked one of the blocks. "Well, crud, I hadn't thought of that."

"Then we have to get over there and break in somehow to find out," Quinn insisted. "Right away."

Corri jingled her keys. "No need for breaking and entering. I have her house key." She eyed her aunt. "You stay here, okay?"

"Fine," Theresa agreed. "But Lucas, go with them."

He nodded. "Yeah, I'll drive. You and Quinn come with me. That way, Quinn can talk to Aiden on the way."

They crammed into Lucas's truck and tore down Vale Road like a bullet, following close behind Corri's car, leaving suburban civilization behind.

Quinn kept moving her phone around the cab. "I have no bars. Where the heck are we?"

Daria peered through the windshield, all the while bracing herself against the dashboard. "I can't answer that, Quinn, because Lucas is trying to eject my spleen out of my mouth."

"Hey, I'm just trying to keep up. I have no idea where Jenny lives, but don't expect any bars on your phone anytime soon. We're headed to the middle of nowhere."

Chapter Nineteen

People's good deeds we write in water.
The evil deeds are etched in brass.
—Shakespeare's *Henry VIII*

Corri inserted the key into the lock. "You know, it just hit me. This is the first time I've ever been to her house." She opened the door and walked in first.

Quinn turned to Lucas and her cousin, her voice low. "How are you friends with someone for so long and never visit?"

"Because she lives out in the sticks!" Corri called out. "I can hear you, by the way."

"Duly noted," Daria mouthed. "By the way, I bet your phones will work now." She pointed to a cell tower right next to Jenny's property. "Let Aiden know where we are. Just in case, and don't touch anything inside. It'll be evidence soon enough."

"Good call." Quinn did have cell service back and left a message on Aiden's voice mail. "He's probably arresting her over at Senya's now."

Walking in, she saw that Jenny's house was just as she'd expected: soft-yellow paint on the walls, one of those shabby chic couches with lovely florals. Pictures of her friends in silver frames.

Corri noticed Quinn gazing at the photos. "I didn't know she had so many snapshots of us," she said with a sheepish expression. "You know, she moved into this place a few years ago. She was so proud. Took her forever to save for the down payment on a teacher's salary. She invited us over so many times, and we promised her we'd do it, but, well, we never did.

"Honestly, Senya, Ella, and I would say, only amongst ourselves, of course, how it would be such a pain to come out here . . . never thinking that maybe we were hurting her feelings?"

Among the framed photos on the shelves were almost as many books as Quinn had in the shop—most of them science related. Lots of kitschy gifts, too, like tons of ceramic figurines with *#1 Teacher* written on them with paint pens and snow globes from zoos across the country. Quinn always said you could learn a lot about a person form their bookshelves and their car bumpers. Both aimed true when it came to Jenny.

Corri noticed the teacher gifts too. "That's weird. I didn't expect she'd have so many."

Quinn regarded her. "Why? It's pretty normal for students to give gifts to their favorite teachers."

That made her balk. "Oh, don't get me wrong—Jenny is brilliant. She knows her stuff and she has her pets. But a lot of students say behind her back it's no wonder her name is Kieval—'cause it rhymes with evil."

"But she seems so nice," Daria countered.

Corri rubbed her eyes with her palms. "Yeah, sure, she is the sweetest, but once in a while, well, let's just say, I've seen Jenny get mad. Real mad."

"I'm going to check out the other rooms," Daria said. "Lucas, come with me?"

Quinn went back to the photos, noticing more of what wasn't there than what was. "So, no pictures of family? Any boyfriends?"

"No one in a long while. Certainly nothing serious." Corri sighed, shaking her head. "And trust me, if you met Jenny's family, you'd understand why she didn't have their photos out. They were kind of a nightmare. That's a whole other story."

"Guys?" Daria called out from the back. "You need to come here. Now."

Quinn and Corri went down the short hall, past a typical bathroom on the left and a bedroom with more stuffed animals than space for them on the right. Daria and Lucas moved out of the way so they could walk into the study.

But there was nothing typical inside this sanctum. Lining one wall were several large freestanding terrariums, all empty except for some leftover shed snake skins. Adjoining these were a couple of installed wooden shelves holding two covered medium-sized terrariums—also empty except for the abandoned spider webs and deflated, silken egg sacs. Next to them were two more medium-sized enclosures, but they were still occupied—by scorpions. A heat lamp had been left on over them.

Knowing she would probably have nightmares for the rest of her life, Quinn nevertheless peeked inside the scorpion enclosure, counting four adults. One of them had egg sacs on her back.

"Jenny's preparing for her next victim," she informed them. In the corner was a desk, on which were stacked a pile of police procedurals and books on snakes, spiders, scorpions, and killer bees. But what was most interesting were the letters on Jenny's desk, not in her handwriting. Jenny had taped birthday and Christmas cards on the wall that Senya and Ella had written to her. On the desk were reams of stationery.

"Jenny had been practicing, trying to copy their handwriting," Quinn said. "She was trying to forge Senya and Ella's handwriting and signatures."

Corri flinched. "You're kidding me."

Without touching anything, Quinn read the top page. "*If you are reading this, it means Ella and I have decided to take justice in our own hands—first by confessing to the murder of Chad Frivole as well as to the attempted murder of Sebastian Caine, and now by taking our own lives. We are two women who seemed to have it all, and yet, we too were used and neglected by the men in our lives, the exception being our families. We will take our methods to our graves and rest in the knowledge that we exterminated some of the viruses that infected this town for so long. We only wish we could have done more.*"

"Don't read any more." Corri covered her ears.

"Those are just the beginning," Daria choked out. "Look in the closet."

All four of them approached together. The double doors were already opened, and inside there wasn't a stitch of clothing or a shelf or even a rod to hang anything.

"What am I looking at here?" Even though it was quite warm in the house, Corri drew her cardigan tight around her, shielding herself from what was plainly on display.

Lucas crossed himself. "*Dios mío.*"

Quinn couldn't believe what she was seeing either. "Chad's photo is crossed out. There's a photo of my brother circled. I don't know who these other men are."

"They're all the men in town who have a reputation for being players," Corri answered while trying to read the tiny writing under each photograph. "She kept a record of all their hookups. She's got names, dates, places, preferences—and how she was going to kill them." She shook her head, eyes wide and teary. "She's one of my best friends. How did I not see this?"

The door to the study slammed open. "Maybe if you'd actually made an effort, come over once in a while, you would've known the real me."

It was Jenny, with a deranged smile and a gun pointed at them.

"Please, Jenny," Quinn pleaded. "Don't do anything you're going to regret."

"Oh shut up, will you? Do you not see how well I've been planning, for years? Regret? I have none! Actually, I'm quite proud of myself.

"I taught myself how to rig car doors to stay locked—thank you, YouTube. I even installed a remote-control feature so I could jam his car doors from yards away. No one even noticed me.

"Everything else was cake. I was the one who snagged some snakes from Ella's restaurant. I was the one who swiped that handmade journal from her house too. Christ, that woman buys so much stuff, she didn't even notice I had stolen it. All pure genius, if you ask me. I've been setting her up for years. You all being here is just a minor inconvenience." With her thumb, she cocked the trigger. "Nothing that a few bullets and a tubful of lye won't get rid of."

"Jenny, why are you doing this? This isn't you," Daria implored. "Can you put the gun down? Maybe we can sit down and talk?"

That got her a derisive smirk. "Out of anyone in this room, *you* should be the one to know why I'm doing this. *Everyone* knows what that guy Raj did to you. Messed you up so bad you locked yourself away in a convent! You're a runner, *Sister*. A coward. But not me. I'm a fighter. I have the courage to do what everyone else wishes they could do."

"You're right, Jenny. I'm a coward. I admit it. But make no mistake: there's nothing courageous to be found in hurting people. You do this, Jenny, and you heal nothing."

Jenny shook her head furiously back and forth, holding the gun with both hands. "At least the smart and handsome men went after you and your cousin. Corri's so beautiful, men didn't care she had half a leg blown off." Jenny's faced turned hot pink. "But none of them noticed me. *Ever*. It was like I wasn't even in the room."

She aimed her gun toward her degrees hanging on the wall and pulled the trigger. Everyone startled, crouching down, the glass in the frames shattering in a high pitch. Jenny kept talking. "It didn't matter that I'm smart." She aimed at her next degree and shot again through the middle. "Or that I volunteer at animal shelters." Another shot at the second master's. "Or speak three languages fluently. None of it mattered. It was never enough. *Why is it never enough!"*

Jenny swung the gun around, aiming right at Daria, a crazed sneer showing her teeth. "Say hello to Jesus for me."

Daria stopped breathing, bracing herself for the shot, but Lucas dove straight for Jenny. "Elizabeth, *run!"*

Another shot rang out, but Sister Daria couldn't move. "Noooo!"

Both Lucas and Jenny fell on the ground as he tried to wrestle the gun out of her hand.

The front door flew open and a SWAT team came barreling through, Aiden in the front.

"Vienna Police! Put your hands in the air!"

In a flash they got the gun, peeling Lucas off Jenny.

"Let me at 'im! I can take him!" Jenny twisted her body, her head flailing back and forth.

Officer Johnson put a knee to her back. "Jennifer Kieval, you are under arrest for the murder of Chad Frivole and the attempted murder of Sebastian Caine." Shae cuffed her hands behind her back and hoisted Jenny to her feet.

"Read her her rights and get her out of here," Aiden ordered.

Sweat streamed down the sides of Jenny's face, all the ire draining away as she swooned at the detective. "See? What'd I tell you, ladies. *Totally* clone-worthy."

Epilogue

Sister Daria was pretty sure this wasn't the time nor the place, but she had to ask:

"Explain to me how you were accused of murder, arrested, drugged by your supposed close friend, and you still managed to open your restaurant on time?"

It was three weeks later, and the entire town had come out to celebrate the grand opening of Ella Diaz's restaurant. Usually a novitiate wouldn't be allowed out except for a family occasion, but since Ella had invited everyone in her Order, the Reverend Mother was more than happy to bend the rules. Once again.

"How did I open the restaurant on schedule? I'm a Diaz, that's how. Nothing gets in the way of something we want."

She had elbowed Lucas when saying that, but Daria pretended not to notice.

"What did I tell you?" he reminded her. "It's standing room only. Everyone wanted to come. And you were worried."

Ella let out a throaty laugh. "Everyone came to see if I was going to serve snake tacos."

Daria pretended to cover her ears. "Please don't mention any of the three *s*'s," she begged.

"What is she talking about, Lucas?"

He frowned. "*Serpientes, arañas, y escorpiones*. Can't say I blame her."

Daria appreciated his saying them in Spanish. Even though she understood the words, it helped to not hear them in her native language. Handsome, considerate, and so, so brave. Plus, he smelled really good. She had to get out of there, without offending Ella.

"Congratulations again on the new restaurant, and for inviting my Order."

Ella shooed away the words. "It is my pleasure." Her expression softened. "You mean a lot to my brother, you know."

In spite of her defenses, Daria couldn't stop Lucas's sister's words from hitting the center of her soul. *Don't go there, lady. Time for a redirect.*

"Well, he means a lot to our Order. The storage building has helped more than you know, as well as your continued dog food donations. Because of your family, we're expanding our operations to include rescues."

Yep, Daria totally ignored the subtext Ella kept offering up, just as she had been avoiding Lucas ever since Jenny's arrest. He had been by every day, either to work on the construction project with Lupe and her crew or to check on her. But as soon as she had given her statement to the police and let her parents know she was all right, Daria had gone into voluntary seclusion at the abbey, refusing any visitors. She would have stayed there, too, but the Reverend Mother had had enough.

"If the Father, Son, or Holy Spirit hasn't answered you by now, then they're not going to, not while you're in seclusion. Time to face what needs to be faced."

At least the Reverend Mother had blocked any reporters from getting to her.

"I think I'm going to try and find Quinn and head home. Thanks again for everything. Have a wonderful night!" she told her friends, starting to move toward the exit before either of them could protest.

Daria had done what she needed to do: she had finally seen Lucas. They had spoken. She had faced him. At least that's what she was going to keep telling herself.

It took a while, but she finally found Quinn outside the restaurant. "Hey, what are you doing out here?"

"Oh, I think I've had enough revelry for one night. Besides, I can't take crowds."

She felt the same way. "Must be a Caine trait. Where's Aiden?"

Quinn's expression saddened. "He's getting the car. I think it's parked back in Falls Church."

Daria chuckled. "I'll keep you company while you wait." She studied her cousin. "Want to tell me what's wrong?"

Quinn let out a sigh. "That obvious, huh?"

"Were you trying to hide it?"

Quinn met her eye. "No? Yes? I don't know . . . It's just that, well, he's been getting a lot of attention in the media, because of the case."

"That's a good thing, right?"

Quinn shrugged. "Usually."

"What, has he been offered his own America's Most Wanted reboot like Senya?"

Sister Daria hadn't been out of seclusion for five minutes before Sister Ceci barraged her with all the news she had been missing: Jenny hadn't wanted to waste taxpayer money on a trial, so she'd pled guilty to one count of murder and one count of attempted murder, and they'd dropped the breaking-and-entering charge. She'd been sentenced to life in prison and was rumored to be receiving letters from a bevy of suitors worldwide. Some had even come to visit her. Between the male attention and teaching science to her fellow inmates, Jenny was quoted in the press as saying she was "living her best life."

Senya had handled the media like a pro, offering the exclusive on her story to the same network that offered her the show reboot. Sister Ceci had been surprised, but Daria wasn't: Senya had always been meant to occupy bigger, grander stages; no surprise she was selling her practice and moving to Los Angeles.

Corri's mother, after seeing her daughter on the news, had shown up unannounced at her doorstep. She said she wanted an explanation, but what she *really* wanted was to stir up a whirlwind of drama that resulted in her pockets full of cash. Corri's mom was this close to selling stories about her daughter to the tabloids, until Sister Theresa stepped in. Who knew what was said between the sisters, but after Theresa was done with Nadine Rypka, the latter offered her daughter an apology and promised never to come unannounced again. When Daria asked for details, Sister Theresa brushed her off with, "Let's put it this way: I know my sister better than anyone. I know where all the bodies are buried. Worth the extra Hail Marys after confession. Should've done it years ago."

Quinn stared off but kept talking. "Anyway, people are impressed with how he handled the case."

"Well, they should be," Daria agreed. "Wait, who are 'people'?"

"The FBI. They're recruiting him, or trying to, and he's seriously considering it."

Daria didn't know what to say. She had always assumed Aiden would remain a part of Vienna. Maybe not a detective forever, but who knew, perhaps police chief. Or running for public office.

"He's outgrown this town. I don't want to be the reason he holds himself back."

Daria slid her hand into her cousin's, giving it a squeeze. "What does Aiden have to say about it?"

"He wants to know, if he decides to take their offer, if I'll go with him."

Daria stilled. "And what was your answer?"

"I didn't have one, at least not yet. He just brought it up tonight, before we came to the opening."

"Impeccable timing," Daria groused.

Quinn laughed. "Right?"

Aiden pulled up in his SUV and rolled down the window. "Hey, thanks for keeping my girl company."

Again with the crap timing. "Always."

Her cousin gave her a hug. "Love you."

"Love you more."

Quinn let her go, opened the door, and hopped in. After fiddling with her seat belt, she lifted her head. "Can we give you a ride?"

A deep voice sounded from behind. "I've got her."

Aiden and Quinn beamed, while Daria closed her eyes. Because she'd know that voice anywhere. It had echoed in her dreams. In her prayers. This man whom she'd been running from since the first day they met.

Needless to say, Aiden took off, probably to talk with his woman about what they were going to do, but she wouldn't put it past him if he was playing Cupid.

They didn't say a word on the way to Lucas's truck. They drove in silence out of the restaurant parking lot, down Church Street and onto Lawyers. That is, until they reached the last, long stretch of road that led to home.

"You've been avoiding me."

She opened her mouth to protest but realized he deserved better. "Yes, I have been avoiding you." She caught her reflection in his side mirror: the fearful expression of a girl, not a woman. A small voice inside her spoke: *Aren't you tired of running?*

"I know. I'm-it's just," she let out a low sigh. "I'm not going to avoid you. Not anymore."

Lucas met her gaze before returning his focus on driving. "I met you, and it was like a juggernaut came out of nowhere, hitting me square in the chest. I knew I should walk away, not set foot anywhere near you. But I couldn't help it, Elizabeth. I still can't."

She reminded herself to breathe. "Why do you call me that?"

He pressed the brake at the stop sign. "You know why."

She did. Yet another truth she hadn't wanted to admit to herself.

He pressed on the accelerator and they were moving forward. The skies had opened wide while they had been at the opening, and she couldn't help but revel in how fresh and clean the road ahead was, how it gleamed bright, even in the dark.

She stared out the window, at everything and nothing. "I've been running for a long time, Lucas."

"I know."

They were in front of the abbey. He parked and turned off the truck.

The air in the truck turned thick. "I would've kept running if it hadn't been for you. Seeing you lunge yourself at Jenny like you did? Telling me to run?"

"Look at me, Elizabeth."

She hesitated for only a couple of seconds before turning to face him.

His brown eyes locked her in. "You didn't run. I told you to run, and you didn't."

"I—I couldn't. I thought . . . I thought she had shot you. For a second there, hearing the gun go off and seeing you lying on the ground? I thought you were dead."

He nodded, taking in her words. "I'm here. I'm not going anywhere unless you tell me to go. Then I will respect your wishes, and you won't see me."

Her chest rose and fell. She was finding it hard to breathe.

"I'm in love with you, Elizabeth."

He loved her—and, more than anything, she wanted to tell him she was falling for him too. But there was still something holding her back.

What was holding her back?

"I don't expect you to say it. All I'm asking for is a chance, for you to consider a different life than the one you planned."

She ran her fingers through her hair, dragging her fingernails against her scalp. "I have about a thousand different thoughts and feelings going through my head right now. I don't even know where to start."

Lucas's focus was outside the truck, his energy suddenly on high alert.

"What's wrong?"

Lucas ran a hand down his front windshield. "Why is there a guy waving to us from the lawn?"

She turned to see what he was talking about, but the windows were fogged up, so she opened the door and hopped out of the truck.

"Who's there?" she called out.

A slender figure came out of the shadows, the sound of footsteps crunching on the wet grass. He stopped under a dim streetlamp.

"It's me, Elizabeth. It's Raj. I've come back for you."

Not-So-Secret Recipes
from Vienna, Virginia

Slingbaums' Never-Soggy Fried Pickles

In order to have the absolute best fried pickles you've ever tasted, you're going to have to combine old-world Ashkenazi Jewish flavors with southern comfort food traditions. If you don't have time to make your own half-sour pickles, I recommend Ba-Tampte Half Sour Pickles or Guss' Pickles. If you can't find either brand, then it's worth it to make your own.

Ingredients
(Part I: Pickles)

5–7 Kirby organic cucumbers

1 half-gallon mason jar

1 piece cheesecloth, cut to fit top of jar

1 teaspoon coriander seeds, crushed

1 teaspoon coriander seeds, whole

½ teaspoon black peppercorns, crushed

½ teaspoon black peppercorns, whole

½ teaspoon mustard seeds, crushed

5 garlic cloves, peeled, sliced, and crushed

2 bay leaves

5 sprigs fresh organic dill

¼ cup kosher sea salt

6 cups water to fill the jar (after all ingredients have been placed inside)

Directions
(Part I: Pickles)

Wash cucumbers and place them in your mason jar.

With the flat end of your butcher knife, crush your coriander, black peppercorns, mustard seeds, and garlic. Leave some of your coriander and peppercorns whole for later. Place in the jar with the cucumbers. Insert the bay leaves and most of the dill sprigs inside the jar too.

On the stove, place sea salt in with three cups of water. Bring to a boil. Once dissolved, remove from heat and add three more cups cold water. Fill jar with salt water, covering the cucumbers, but leaving some air space at the top. Add whole peppercorns and coriander along with sprig of dill to the top. Cover the jar with a piece of cheesecloth cut to cover the top, allowing some room, and secure with a rubber band. Only partially tighten the lid.

Place in a cool, dry place (around 64 degrees) and leave for four days.

A Midsummer Night's Scheme

Check it daily. You will see some bubbles in the jar—that's carbon dioxide and totally normal. The water may get cloudy—that's okay. If it's gets dark or so cloudy it's hard to see the pickles, discard immediately (could be mold). Otherwise, after four days, drain and reserve the brine. Pat down the pickles with a paper towel.

Ingredients
(Part II: Fried pickles)

5–7 pickles (make sure they're really dry!), sliced to thickness desired

1 egg

8 ounces club soda

1 tablespoon baking powder

1 teaspoon kosher salt

2 cups all-purpose flour

Canola oil for frying

Deep fryer thermometer

Salt and pepper to taste

Directions
(Part II: Fried pickles)

In a large bowl, combine egg, club soda, baking powder, and kosher salt. Keep flour in a separate bowl. Add salt and pepper to flour.

Coat pickle slices in flour, then lightly dip in egg mixture, then in flour again.

Heat oil in a large pot until it reaches 375 degrees. Make sure to check the temperature of the oil regularly. Fry in small batches for about 3–4 minutes or until golden brown. Expect the oil temperature will drop when you place slices into the pot, so adjust accordingly. Do not fry all the pickles at once; otherwise they will get soggy.

Drain on paper towels and serve immediately. Add dip of choice ☺

Slingbaum Family Homemade Chopped Liver With Caramelized Onions

This is a recipe that's been handed down in my family for generations, but when I grew up and had my own home, I added my own flare—the caramelized onions—to add some sweetness to the savory. For those of you who hear "chopped liver" and want to cringe, let me say this: once it's done, it is absolutely one of the best spreads out there. Really. But I will admit, making it isn't for the faint of heart—or stomach.

Ingredients

1 pound organic chicken livers

Kosher salt and freshly ground black pepper

½ cup duck fat, melted in a pan

1 large onion, diced

3 hard-boiled eggs

Directions

Season the chicken livers with salt and pepper. Heat the duck fat in a pan over medium-high heat until melted into a clear or golden liquid. If you don't have duck fat, that's fine; use chicken fat (called schmaltz in Yiddish)—ask your butcher for some or find in the kosher frozen section. Slice up the chicken livers and sauté until the livers are lightly brown and still pink in the middle. Remove with a slotted spoon and let cool.

Turn down the heat to medium, keeping the residual duck fat from making the liver in the pan. Add the onions, season with salt and pepper, and cook, stirring often, until the onions are caramelized. Remove from heat and let the onions cool to room temperature.

Add the livers to a food processor and pulse until smooth or until the desired consistency is achieved. Transfer to a large bowl. Dice the eggs, allowing the yolks to crumble. Add the eggs and the onions and whatever cooking liquids remain in the pan to the pureed livers. Mix it all together and season with salt and pepper to taste. Serve cold with crackers or bread.

For the burger recipes mentioned, I encourage you to pick up a copy of the first book in this series, *To Kill a Mocking Girl*. Recipes in the back.

Acknowledgments

This series wouldn't be out in the world without certain people's help and vision. First and foremost, my love and thanks to my family, especially my daughters, Hunter and Samara. You are everything to me. Your insights and suggestions have guided me beyond measure. I love you both, and I respect you both as much.

I am fortunate enough to have an amazing editor in Faith Black Ross. Your patience, expertise, and encouragement served as a comfort to me during the pandemic, and I thank you. I also need to thank my best friend, Lisa Waldorf-Lee. No one proofreads like you do. Thank you for your unbridled enthusiasm and your eagle eye. You are my own personal angel.

Thank you to my mom, Genie Appel Cohen. You taught me how to write, my first art medium. I still learn from you every day, and I'm so blessed because of it.

Thank you to my agent, Jill Marsal. You've become a real partner in my process through the years, and I count on your counsel more than I say. So grateful for you!

Acknowledgments

And last, but never least—to you, the readers. I am honored you have taken the time in your life to share my imaginative world with me. I appreciate your emails and letters and gifts. I appreciate the love you have for the characters on these pages.